GW00982869

Praise for *Fractured Soul*

"*Fractured Soul* is a brilliant sequel, exceeding even the remarkable first book in the series. It will haunt your every waking moment between the times you're reading it, and it will stay with you long after you've finished. It's an amazingly well-written and engrossing story that I highly recommend—after you've read the first one, of course."

—**Cindy Bennett**, bestselling author of *Geek Girl* and *Rapunzel Untangled*

"Rachel McClellan delivers a stunning sequel to *Fractured Light*. The romance remains as passionate and pure as ever, the characters achieve even greater depth, and the action is absolutely unrelenting. McClellan's world is frightening and beautiful, a realistic and fascinating mix of darkness and light. Do yourself a favor, and clear your schedule before you start reading—you won't want to stop!"

—**Heather Frost**, author of the Seers trilogy

"When I read *Fractured Light* by Rachel McClellan, I was intrigued by the original story line and engaging writing. *Fractured Soul* picks up where *Fractured Light* left off and Llona is a strong heroine. I loved following her throughout the book as she learns more about herself and her powers. Lucent Academy was not what I expected it to be. Instead of being a safe place for Llona to train, it is filled with clueless girls and leaders that don't want to face the truth of their existence. Full of heart-pounding action, breathless romance, and killer drama, *Fractured Soul* by Rachel McClellan has it all, and I can't wait to read *Fractured Truth*!"

—**Christie Rich**, author of the Elemental Enmity series

"I love these books! A kick-butt heroine and a hottie love interest, with a refreshingly original concept. Be prepared—once you start, these are hard to put down."

—**Paula Cotton**, book reviewer at ReadingLark.blogspot.com

"Rachel McClellan's *Fractured Soul* is a masterfully executed sequel—it's built upon the foundation laid by its predecessor, but instead of merely living up to expectations, it chooses to redefine them in creative and compelling ways: new characters threaten to outshine the old, tension and action are interwoven with exquisite skill, and the story line is nothing short of inspired. Fans will clamor for the next book."

—**Thomas Winship**, author of the
Vaempire Revolution series

"*Fractured Soul* is a mysterious, engaging follow-up to *Fractured Light* that will keep you on the edge of your seat till the very end."

—**Alicia K. Leppert**, author of *Emerald City*

RACHEL McCLELLAN

A NOVEL

FRACTURED SOUL

Sweetwater Books
An Imprint of Cedar Fort, Inc.
Springville, Utah

This is a work of fiction. The characters, names, incidents, places, and dialogue are products of the author's imagination, and are not to be construed as real.

ISBN 13: 978-1-4621-1180-0

Published by Sweetwater Books, an imprint of Cedar Fort, Inc.
2373 W. 700 S., Springville, UT 84663
Distributed by Cedar Fort, Inc. www.cedarfort.com

LIBRARY OF CONGRESS CATALOGING-IN-PUBLICATION DATA

McClellan, Rachel, 1977-
Fractured Soul / Rachel McClellan.
pages cm
ISBN 978-1-4621-1180-0
I. Title.
PS3613.C3582F737 2012
813'.6--dc23

2012041533

Cover design by Rebecca J. Greenwood
Cover design © 2013 Lyle Mortimer
Edited and typeset by Emily S. Chambers

Printed in the United States of America

10 9 8 7 6 5 4 3 2 1

I will love the light
For it shows me the way.
Yet I will endure the darkness
For it shows me the stars.
—Og Mandino

ONE

People told me life would return to normal, but how could it after you'd killed someone? Or some*thing.* Life would never be the same again, apparently starting with my new dorm room at Lucent Academy.

"Why does it smell like blood in here?" I dropped my duffle bag on the perfectly made bed. The pink floral bedspread wrinkled its way out of perfection.

"What a silly thing to say," my aunt Sophie said. "This room is practically brand new."

I looked under the bed. "I don't think so." Where was the smell coming from? "Did a butcher live in here?"

May, my best friend, walked through the door. "What butcher?"

"The butcher who killed a cow in my room." I looked around. My dorm room was twice the size of my bedroom back home but not nearly as comfortable. The wild-rose-colored walls and heavy wooden chests screamed pretentious. So not my style.

"There was a cow?" May asked.

Sophie frowned. "Really, Llona. You have such an imagination." She turned to May; her long and ruffled blue skirt followed. "Did you find your room satisfactory?"

"I did. And thanks again for inviting me here."

Sophie placed a hand on her shoulder. "Lucent's glad to have you. We always look forward to having new Furies."

"When's dinner?" I asked. May and I had been traveling for a week since leaving Utah. Sophie thought it would be fun to let us sightsee before we started school again. At first I thought it was a great idea, but by our third museum and our tenth fast-food restaurant, all I wanted was a good meal and a place to call home.

"In about twenty minutes," Sophie said. She swiped her finger along the edge of the chair rail, obviously inspecting for dust. "Why don't you get settled, and then come on down when you hear the chimes. Do you remember where to find the dining room?"

"Um, first floor, all the way at the end," I said. Sophie had given us a quick tour on the way up. There were so many rooms, I was surprised I'd remembered.

Sophie smiled. "Good. I'll see you girls down there. Oh, and by the way, Llona, even though Auras aren't normally unkind, just remember that they're still teenagers trying to discover who they are. Sometimes they say things that surprise even me."

"What's that supposed to mean?"

She paused. "You've been on the outside your whole life. They may view you as different."

"Fantastic. So I was a freak before and now you're saying I'm a freak here too?"

"No, it will just take a while for the girls to get to know you. I'm sure once they do, they will love you just like I do."

Uh-huh, sure. 'Cause that's how girls are. "I wish Christian was here," I mumbled and turned my attention to my bag so she wouldn't see me scowling. It was amazing how easily adults forgot what it's like to be a teenager.

"What did you say?" Sophie said.

I looked up, surprised she'd heard me. "Nothing," I said.

Sophie pursed her lips like she wanted to say more. Finally, she said, "Try not to be late, girls." The door closed.

May jumped onto my bed. "Can you believe this place? It's like right out of a fairy tale. I feel like a princess!"

I forced a smile and shoved clothes into the nearest dresser.

"What's wrong?" she asked.

I stopped moving. "Nothing, really. I'll get over it." I crinkled my nose. "Except for this awful smell."

"What smell?"

"You really don't smell it?" I opened the closet doors and—with just a thought—turned on the light. The walk-in closet was bare except for a thin layer of dust covering the wooden floor.

"It might smell a little musty," May offered. "Do you really think the other girls will be mean to us?"

I shrugged. "Probably not to you. From what I hear, Furies are a rare find. I'm sure they'll treat you like the diamond you are!" I grinned and sat down next to her, but I secretly wondered how things would be different if I were a Fury instead of an Aura. May's ability to create and control fire was pretty cool. Not only that, but Furies—especially good ones—were rare. That's why Auras were always excited to have one around. But then again, being an Aura had its perks too—if I could use my ability to control Light the way I wanted, which was to defend myself. At Lucent, Light was only to be used to edify and beautify the world around us.

May laughed. "You sound just like your aunt."

I sighed. "This place is going to take some getting used to."

May nodded.

"How are you doing?" I asked. She had been quiet on the drive over from New York City, but I didn't dare ask her what was wrong in front of the man who had escorted us to Lucent.

May looked down, and my eyes followed her gaze. Her fingers traced the floral pattern on the quilt. "For some reason, I thought I'd feel better putting all this space between us and Highland, but I almost feel worse. It's like I've run away or something." May looked at me, searching for understanding. "Does that make sense?"

"It does. It feels like we're betraying Tracey by being here. We get to live our lives while she's six feet under." Beneath the pillow on my lap, I dug my nails into my palm, remembering how Mr. Steele, a Vyken posing as my math teacher, had sliced my friend's throat. And even worse, it was my fault. My selfishness had left Tracey dead, May injured, and many others traumatized. If only I would've left for Lucent sooner.

"Are you going to call Christian tonight?" May asked, like she thought mentioning the name of the boy I loved would help me forget about what happened.

I forced another smile. "I'll try. I have to call my uncle Jake first to let him know I'm finally here, and if I don't have someone standing over me, I'll call Christian."

"I can't believe they won't let you talk to him," May said.

"Oh, I can talk to him, but it's"—I made air quotes—"'frowned upon.'" Christian wasn't my official Guardian anymore, but it still wasn't considered proper for us to speak informally to each other.

May chuckled and stood up. "I better finish unpacking before we have to go downstairs. Come grab me when you're ready."

After May shut the door, I opened the window to let in fresh air. I was looking forward to the cooler New York weather. I didn't think I could've handled sunny and warm at this point in my life. There was nothing bright about it. Every night for the last week, I'd been having nightmares like nothing I'd ever experienced before. I kept dreaming of death; vivid pictures of people drowning, burning, being strangled. I inhaled deeply and shook my head, shaking the images from my mind.

A window screen prevented me from seeing the full extent of Lucent. I traced its edges until I found the latch. I popped out the screen, slid it under my bed, and then returned to the window. Leaning out as far as I could, I scanned the area.

My room was located in the right wing of Chadni Hall. I was on the third of four floors, which was for sixteen-year-olds and upperclassmen. When we had first arrived, I was in awe at the size of the school, but now looking at everything from this high in the air, Lucent seemed so much bigger.

The sun was setting, taking the shadows of trees and buildings with it. They stretched long and thin, crossing into each other until they blurred into the forest just beyond a tall rock wall surrounding the school.

Behind the main building were three more buildings almost as big as Chadni Hall. If I remembered correctly, the square, three-story building to my left was Denelle Hall where all the classes were held. To the right of it was a circular, red-brick building with tall, white columns. Sophie had called it Risen Auditorium. That's where the theatre and the music rooms were. And in between these two buildings was the tallest structure of all: a gray stone clock tower. Finally, toward the rear of the school grounds, the square shape of Lambert House stood, which Sophie said were living quarters. She didn't say for whom though.

From Denelle Hall, a steady line of people headed toward my building. I took a deep breath. That was a lot of teenagers. Just then, one of the girls' faces turned up in my direction. I quickly ducked back in my room and away from the window.

Already the fresh air was making a difference on the smell. Either that or I was getting used to it. I sat down at the vanity and ran a brush through my hair. Maybe someone at Lucent could show me how to change it, I hoped. I was tired of its blonde, almost white, color. I always thought I'd look better with brown hair, like May's, but dye never worked on my hair.

A tinkling sound, as if someone had waved a magic wand, chimed. I assumed it was the dinner bell Sophie had talked about.

I swept my long hair to the side of my neck and examined the two small holes where Mr. Steele had bitten me. They were still there, as if it happened yesterday. The red, swollen edges around the wounds made them look like eyes. I quickly applied concealer. I hated the way the marks stared at me, accusingly.

I leaned back in my chair, thinking. How could I have not recognized that something was wrong with Mr. Steele? Every time he came near me, I got all dizzy-headed and confused. At the time I'd thought it was because of some weird attraction, but, looking back, I could see how stupid that was. For months Mr. Steele secretly terrorized me, forcing the Light within me to mature early just so he could steal it from me like he did when he'd killed my mother.

The Light in an Aura's blood was the one thing Vykens wanted most because it gave them many powers, including the ability to change their appearance. But Mr. Steele had underestimated my abilities. With the help of Christian, I learned to use my ability over Light as a weapon—a weapon that ultimately destroyed Mr. Steele.

However, my victory came with a price.

Mr. Steele had bit me, and ever since then I felt something growing inside me. It was dark and contentious, and its evil pressed on me from the inside out. I'd never felt dirtier, like I'd been touched by the worst kind of monster imaginable.

I turned away from the mirror and pulled a pink beanie over my head. Enough of the past. I stood and was about to open my door to go get May when I saw something move out of the corner of my eye. I glanced to my left, to the corner of the room where it was the darkest. There was nothing there—only an old dresser. I waited a second, but nothing happened. Strange.

May opened my door, startling me. "What's with the weird chimes?" she asked.

"I don't know, but if I have to hear that every day, I think I'll go crazy."

"I know, right?" May turned to the mirror and adjusted her hair. She was wearing a different outfit—it looked brand new—and she had reapplied her makeup. *She must be nervous*, I thought. I never considered how hard this must be for her. She had guarded her secret of being a Fury for so long that to all of a sudden be surrounded by people who knew the truth might be overwhelming.

"Everyone is going to love you, and I'm not just saying that." I wrapped my arm around her shoulder. "Come on. Let's go be the new kids," I said.

May, with her easy-going personality, would fit right in, but I wouldn't, nor did I care to. I was here for one reason only: to learn as much as I could about my ability, then I was out of here. I didn't want to be a part of the Auras' strange culture that didn't allow us to reach our full potential. I wanted more.

We were almost to the end of the hall when a door opened and four laughing girls appeared, but when they saw us they stopped. May said, "Hi, guys!" as we passed. They said nothing—just stared like we were a new zoo exhibit. But before we turned the corner, my sensitive ears, which I'd inherited from my Guardian father, heard one of them whisper, "I can't believe they put her in that room. I'll bet she's dead by the end of the month."

TWO

I PAUSED FOR JUST A MOMENT, WONDERING IF I'D HEARD CORrectly, but when May glanced back at me, I ignored the cold chill rooting itself in my spine and continued downstairs.

The dining room wasn't at all what I expected. It looked more like a grand ballroom inside a five-star hotel. Ten chandeliers hung from a white-trimmed ceiling, and in between square moldings were paintings of what I imagined heaven would look like. It should have made me feel all ethereal, but instead I felt unworthy.

Positioned perfectly throughout the room were dozens of circular tables, each decked out like Martha Stewart had decorated them. Even the tall glass vases in the center of the tables held real flowers. I glanced down at my attire—jeans and T-shirt. "Do you think we should go back and change?" I asked May.

"No, we're good. Everyone else is dressed casually too."

I looked up, seeing the other girls for the first time. Most of them were already seated, but they were so still and quiet, it's no wonder I had missed them. I would've thought they were statues if it hadn't been for their eyes, which were darting around the room meeting the gazes of other girls as if they were silently communicating.

"Where should we sit?" May whispered. We were standing in the doorway, off to the side.

"Let's go sit—"

"Can I have your attention, please?" Sophie's voice boomed through a speaker nearby. I jumped and grabbed May. Everyone turned to the front of the dining room. Sophie was standing at a podium speaking into a microphone.

"I know we normally don't interrupt your dinner," she said, "but we have a couple of new girls we'd like to introduce."

I moaned. *Nice, Sophie. Couldn't you have waited a day?*

Sophie eyed us huddled in the doorway and motioned us over. May and I looked at each other.

"Come on now, don't be shy," Sophie said, like we were first graders at a new school. I could strangle her.

May moved first; I followed her lead through the maze of tables up to the front. The hard stares of the girls drilled holes right through me. When we reached the front, Sophie said, "This is Llona Reese, and this is May Cellini. Llona is an Aura, and May is a Fury."

A unison gasp broke the silence. Their eyes moved to May, relieving me of their cold stares.

"Let's make them feel welcome," Sophie continued. "It's not often we get new girls." She turned to us. "Welcome to Lucent Academy!"

A polite applause, like the gentle pitter-patter of a spring rain, echoed across the great room. I bowed my head slightly in acknowledgment, but wondered if I should have curtsied or something. As soon as their clapping slowed, I dived toward the nearest seat. May followed.

The table was almost full. I smiled at the other girls, who I just now recognized as the ones who'd joked about my room and me turning up dead inside it. Awesome.

The girls didn't say or do anything—just remained in their

statue-like stance—but then the magical chimes sung their song, and it was as if the sound woke the girls. The room burst into an array of sounds all at once: girls chatted and laughed, dishes clanked together as many poured water into their glasses, and doors at the side of the room flew open, letting in a steady stream of people in uniforms, carrying platters of food. From where I sat, I smelled chicken and broccoli.

A girl across the table said, "So, May, Llona," there was contempt in her voice when she said my name. She'd obviously heard something about me she didn't like. "I'm Ashlyn and these are my friends, Valerie, Anna, Jan, and Katie." The girls smiled and said hello.

"Welcome to our school," Ashlyn said. "It's always nice to have a Fury among us."

Ashlyn was very pretty with petite features and long strawberry-blonde hair that fell past her shoulders in big curls. I wondered how she was able to get curls that big. I reached up and tugged at my own hair.

"Where are you from?" Valerie asked May. Valerie's blue eyes were the same navy blue color as her baby-doll T-shirt.

May looked at me. "We're from Utah. We both went to the same school."

"Really?" Valerie said. "I wonder what the odds are of that? A Fury and an Aura."

"How did you discover each other?" Anna butted in. Her voice was small and mousy, matching her short dark hair and upturned nose.

"It was by accident, really," I began.

"Anna was asking May," Ashlyn interrupted.

I visibly jerked. "Oh, okay." *And so it begins.* I grabbed my glass and took a sip of water.

May looked uncomfortable, but she continued where I'd left off. "We were lab partners. I accidentally exploded a beaker of oil and it caught her hair on fire."

A couple of the girls giggled.

May ignored them. "Llona had seen me start the fire, and I noticed her hair grow back, so we both knew we were different. We were pretty much best friends after that."

Ashlyn tilted her head. "What do you mean her hair *grew* back?"

May glanced over at me nervously, hoping I would answer, but if they didn't want to talk to me, I wasn't going to start.

May hesitated before she said, "Her hair can't be cut or colored. It's always the same. Isn't that how all Auras' hair is?"

The girls paused and looked at each other before they burst out laughing. I took another drink; my eyes settled on Sophie sitting three tables over. She gave me an encouraging smile. I didn't return it.

Ashlyn was the last one to stop laughing, unfortunately. The sound hurt my ears—it was loud and high pitched, sounding more like a chipmunk on crack than an actual laugh. I stared at her coolly.

"So you're telling me," Ashlyn said, addressing me with a stupid grin, "that your hair won't ever change?"

"Are you giving me permission to speak now?" I said.

The table grew quiet.

Ashlyn turned to Anna and said, "This is what the outside does to you, turns you into a heathen."

I was about to show her how a heathen curses when three waitresses brought food to our table. Two of the servers looked like they were around twelve, and the older one looked more my age. When the older one set a plate of food in front of me, I glanced at her and said, "Thank—" Then the water in my throat caught, and I began to cough, making the girls at the table laugh again. I did a double take at the waitress's face to see if what I'd just seen was real.

It was, but I still couldn't believe it. On the side of the girl's face and partway down her neck were light green scales. They were shinier than the rest of her skin, and if I looked at them at a certain angle, they had a rainbow glow to them. The girl met my stare but then quickly looked away, her face reddening.

As soon as the waitresses were gone, Ashlyn said, "Is that your first time seeing a Lizen?" She seemed pleased by my ignorance.

"A what?" May asked.

"A Lizen. You know, half man, half . . . lizard." The other girls looked at her in shock as if she'd said something forbidden.

It was my turn to laugh. "Lizard people? It's just a crazy birth deformity."

"You really don't know a thing, do you?" Ashlyn straightened in her seat as if she were a teacher preparing for a lecture. "Lizens have been around since the dawn of time. While other species were evolving, Lizens didn't quite make it. Their *deformity* stuck, and when they bred with each other, it only made it worse."

"Where have they been this whole time?" May asked, eyes wide.

"In hiding of course. Wouldn't you hide too if you had scales on your body?" She tossed a disgusted look in the direction of the ever-moving waitresses.

Valerie looked at us conspiratorially, adding, "Their race almost went extinct until the Auras brought them here to serve us. They live on campus in Lambert House. The women work inside and the men take care of the grounds."

"And they like this?" I wondered out loud. From what I'd seen and experienced so far, serving pampered Auras was the last job I'd ever want.

"Like what?" Ashlyn said.

"Serving Auras," May said, apparently thinking the same thing.

Ashlyn looked at us like we'd just told her the world was flat. "Of course they like it. We've made their lives dramatically better. What more could they ask for?"

I glanced around, still in shock. "Yeah, what more."

Throughout the rest of dinner, the girls spoke mostly to May. I was surprised by how boastful and prideful they were. No wonder my mother had left early and refused to be a part of their organization. Some people thought she took it too far by marrying her Guardian, a big no-no, but I didn't.

"You should take that," Valerie said while Ashlyn was speaking to May.

I followed the direction of her pointed finger. Next to my glass was a blue pill. "What is it?"

"It's our vitamin. We all take it. It keeps us at optimum health."

I picked it up and looked at it. "Really?" A memory stirred. My mother used to take them too. I wondered why my father never gave them to me. Maybe he was too proud to ask the Council for them, or maybe he had and they'd refused.

"Isn't that right, Valerie?" Ashlyn said, interrupting us.

Valerie turned away from me and joined in their conversation. Whatever. If these vitamins were good enough for my mom . . . I popped the pill into my mouth and washed it down with water.

My attention wandered away from the Auran girls and over to the Lizens who were lined up against the walls, hands behind their backs, waiting for us to finish. They looked like regular girls, no different than the rest of us, except for the occasional patches of scales, some more noticeable than others.

I studied them for a moment, specifically their eyes, which always seemed to be looking down. And none of them were smiling.

"Llona?"

I turned around.

Sophie was standing behind me, smiling. "There are some people I would like to introduce you to. Are you about finished?"

I glanced down at my half-eaten chicken. Usually I had a great appetite, but the atmosphere in the dining room made me ill. "Sure." I stood up and followed Sophie back to her table.

"Everyone, I'd like to introduce you to my niece, Llona," Sophie said.

All eyes turned on me as if in slow motion. They all looked friendly enough, smiling and nodding their heads, but something about the way they did it looked forced.

Sophie motioned around the table. "Llona, here are a few of your teachers. Ms. Ravitz, Ms. Crawford, Ms. McBride, and Ms. Haddy. And over there next to the podium," she pointed to an older-looking Chinese man who was speaking with a student, "is Dr. Han. He sits with me on the Auran Council."

The Auran Council. I almost grimaced. They were a group of nine people, three overseeing each Auran school, who set the rules. As far as I was concerned, they were responsible for the Aurans' weakened state. "Nice to meet you all."

"You'll have an opportunity to get to know each of them in your classes," Sophie said.

"We're glad you're here, Llona," said Ms. Crawford. She was a beautiful African American woman in what looked like her thirties. Her smile actually seemed genuine.

Sophie turned me around and said quietly, "After dinner I want you to go to the medical room on the first floor to have your blood drawn."

"Why?"

"An Aura's blood is special. If something were to ever happen to one of us and, heaven forbid, someone needs blood, we store it here. We draw everyone's blood once a month."

"That seems like a lot. Can I refuse?"

She took hold of my hand and squeezed. "Of course you can, Llona, but it's frowned upon. We do things here that you may not like, but they are for your protection, and the protection of the whole Auran race. Because we are so few, we have to be careful. We must survive."

Funny. That's what I had always tried to do too, convincing my uncle Jake to move from one place to another to keep me safe, but I was different now. I could protect myself. I'd killed a Vyken, and I knew I could do it again. That made me feel safer than anything Lucent could ever do for me.

With my voice low, I ventured, "Maybe instead of just trying to survive, we should be trying to kill Vykens."

Sophie reared back with such disgust you'd think I'd barfed on her. "What a horrible thing to say!" she gasped.

"What is so horrible about wanting to save our race?"

"Light does not kill, Llona." Her voice was growing louder. "You have no respect for Light and its power!" Sophie's mouth closed tight, and she looked around as if she'd just remembered where we were. "We'll discuss this later," she hissed and walked away.

I stared after her, a new and foreign heat burning my insides. The feeling was so intense that the lights in the room flickered. I almost considered plunging everyone into darkness so I could escape unnoticed, but when several people looked up, specifically the teachers, I inhaled deeply and forced myself to relax.

I returned to the table. "I'm going to head back to my room. Do you want to come?" I asked May.

May glanced at the other girls and then to me. "Of course." She quickly stood up. "I'll see you guys later."

Her good-bye was followed by, "Bye, May!" and "It was nice to meet you!" and "I'm glad you're here!"

I kept a perma-grin on my face until the dining room doors

closed behind us. Before I could stop myself, I made a lighted-up fist and punched a wall, spraying what looked like electricity all around us.

THREE

May jumped, barely missing a jolt of light. "Llona!"

I glanced down at my bloodied knuckle as shocked as May looked.

"Why did you do that?"

I shook my head. "I'm not sure. I guess it's this place, my aunt, those girls . . ."

"Some of them were okay," May said, her voice quiet.

I was about to disagree with her, but thought better of it. May was right. They were kind, to *her*.

May traced her finger on the wall where I'd punched it. "I know there are some weird things here, like the chimes and the fancy meals, but it feels good to finally belong somewhere and not have to hide who I am."

"They seemed to like you. I'm sorry I left early. Why don't you go back?" I stared at a drop of blood trailing down my finger.

May looked toward the closed doors. "That's okay. I want to hang out with you. I think you could use the company."

"Actually I'd like to be alone for a while. You know, clear my head and stuff."

"You sure?"

I nodded.

"Okay. I'll come see you after dinner."

Back in my room, I sat on the bed and blotted a tissue against my knuckles. Where had that rush of anger come from? Sure I was upset, but enough to punch a wall? I'd never done that before.

I sat up. There was only one thing I felt like doing right now, and there probably wasn't much time to do it. I opened my door and went down the long hall to the commons area. It was a large room in the center of Chadni Hall, filled with chairs and tables for studying. Four halls, two on each side, led to the girls' dorm rooms.

I'd spotted a phone here on my way up, but looking at it now, I decided it was too public. Another stupid rule of Lucent's was no cell phones. I glanced around. Not far away, near the elevator doors, was another room. A plaque on the wall next to it read "Nurse." I tried the doorknob, but it was locked. *Figures.*

After making sure I was alone, I produced a small ball of light and held it up to the doorknob for inspection. It was just like my lock at home. Steadily, I used my fingers to shape the light into what looked like a nail and then guided the small spear into the hole of the doorknob until I heard a *click*. I smiled.

Flipping on the lights, I went inside and closed the door. The small white room looked like a miniature doctor's office with a single hospital bed, swivel chair, and clear jars filled with cotton balls and wooden sticks. A phone hung on the wall to the right of me.

I glanced at my watch. It would be 3:30 p.m. in Oregon. After I left Bountiful, Christian flew out to Portland where he would go back to training younger Guardians. This is what the Auran Council wanted while they figured out what to do with him. They were still upset that I'd killed the Vyken when it was Christian's responsibility. Completely stupid.

I picked up the receiver and dialed his cell. I couldn't wait to talk to him. He was the only one who really understood me. I would've called him sooner, but I couldn't ever escape our escort. It had been almost a week since I'd heard his voice.

After six rings it went to voice mail. I listened to the sound of his voice until I heard a beep. I debated whether or not to leave a message, but decided against it and hung up. As much as I hated to admit it, maybe it was better if we didn't speak for a while, at least until I figured out what was going on with me. I grimaced at a sudden pain in my heart.

Just then I heard laughter coming from down the hall. My sensitive hearing heard them talking about May, but in a good way. "Another Fury, can you imagine? Vykens will never bother us now," a girl said. I chuckled to myself. If only they knew the real power inside them.

I held still and waited for girls to pass by before I quietly opened the door and stuck my head out. The hall was empty. I stepped out and returned to my room. *I can do this*, I reasoned. This was only temporary, a few months, maybe a year of my life. I'd fix whatever was wrong with me, learn what I could at Lucent, and then get out of here and back to Christian.

I touched my lips, remembering Christian's kiss good-bye. It went beyond a kiss of lustful passion; it was tender, kind, and, although we had never said it to each other, full of love. I fell sideways on my bed, clutching a pillow to my chest. Guardians aren't supposed to get involved with their wards, but the moment I met him last year, I felt a connection. And as much as he tried to deny it at first, he did too.

But what if Christian received even a glimpse of my recent nightmares? Would he feel differently? A sharp knock at my door interrupted my thoughts.

"Llona?" a woman asked when I opened the door. She was older, maybe in her fifties, wearing tan slacks and a blue polo shirt. In her left hand she carried a black bag.

"Yes?" I replied.

"I'm Abigail Watts, the school nurse. I believe you missed an appointment."

I scrunched my face. "Right. Sorry. I completely forgot."

"No problem. I can draw your blood in here."

I hesitated. I don't know why I was afraid to have my blood drawn. It wasn't because I feared needles; I just felt funny giving away my blood to people I didn't know.

Abigail must have noticed my hesitation because she said, "Did Sophie explain why we need it?" She moved a short brown curl off her forehead. Dark circles hung under her eyes. I wondered what could cause a nurse to look so worn out in a school where students rarely got hurt.

"She did. Come in, Ms. Watts," I finally said.

"Please, call me Abigail. Have a seat on the bed, dear."

Abigail scooted over my vanity seat and sat across from me. From within her black bag she removed an IV bag, tubing, and a needle. "Rest your left arm on your thigh, face up, please."

I did as she asked. "So all the girls give blood once a month?"

Abigail nodded. "For several years now." She looked down. "What did you do to your knuckles?"

"Scraped 'em," I answered quickly and snuck my right hand under the pillow on my lap

"It looks bad. Do you want a bandage?"

"No. It's fine. Doesn't even hurt."

She gave me a strange look. "You look like her, you know."

"Who?"

"Your mother."

"You knew her?"

She paused, and I swore I saw sadness in her eyes, but just as quickly as it had come it was gone. "I did. I was a nurse when she was here years ago. You may want to look away."

I flinched when I felt the needle pierce my arm. "What was she like?"

Abigail plugged the IV tubing into the needle. Blood flowed from my arm into the clear plastic bag. "She was very kind, but difficult too," she said.

"How so?"

Abigail smiled. "Let's just say she had a mind of her own."

"Isn't that a good thing?"

"Not when you have a dying race you're trying to protect. Auras who try to do things their own way usually end up dead."

"But she was happy, more so than I've ever seen anyone else."

Abigail squeezed my hand gently. "I don't doubt that. I guess what I'm trying to say is, sometimes Auras have to think of themselves as part of something bigger. Just like a clock won't work if it's missing a gear, we can't afford to lose a single Aura. We mourned for your mother, truly, we did."

I stared at the blood leaving my arm. I had a sudden urge to draw it back into me.

"You've been through a lot, Llona. If you'll let us, we can help."

I considered this. I desperately wanted someone to talk to, and since no one else was around, I might as well try Abigail. She seemed nice enough. I started with the one question no one ever seemed to know the answer to: "Why can't I change my hair?"

"Excuse me?" she asked.

"My hair. It's always the same. I can't cut it or color it."

She laughed, but it was a kind laugh and not at all mocking. "It's the Light in our DNA. It affects some of us physically, changing certain parts of our makeup." She held up her left hand, revealing a sixth finger. "I think it did this to me." She curled it back up and placed her hand in her lap. "We all have things about us that we would like to change. Very few of us are ever happy with our appearance. Personally, I think your hair is lovely. There are lots of people who would love to have your hair, especially those who have lost theirs to cancer."

"I guess if you put it like that," I said, feeling stupid for asking the question.

"You're a special girl, Llona. Whatever happens here, just remember your focus: to become a better and stronger Aura. There are so few of us."

I was about to ask her what she meant when a head popped in the door.

"Am I interrupting?" May asked.

Abigail looked down at the bag, which was almost full. "Nope. I'm finished. Come on in." Carefully, she pulled out the needle and pushed a cotton ball onto my arm. "Hold this, please," she told me.

"How was dinner, May?" I asked. Abigail placed a Band-Aid over the cotton ball.

"Not bad."

"So, you're May?" Abigail asked. "The recently discovered Fury?"

"That's what everyone keeps saying," May said.

Abigail went to her and, inches from her face, said, "Be careful and know exactly who you are." She leaned away and smiled. "You girls have a good night and remember, if you ever need to talk to someone, my office is near the commons room."

As soon as she closed the door, May said, "That was weird."

"Completely," I agreed.

May slipped off her sandals and wiggled her toes into the tan carpet. "You're lucky you have carpet."

"Don't you?"

"No. I have the same hardwood that's in the halls."

I found it odd that my room would have carpet when our

rooms were so close. "Yeah, well I would rather have hardwood floors than a stinky room."

May inhaled deeply. "I don't know why you keep saying that. It smells fine in here. How's your hand?"

I looked down at my right knuckle and was surprised to see that it was almost healed.

May noticed too. "Wow! I can't believe how fast Auras heal."

"Neither can I," I said, knowing I had never healed this fast before.

Before I could think too much about it, May asked, "Have you called Jake yet?"

"Not yet."

"I still need to call my mom too. Some lady in the dining room said we could use the phone in the commons room or downstairs in the lobby after seven."

"Cool. Let's go. I'll try calling Christian after Jake." I turned around and almost ran into Sophie, who was standing in the doorway. I gasped.

"Call Christian?" she said, her eyes narrowing.

I stuttered. "I just wanted to see how he's doing, that's all."

Sophie closed the door. "I think we should have a talk, Llona."

May looked from me to her. "Maybe I should go—"

"Stay," Sophie said. "Llona may need to be reminded of what I'm about to tell her. Sit down, please."

Both May and I dropped to the bed and looked at each other.

"I have a confession, Llona. About you. And Christian." Sophie walked to the window and peered out. "I know Christian was staying at your house for a while—"

"It wasn't what it seemed!" I blurted. How could she have known? Jake wouldn't have said anything. I didn't think anyway.

Sophie turned around and gave me a kind smile. "I know, Llona. It was your special circumstance, I understand. You felt you were being hunted and thought a Vyken was after you. Having Christian close by made you feel safer. I know all about it."

I shook my head. "I didn't just think a Vyken was after me. I *knew* it."

"It's true," May said.

"Of course it is. Christian's report was very detailed, including the part where you—not him—killed the Vyken."

"That wasn't his fault," I said, my hands tightening into fists. "I snuck out of the house while he spoke to the police about . . ." I swallowed, unable to say Tracey's name. May looked at me sympathetically.

Sophie sat down on the vanity chair and placed her hand over mine. "This isn't about what happened. This is about your future."

"My future?"

"You formed a bond with Christian. Most Auras do with their Guardians, but I'm worried that your bond, because it was created under unusual circumstances, might be different than most."

My pulse began to race. Did she know we'd kissed?

Sophie took a deep breath. "I'm afraid you may feel more strongly for Christian than you should. It's only natural, after all. You haven't been properly trained, and you might think it's acceptable because of your parents' relationship, but," she motioned for me not to interrupt, "I want to reiterate that a relationship between an Aura and her Guardian is dangerous. Your mother knew this, but she ignored it."

"What are you talking about?"

Sophie withdrew her hand and looked away. "Laura came to me the night before she was married. She was having doubts about your father, Mark."

"No way," I said, knowing how much my parents loved each other.

"It's true. You see your mother kept having dreams—nightmares is more like it. In it she would see Mark dying, a hundred different ways. At first she thought she was just nervous because they were going against everything they'd been taught, but after a while, she became convinced it was a premonition. I told her if she felt that strongly about it, then she shouldn't marry him."

My mouth dropped open, but Sophie continued, "When we finished talking, Laura had decided to do just that. She told me that if their union meant Mark might die, then it wasn't worth it. However, the next day they were married. Mark must've said something to convince her otherwise."

"My parents were happy."

"Of course they were, but both of them are dead now, and I know that if they hadn't married, they'd be alive today."

"You don't know this."

"Maybe not, but I feel it. The only good thing to come out of their union was you."

"Why are you telling me all this?"

"Because I don't want to see what happened to her happen to you or Christian."

"But nothing's going on with me and Christian."

She stared at me for what felt like a very long time. "Good. Let's keep it that way."

"Well that should be easy to do, seeing how he's not here, right?"

Sophie tightened her lips and stood up. "Just remember what I said." She went to the door and opened it. Before going through it, she said, "If you're really in love—" Sophie stopped and cleared her throat, "I mean, in the future, when you think you've found your one true love, you will sacrifice everything for their safety."

The door closed. I stared at the back of it, trying to process Sophie's words.

May spoke first. "I'm sure your mom never regretted her decision to marry your dad."

I nodded, feeling numb. The smell of blood in my room smelled stronger somehow.

"Are you okay, Llona?" She rubbed my back.

I jumped up and inhaled deeply. "I'm fine. Just weirded out by my aunt. She can be so dramatic sometimes."

"Do you believe what she said?"

I turned my back to her. "I don't know. I don't really want to think about it."

May was quiet for a minute, then, "Do you still want to call Jake?"

I looked down at a full suitcase on the floor. "I'll call him tomorrow."

May stood up and nodded. "Will you be okay?"

"Of course."

She gave me a hug. "See you in the morning?"

I nodded.

* * * * *

After May left, I thought more of what Sophie had said while I unpacked. Could my dreams be some sort of premonition? But I hadn't seen Christian in them yet, and I hoped I never would. They were just crazy nightmares, that's all.

I resolved not to think about it anymore and finished unpacking my clothes into the small closet. I showered and got ready for bed. Still not tired, I began to read a book May had let me borrow. I was hoping it would put me to sleep, but when I finished at two in the morning, I knew it was useless.

Since that day I killed Mr. Steele, I hadn't been able to sleep.

Jake had bought me over-the-counter sleep medication when I was at home, but now even that didn't work. I swung my feet over the edge of the bed. The full moon spilled in through my window in great ribbons of light, pushing the darkness to the corners of the room. Seeing the moonlight was like remembering an old friend.

I dressed quickly and opened my window. Other than a few street lamps lighting up the sidewalks between buildings, Lucent was dark and quiet. I leaned out the window and scanned the side of the brick building. Within arm's reach was a fat pipe attached to the brick wall. I gave it a hard jerk to make sure it was sturdy. The last thing I wanted was to fall to my death on my first day.

I carefully slipped out the window and wrapped my hands around the pipe. My feet fumbled in the air until they found the metal clips that held the pipe to the bricks. *Now what?* I glanced down. I had at least thirty feet to go. Using arm strength, I slowly began to slide down the pipe until I could jump to the ground.

I kept to the shadows as I made my way between buildings, even though Sophie had said I could come and go as I pleased. Something told me that wandering around in the middle of the night wouldn't be approved. But the moment I was clear of the lights, I sprinted toward the wall surrounding the school. The light from the full moon made the muscles beneath my skin hum with energy, but it did nothing to increase my strength like it used to do. Christian had taught me months ago how to control my power so I could always have Light's full strength, regardless of the moon's cycle.

The wall's dark form grew taller the closer I came, making me feel claustrophobic. I ran faster alongside the wall, searching for an opening. It must have been at least a mile long. The only opening I found was where the wall came together at the front gates, which were, of course, now closed and, after a quick examination, impossible to climb due to their long vertical bars.

I was trapped. I took a deep breath and took off running again, this time toward a shed I had passed earlier. It was in the rear of the property and right next to the wall.

I turned around to make sure I was alone. The shadows of the trees and building stretched long until they disappeared into the moonlight. I moved to face forward, but just then swore I saw a shadow detach from another and move behind me. Stopping briefly, I turned around but saw and heard no one. *Chill out, Llona. No one is following you.*

I started forward again, spotting the shed's dark silhouette up ahead and picked up my pace. I was going to need a lot more speed to accomplish what I wanted to do.

Within feet of the shed, I leapt as high as I could. My fingers just barely caught the edge of the shed's roof, and I used my arms to pull me up the rest of the way. I straightened and looked out over the wall. Moonlight drenched the top of the forest, but none of its light was allowed through. The trees clung to the darkness as if it were its lifeblood. I suddenly wanted to be a part of it, to discover what lay hidden within.

I scooted back as far as I could on the shed's small roof, took a deep breath, and then sprinted five steps. In one giant leap I jumped from the shed and landed on top of the wall, swinging my arms hard to keep me balanced on its narrow top. As soon as I was sure I wasn't going to fall on my face, I let out the air I'd been holding.

The air was cool, and, as I breathed in, it raced into my lungs. The feeling of suffocation no longer plagued me. Smiling, I didn't just jump from the wall, I dove. And just before I reached the ground, I turned my dive into a summersault and rolled into a standing position.

I focused on the darkness ahead of me. I should be frightened. I shouldn't want to go in there. But I did. A sudden fierceness I couldn't explain propelled me forward. I was almost there, about to take a step into the inviting black, when I heard, "Stop!"

FOUR

I TURNED AROUND, STARTLED TO HEAR A VOICE. A BOY RAN toward me, but as he drew closer I could see he was hardly a boy. He looked to be nineteen, maybe twenty, with a buzz haircut. His eyes were big and dark, shadowed by thick eyebrows.

"What are you doing out here?" he said. His posture was stiff, upright, like a drill sergeant.

"Running. What are you doing out here?" I countered.

"Guarding the school. How did you get out here anyway?"

"I jumped over the Great Wall of China, and not too easily, I might add."

His demeanor relaxed. "I would have liked to have seen that. Now, really, you should go back inside. It's not safe for you."

"Not happening. I need to go running."

"There's a track on the inside. Go there."

I shook my head again. "Too confining."

He looked me up and down as if searching for another reason I'd be out here other than sheer desire. "Who are you?"

"Llona Reese. I just got here today."

He smiled or smirked—the faint moonlight held the truth from me. "The special Llona Reese. My name's Jackson. I knew your father."

"How's that?"

"He trained me for a short time when I was younger. Good man. Very talented."

A Guardian. I should've known they'd be around with their special hearing and amazing eyesight. "So you're out here patrolling?" I asked.

Jackson glanced behind me. I couldn't help but admire his strong Roman nose. "That's right. It's not safe out here for Auras," he said.

"I was told I would be safe."

"You're safe in there," he said, nodding his head toward the school.

"Why not out here?"

He looked at me like I was an idiot. "This is a school for Auras. Don't you think a Vyken might want to hang out, looking for, um, I don't know, someone like you—an Aura who doesn't like to follow the rules?"

"I'm not afraid of Vykens," I said. The weird thing was I wasn't. Knowing I could kill one was strangely comforting.

"Just because you killed one, doesn't mean they aren't dangerous."

I looked at him, surprised.

"Yeah, I know what you did," Jackson said. "The other Auras may not, but most Guardians do. We're all aware of how Christian screwed up."

Heat rose to my face. "He did not screw up! I snuck away so no one else would get hurt." *Calm down*, I told myself. *I don't have to tell this guy anything.*

"It doesn't matter what you did. Christian should've been there. It should've been him who killed the Vyken, not you."

"Why?"

"Because you're an Aura. You're incapable of killing."

It was my turn to look at him as if he were the idiot. "But I did kill one, and I was just fine. In fact, I liked it." Hearing myself say this was the one thing tonight that had managed to frighten me.

"Then there's something wrong with you," he said, as if that was the only explanation.

"I don't have time for this." I took a step toward the shadows.

Jackson grabbed me by the arm. His grip was incredibly strong. "I can't let you do that."

I shrugged his arm away. "You don't have a choice. I'm not a prisoner."

He considered this. "Fine, but if you insist on running out here then I'm going with you."

"You sure you can keep up?" I took off before he could answer.

Darkness swallowed me the moment I entered the old forest. There was something strangely seductive about the way the dark felt against my skin, cool and tingly, and I liked the way it made me feel as if I was running faster than I actually was. Before I could stop myself, I began to giggle.

I raced through the trees, sometimes swinging from a branch to help myself over thick shrubs or dips in the landscape. There was nothing to slow my pace except for Jackson, who wasn't doing too bad of a job keeping up. I turned a sharp corner into a small clearing and stopped abruptly. The forest felt different here, even smelled different, like burnt pine needles, and I had the strange feeling that I'd crossed over into someone else's territory.

Behind me, Jackson said, panting, "That was incredible! I never run like—" he froze as if he were sensing the same thing I was. He stepped in front of me and returned to his soldier-like stance.

Not more than twenty feet in front of us, a wall of trees, black as night, appeared to shift. Something moved within it. My pulse quickened when a throaty growl, low and deep, filled the air around us. The hair on my arms rose.

"Run," Jackson whispered.

I was about to take him up on his offer when a voice said, "I wouldn't do that if I were you." From the shadows, a Vyken in his pure form stepped out. Air caught in my chest, and I almost choked on it.

The Vyken wore normal clothes, jeans and a dark T-shirt, but there was nothing normal about him. A leather-like skin, black in color, pulled tight around his face, but in some areas the skin stretched too far, creating cracks and spaces where yellowed bone, specifically on his cheek bones, shined through.

As horrible as his appearance was, it was nothing compared to his dark, sunken eyes. They begged for an audience, a theater production of the worst kind of violence imaginable. I stumbled back, a wave of nausea threatening to collapse me, but Jackson caught my arm.

"Get back, Vyken," Jackson said.

I forced my gaze down and stared at the ground while I tried to overcome the effect the Vyken had over me. I shook my head, wondering again why this was. Auras couldn't "feel" Vykens. At least that's what Sophie had told me, and my mother had been killed by one whom she considered a close friend, so obviously she couldn't. Christian once spoke of an Aura in the thirties who could do the same thing as me. "It's a gift, Llona," he'd told me. Looking at the Vyken in front of me, I wondered if it was more of a curse.

The Vyken raised a leathery finger toward me. "I want that one." A string of saliva dripped from his deformed lip.

I straightened, my strength returned, and stepped next to Jackson. "I'm all gristle," I said, "but you're welcome to try."

Jackson glanced at me sideways. "Shut your mouth, Llona."

I looked at Jackson and then at the Vyken. A searing heat,

much like before, began to course through my blood until I felt like killing them both.

The Vyken parted his lips and attempted a smile, but his worn skin wouldn't stretch that far. "I like you," he said.

I opened my mouth, all set for a perfect, sarcastic retort, when the Vyken lunged for me. I fell backward with the Vyken practically on my chest. His face was inches from mine, and he snapped his jaws wide, tearing the skin on his face. I barely managed to hold him back, giving Jackson enough time to kick him off me.

As a Guardian, Jackson was strong, more so than a normal man. This strength, handed down from father to son, matched most Vykens.

The Vyken rolled into a crouching position, and when he looked up, he saw only me. I scrambled backward as he leapt into the air, but before he could touch me, Jackson tackled him. They tumbled to the ground, the Vyken kicking and clawing at every part of Jackson.

I jumped to my feet, angling for a position where I could be of some use, but the two were too tangled for me to do anything but watch in horror. Finally Jackson kicked the Vyken from him, and I prepared to throw a ball of Light the size of my fist into his chest, but Jackson got in my way again.

"Move it, Jackson!" I said.

He looked back at me and grinned. "I've got this." He swung his fist, connecting it with the Vyken's jaw, but when he swung again the Vyken disappeared only to reappear behind him in less than a blink of an eye. The Vyken picked up Jackson and tossed him into a nearby tree. Jackson fell to the ground, moaning.

"You were saying?" I mumbled and crouched low ready to fight the Vyken who had refocused his attention on me.

"I can't wait to taste you," he said. Part of his torn flesh flapped as he spoke.

I didn't bother with retorts. I just wanted to fight.

Before the Vyken could lunge for me, I attacked him, proud to see his eyes widen in surprise. I swiped his legs out from under him, and dropped my elbow into his face. He cried out and shoved me away. I stumbled forward, almost tripping. I was about to turn around when the Vyken took hold of my hair and jerked me onto my back. He pounced onto my chest, forcing all the air from my lungs. I sputtered and gasped as I tried to suck air back in, but I was also trying to keep the Vykens hand from squeezing my throat.

And then everything changed.

A voice I never thought I would hear at Lucent, said, "Have you forgotten everything I taught you?"

Through my struggling, I looked over. Christian was leaning against the same tree Jackson had been thrown into moments ago. My Christian. Here. Jackson was standing next to him, rolling his shoulders back. I wanted to smile, to laugh, and to cry, but my emotional moment was ruined when I got punched in the face.

"Aren't you going to help her?" Jackson said.

"Nope. She's got this. Right, Llona?"

I smiled inwardly. *Of course, I've got this.* With the Vyken still straddling me, I bucked hard, knocking him off balance just enough for me to squirm out from under him. When the Vyken looked back at me, I kicked him hard in the jaw and then jumped to my feet, giving me a few precious seconds to create three tight balls of Light. When the Vyken charged me, I tossed them, drilling each one into his face.

By the time he reached me, his face was smoking and one eye was melting from its socket. I flipped forward, my hands landing on the ground just in front of the Vyken, and when my feet locked around his neck, I used my momentum to swing me up so I was sitting on the Vyken's shoulders. I ignited my hands with Light and clutched the Vyken's head, forcing Light into him. The last time I tried this was on Mr. Steele, and to do it I had to suck the lights from the school to have enough power to kill him, but, feeling the way I did right now, I knew I had plenty without having to borrow it.

Light poured into the Vyken until he began to crack and peel. It wasn't long before he exploded into dust, and without him under me, I fell to the ground.

Christian laughed. "That was the coolest thing I've ever seen! Good job."

Jackson turned to him, his chest heaving. "Are you mental? She could've been killed."

Christian shook his head. "I wouldn't have let that happen. Besides, this was something Llona could handle."

I brushed myself off and stood up. I couldn't stop smiling. Christian stood less than ten feet away. I wanted to throw my arms around him, feel my lips against his, but I was all too aware of Jackson. "What are you doing here?" I asked, barely containing my excitement.

"Change of plans." The corners of his mouth were twitching like he was trying to keep from smiling, but he failed. The dimple I'd fallen in love with almost a year ago appeared on his cheek, and it sucked me toward him like a black hole. I stumbled forward and reached for him, no longer caring who was around, but when I did, his eyes grew big and he shook his head, just barely enough for me to notice. I brought my arms back to my side.

"Good to see you again, Llona," he said and held out his hand.

I looked down at it. A handshake? Is he serious? I searched his eyes. He was very serious. Fine. I could play this game.

I cleared my throat and said in my most formal voice. "It's good to see you too." I shook his hand. It was warm and gripped my palm tight. Only when Jackson began to speak did he let go.

"Since when did a Guardian's job involve teaching an Aura to fight?"

"She mostly taught herself, and it took me a while to admit it, but Llona's a very capable fighter." Christian's eyes never left mine. "What's wrong, Jackson? Afraid of a little competition?"

"Hardly, but when the Council hears about you encouraging Llona to kill a Vyken, you'll both be gone."

This made Christian turn away from me. He looked at Jackson, worry lines creasing onto his face. "Come on, Jackson. No harm was done. Please don't tell them."

"What's the big deal?" I said.

Jackson looked at me. "Are you kidding? You just killed a Vyken." He waited for me to say something, but when I didn't, he continued, "By fighting. Auras aren't supposed to fight, let alone fight a Vyken. It's the Guardian's job." He glanced at Christian. "Seriously, C. The Council is going to skin you alive."

"Actually, Jackson," I said, "you were here too. Why didn't you kill him?"

This made him pause, and he blew air through his nose. "Fine. I won't say anything this time, but it better not happen again. And you need to stay in the school. It's not safe out here."

"I'll go out whenever I want," I said but instantly regretted my words. Where had that come from?

Jackson smirked. "You must've had your hands full with this spoiled one, C. I'm surprised they let her come to Lucent with that mouth."

Christian balled his hands into fists, but before Jackson could notice, I turned around and started for the school. "I'm going back. Enough fun for one night."

Jackson laughed. "I knew you were scared."

I kept walking.

Behind me I heard Christian say, "I'll see her back."

"She's all yours," Jackson said.

A moment later Christian caught up to me. "Sorry about that. Jackson's always been a little rough around the edges, but he's harmless."

"How long have you known him?"

"Since we first started training together when I was eight. He's a year older."

I didn't say anything else, wanting to put enough distance between us and Jackson to where he wouldn't be able to hear us. After a minute I glanced behind me. When I didn't see Jackson, I asked again, my voice low, "Seriously. Why are you here?"

He glanced behind us, seeming to share my thoughts, and whispered, "Right before I was to leave for Oregon, I got a call from your aunt. She told me to come out here instead of returning to the training facility."

"Why?"

He shrugged. "I don't know. Maybe I'm in more trouble than I think." He smiled like it wasn't a big deal.

I stopped and looked at him, really looked. He was the same Christian, but he seemed stronger somehow, more sure of himself. When I noticed he was staring back at me the same way, I quickly glanced away, afraid he'd see something new he didn't like. "Are you sure it's a good idea for you to be here? With me?"

He looked around one more time before he took me in his arms, hugging me tight. "It's the best. It about killed me to say good-bye to you."

"I know the feeling." I breathed him in. The smell of cologne, mixed with the smell of cotton and Tide, filled my nostrils. Instead of wondering how I was able to smell his laundry detergent, I remained still, my head resting on his shoulder.

We stood like that for a while, alone in the dark, listening to the quiet rustlings of the forest. He sighed and leaned away. "This is going to be harder than I thought."

I panicked. This was it. He could sense that something was wrong with me. "Please don't say it. I know—"

Christian's mouth found mine. His lips were warm and soft, moving over mine, yet the deep kiss held more passion than ever before. I melted into his arms, held in place only by his tightening grip, pressing me closer to his chest. When we finally broke apart, he said, "I wish we had more time, but I have to go."

I barely nodded, my knees weak.

He kissed me again. "We have to be careful, Llona," he said when he let me go. "No one can know we're together or they'll kick you out."

More secrets. My hand went to my neck, to rub or hide my bite marks. "Maybe we should stay away from each other while you're here."

His eyes widened, and he took my hand. "What? No, that's not what I mean. I've missed you so much. I don't want to be apart anymore. We just have to be careful is all. That's something we're used to, right?"

I didn't know what to say. My brain and my heart were fighting each other.

Looking into my eyes, Christian raised his hand to push aside my hair, but when I realized he was about to expose my bite marks, I panicked and stepped back.

"What's wrong?" he said

I quickly smiled and started walking again. "Nothing. I should probably get back too. Vykens outside of the school and all." How could I ever tell him about the poison inside me? If it repulsed me, what would Christian, or anyone else for that matter, think?

After a moment I realized Christian wasn't following me. I stopped and turned around. He was a ways back studying something on the ground. "What is it?" I asked.

Christian stood up, holding something plastic in his hand. His face was pale, but I couldn't tell if it was from the moonlight spilling in from the tops of the trees or something else. "Do you know what this is?" he asked, moving toward me.

As he drew closer, holding the object up, I knew exactly what it was. "Sure. It's an IV bag. The nurse used one on me tonight when she drew my blood. How did it get out here?"

"I don't know, but I don't like it."

I took it from him and held it to the light. "There's still a little blood in it," I said and shivered. "You don't think a Vyken has access to our blood, do you? 'Cause that would be really bad."

Christian looked all around us, his face serious. "It would be bad. Even worse than finding a Vyken outside of the school."

"I take it that's not normal?"

"It happens, but it's rare. Looking back, though, Jackson didn't seem surprised. I'll ask him about it." He took my hand. "Come on. Let's get you back."

"So how'd you know I'd be out here?" I asked, walking alongside him.

Christian chuckled. "Your first night in what you would consider a strange place? I knew you'd escape. I just wasn't sure what time. I've been out here for a while."

"Did Jackson know?"

"No. I got here at about eleven. He was already out patrolling."

The wall was just ahead.

"I bet Guardians love being our babysitters."

"It's not like that." He smiled and squeezed my hand.

When we reached the wall, he turned to me. "I'll be

looking for you, and we'll meet whenever we can."

I forced a smile, wondering how I'd be able to keep everything from him.

Christian looked up. "You want help over?"

Because I was still buzzed from killing the Vyken, I felt like I could jump over myself, but I wasn't about to tell him that. "That'd be great."

He pulled me in for one more hug and a quick kiss. "I'll see you soon. And please don't come out here again, at least until I know more about the Vyken situation."

"Sure," I said and stepped on his clasped hands. He lifted me to the point where I could reach the edge of the wall. I pulled myself up the rest of the way. "See you," I said and jumped to the other side. I didn't want our good-bye to linger. It only made me that much sadder.

That night, when my eyelids closed and the sandman, who looked a lot like a Vyken, invaded my dreams carrying a severed head in one hand and dragging a headless corpse in the other, I began to scream. Not because of the horrifying image, but because it was Christian's head he held, his blue eyes open and his mouth forming the word, *Oh!*

FIVE

"There must be a mistake," I told Ms. Ravitz the next morning. *Please let this be a mistake*, I prayed. There were at least twenty twelve-year-old girls in the classroom staring at me.

She looked down at my paper, tapping it with a pen. "No. This is the right class: Nineteenth Century Auras."

"But Ms. Ravitz," I said, "I'm eighteen and these guys are . . . little. This has to be a mistake."

"Have you ever taken this class before?" The glasses on her face slipped to the end of her nose. With one push of her middle finger they returned to their rightful place, making her brown eyes appear bigger than they really were.

"I've never had this class before. Remember? I'm new here." I had met her just a couple of days ago at dinner, but now she acted like she didn't know who I was.

She looked down at my schedule again. "Llona Reese. That's right! Of course you're in my class. I know it may seem awkward with these younger girls, but this class is important. Please take your seat."

I turned slowly, still not fully recovered from last night's nightmare, which seemed to have drained me mentally. My only defense was forcing myself not to think about it. I stared at the girls. They were all dressed the same: brown slacks and navy blue polo shirts. I looked down at my own Levis and white cotton shirt. I didn't remember anyone saying anything about a dress code.

Ms. Ravitz seemed to have read my mind. "Girls over eighteen can wear what they want within reason," she said. "Now please sit down so we can get started."

I went to the only desk available in the middle of the classroom. As soon as I sat down, the girl in front of me turned around, eyeing me with her green eyes. Her blonde hair was pulled back into a French braid. She was very beautiful.

I was about to smile at her, when her small mouth opened and said, "Sorry we're not good enough for you." The girls around her giggled.

"What? No, that's not what I—"

"No talking please," Ms. Ravitz said. "Please open your book to page eighty-seven. Llona, you're a little behind, so I want you to try and catch up during the next few weeks, okay?"

I nodded my head, wondering if this was how all my other classes were going to be.

It turned out it was. Sophie had crammed as many classes as she could into my schedule. Most of them were with younger girls except for PE, Advanced Light Techniques, and Auras and Their Guardians.

I was looking forward to PE, but when I got there, the teacher, Ms. Haddy, handed me a manual and told me to read. I stared at it in total shock. A manual on physical education?

While Ms. Haddy and the rest of the girls began aerobics, I sat down and skimmed its pages. Basically all it talked about was how *not* to be better than others and how being competitive was wrong. We were all equal, the book said. We should support each other and always work together. *Right.*

I opened the cover and searched the publication information

for a date. 1941. I couldn't help but wonder what Auras were like before then.

The day finally ended. I was in my room reading a history book, or really, trying to distract myself from remembering the nightmare, when I heard a knock on my door. "Come in," I said.

The same Lizen girl who served me at meal times entered my room. Her brown hair was pulled into a tight ponytail, and her aqua-colored eyes matched the shimmer of a thin strip of scales that ran from the top of her right temple all the way to her chin. It was actually pretty cool looking.

The girl wrung her hands together, and she looked everywhere in the room except for at me. "I've come to see if you need any fresh towels," she said. She was almost my height and, if I had to guess, a little younger than me.

"Um, no, I don't think so," I said looking toward the bathroom.

She bowed her head and then turned to go.

"Wait!" I called after her.

She turned around. "Yes?"

"What's your name?"

She hesitated. "My name?"

"Yeah. I'm Llona and, as you probably already know, I'm new here."

"Yes. I know. My name is Tessa."

"Do you like it here?"

"It is satisfactory."

"Do you ever go out?"

"Out?" She finally looked at me. "Out where?"

The hopelessness in her eyes created a pit in my stomach. "Out. You know, to the library, movies, mall?"

She shook her head. "Our appearance would not be accepted."

I sat up straighter on my bed. "Of course it would. Believe me, I've seen stranger."

"You have?"

I nodded. "I met a guy once whose entire face had been tattooed blue."

A saw a spark in her eye, but as soon as it appeared it was gone. "I must return to my duties," she said.

"Okay. Thanks for stopping by."

She turned to leave, but I stopped her again. "Wait, Tessa. One last question."

"Yes?" She kept her hand on the door.

"Does it smell like blood in here?"

Her face turned a pale shade of white, and I thought she was going to pass out. Before I could get to her, she was already out my door and rushing down the hall.

SIX

The next couple of weeks passed quickly. When Christian had said I was behind, he wasn't kidding. I didn't know a thing about Auras. Most of my class time was spent trying to look up terms I'd never heard before like *resplendent* and *ebullient*, or other times I was scrambling to look up certain events in our history just so I could follow a conversation. There was so much to absorb that by the weekend, I was numb.

It was probably good that I was busy. Whenever I was around others, my temperament was short, and I often snapped at people. It took all the strength I had not to get into fights with the other girls, even though they hadn't really done anything to me. This gave fuel to the fire that I was a freak. Sometimes I found it easier to just stay in my room, where I wouldn't have to worry about the anger that seemed to come out of nowhere.

Christian had tried to get together with me several times, secretly of course, but I always found an excuse to stay away from him. This hurt a lot, but every time I saw him, even in passing, I was reminded of his severed head, a nightmare I continued to have. If there were even a chance of something bad happening to him because of the way he felt about me, then I wouldn't risk it. He meant too much to me.

At least I had his letters. I should've asked him to stop, but

I couldn't. Every day Christian had somehow managed to leave one under my pillow. I suspected Tessa had something to do with it.

I picked up the most recent one and read it again:

Leona,

I saw you today, but you didn't see me. You were outside with May at lunch and it took every bit of strength I had not to go to you, scoop you up, and carry you away. I need to see you and soon. Can you meet me tonight? Jackson and I have been patrolling every night and haven't come across another Vyken. Jackson said it doesn't happen often, so . . . if you think you can get away, come at 2:00 a.m. on the south end of the wall. I'll be watching for you.

Can't wait to see you,

Christian

I folded the note and clutched it tightly. I couldn't avoid him forever. Maybe I could think of something to say or do to make him not want to be near me. I wished he could see inside my head, feel the darkness lurking there. That would be enough to drive him away forever.

Because I had too much to do, I skipped the outing the girls were going on to New York City and stayed in my room, even missing lunch. It was well into the afternoon when I heard, "Can I come in?"

I looked up. May was standing in my open doorway. "Please do," I said. "It's so good to see you. I've been going crazy." I tossed my book to the side.

May sat on my bed, staring at a stack of papers, my homework. "I know. I've barely seen you all week. Not even at meals."

"I've been eating either in my room or the commons area while I study. How do you like Dr. Han?"

Her face brightened. "He's amazing! I can't believe how much I've learned. Watch this." She swirled her hand in a complete circle until a ball of fire appeared in her palm.

"Whoa! That is awesome."

She blew it out. "Right?"

"What are your other classes like?"

"Not as good as the class with Dr. Han. There are only a few other Furies, so our classes are small, and the other girl and two boys are a few years younger than me."

"Boys? Where do they stay?"

"With the Guardians just outside the gates in Waverly Hall. Do you like your classes?" she asked.

"Most of them are okay. It's PE I can't stand." I stretched my legs out.

"Really? I thought that would be your favorite."

"Not here. All we're allowed to do is either run, aerobics, or dance, nothing competitive. It sucks."

"Running is competitive."

"Not the way we do it. We have to run in strict formation. I can barely stand it."

May laughed. "How lame!"

"I know."

May picked up one of my books and flipped through its pages. "How about you put off studying for one night and come hang out in my room? We'll watch a movie or something."

I didn't hesitate. "I'd love to." I needed a distraction before 2:00 a.m. came.

"Too bad we can't invite Christian," May said. She saw him the day after I had and was super excited to have someone from home at Lucent. She spoke to him quite often. "I mean, unless you believe everything Sophie said, which I think is just crazy. You guys are meant for each other."

I stared down at my homework. "I don't know."

"He asks a lot about you," May said. "I think he suspects something's up."

"I just need some time to sort things out, you know?"

May nodded. "Maybe the dance next weekend will help you figure out what you want."

I looked up at her. "Dance?"

May grinned. "I forget you weren't there. The other morning Sophie announced that one of the all-boy schools from New York City is coming for a summer dance. I can't wait! I bet they're gorgeous."

I stood up and grabbed a blanket to take to May's room. "Sounds like fun," I said and meant it. Maybe that's just what I needed to get my mind off Christian.

On the way to her room, May asked, "Are you sleeping any better?"

I had confessed my sleeping problems to her on my second day at Lucent. "Actually, it's getting worse. I can't fall asleep before four in the morning."

"How do you get up for class?" She opened the door to her room.

"I don't know. You'd think I wouldn't be able to, but surprisingly it's not that hard. I think I might just give up on sleep all together."

"Why don't you talk to the nurse about it? Despite her weirdness, she seemed nice enough." May turned the television on and tossed some pillows onto the floor.

"Maybe I will. Speaking of weird . . ." I told her about Tessa and how she had almost passed out when I asked her why my room smelled like blood.

"What did she say?"

"Nothing. She just turned around and ran off. I've been so busy that I haven't had a chance to talk to her since."

"That's odd, but really, Llona, I don't smell anything."

"I guess it's just me," I said, making a mental note not to bring it up again.

I contemplated telling May about what had really happened with Christian the night we arrived, specifically about me fighting the Vyken, but decided against it. No point involving her in my "crime." Besides, it would probably scare her to know that a Vyken was so close to the school. I knew she was still having her own nightmares about Mr. Steele. Just last week I'd heard her screaming at two in the morning. I'd gone to her and insisted on staying in her room until she fell asleep. No, I wouldn't worry her.

At ten o'clock the bells chimed, indicating that it was time to turn out the lights. I looked over at May who was already asleep. Very quietly, I turned off the TV, tucked her in, and left the room. The halls were dark and empty. I could hear voices from within a few of the rooms, as girls were still awake, enjoying the weekend. And by the smell of it, a couple of them were painting their nails.

I picked up my history book and began to read, but by midnight, I needed a major break. I only had a couple of hours before I was to meet Christian. My apprehension grew. Over and over I practiced what I'd say to him. "We need some time apart. It's best for everyone." I dropped my head into my hands. That sounded so stupid. He'd see right through it.

I stretched out on the bed and shook my hands. My muscles were tingling like they normally did when it was a full moon. I stood up and went to the window, but when I stuck my head out and looked up, the sky was black. No moon. Odd.

The forest's dark, uneven silhouette against the night sky

made it look like a sleeping monster with spikes on its back. It was a monster I was drawn to. It had taken all the strength I had to avoid the forest since that night with Jackson and Christian, despite the fact that we had encountered a Vyken.

I quickly closed the window and moved back, but even as I did so, I knew my attempt at staying away was futile. It had been too long, and my burning desire to be a part of the darkness needed to be quenched.

I didn't think. I only escaped. I headed straight for the shed and this time easily jumped to its roof and over to the top of the wall. I inhaled deeply. The smell of pine and something else tickled my nose. I jumped from the wall and breathed in again. Blood. Fresh blood. Not like the odor in my room. And it was everywhere, all over. Somehow I was smelling the lifeblood of every creature in the forest. What was happening to me?

I glanced behind me, back to where the sleeping Auras lay. I should be with them.

The cry of an animal rose from the forest floor. I could no sooner ignore it than a lion could spare its prey. Something inside me, dark and foreign, needed to feel its life in my hands. I sprinted away from Lucent. My muscles hummed with Light's energy but also with something else. A new strength like nothing I had ever experienced before.

The temperature inside the forest was a few degrees cooler. The cold and the darkness pressed against my skin, as if it were trying to get inside me. I fought it for just a moment, before I relaxed.

It was then that my whole perspective changed. I was no longer *looking* at the darkness; I was inside it, an actual part of it, like the forest was one giant organism. I could feel the night's pulse. Its beat pulled creatures from their holes, from their caves, from all the black crevices that protected them from day's light. Here in the blackest of black, hidden beneath the shadows of the old trees, creatures ruled the forest, and I was a part of them.

I stopped abruptly, my heart pounding, palms sweating. I was terrified. What was wrong with me? I slumped against a tree and reached up to the two little holes in my neck. They felt swollen.

My sensitive ears perked. Not far away two voices spoke. I welcomed the distraction and headed in their direction. Maybe it was Jackson or Christian.

I moved as quickly and quietly as I could through the thick brush. Peering around a tree, I listened closely. I no longer heard voices talking. Instead, I heard the faint sounds of something moving in the forest toward me. A moment later a Vyken appeared, at least I think it was a Vyken. My body had reacted but not by much, sort of like I'd just spun around a few times.

I didn't take the time to wonder why this was; I was too busy focusing on his human-like appearance. If he looked normal than he must've had an Aura's blood recently. I inhaled deeply, my whole body filling with an intense rage.

I looked around for whomever he had been talking to but saw no one. The Vyken passed by me, unaware of my location just twenty feet away. I moved out of my hiding place, my footsteps as quiet as his, and with each step, my anger grew. Whatever was happening to me was because of a Vyken. I had killed two before and felt confident I could do it again if given the chance.

I really wanted that chance.

SEVEN

"YOU LOOK LOST!" I CALLED, AND I SMILED WHEN THE VYKEN visibly jerked.

He turned around. His face was narrow with a long thin nose and high nostrils that were flaring—unless this was his permanent expression. I didn't plan on letting him live long enough to find out.

His mouth opened, revealing a growing set of fangs. "You're the one that's lost, Riding Hood. Didn't your grandmother tell you to stay away from the woods?"

"That's all you've got? Your Nana's bedtime stories?"

The Vyken began to circle around me. He was at least a head taller, and for a brief moment I wondered if maybe this had been a mistake—an awful impulsive move that might have severe consequences.

Oh well. Too late now.

The Vyken looked toward the school. His head tilted. "If it wasn't for your foolish behavior, I'd guess you were an Aura."

"That's for me to know and you to find out."

He glanced around. "Do your little Light buddies know you're out here picking a fight?"

I snorted, then laughed. "You think any of them would come out here in the dark?" There I go again. Why was I bashing the Auras, like I was better than them?

The Vyken frowned, forcing his nostrils up to an impossible length. "If you aren't an Aura, then what are you?"

I brought my fists up. "What does it matter? Just fight me already!"

"You want death?" He took two steps toward me.

"Yes. Yours."

He laughed. "You couldn't kill a rat."

In one leap, I cleared the distance between us and kicked him in the face. He stumbled backward, startled, but quickly regained his composure. "I don't have time for this," he said. He attempted to connect his hardened fist with my face, but I easily dodged it. I swung my leg around toward his back, but he was ready. He ducked and used both hands to shove me into a tree.

I gasped as air exploded from my chest. While I sucked air back in, I created a tight ball of Light and tossed it at him. It cut through his jacket and into his side. He doubled over. "What the—"

Rushing him again, my earlier anger now turned to jubilation. I was actually enjoying this!

In my mind, I calculated my next move, sure it would end the fight in my favor. I was about to execute the plan when the Vyken caught me off guard. Faster than I could blink, he appeared behind me, and a hairy, cold arm wrapped around my throat.

I frantically reached behind me in an attempt to get at his face, but he leaned away. Unable to reach his head, I placed my hands on his arm and ignited them with Light. He cried out, but instead of loosening his grip, he tightened harder, making my Light sputter until it died.

His elongated face was inches from mine, and his hot breath steamed my neck. Long fangs extended in his open mouth and his head drew back like a cobra preparing to strike.

A burst of red exploded behind my eyes, and I felt myself losing consciousness. I was about to throw my head back as hard as I could in hopes of breaking his nose, when all of a sudden his body was pulled off me. I collapsed to the ground, gasping for air.

I thought it might've been Christian, but then I heard a deep and unfamiliar voice say, "You've made your last mistake, Kull."

The Vyken stood up and brushed himself off. "Liam. I heard you were around."

"I see you're still getting yourself into trouble," the other man, Liam, said.

Kull said, "I didn't start this fight."

Liam stepped next to me. "Do you expect me to believe that?"

When my vision cleared, I looked up. Liam was tall with broad shoulders. He looked young—early twenties maybe—with short black hair and strong features, but his powerful presence suggested he was much older.

"Believe what you want," Kull said. "I was only defending myself."

Liam studied Kull for a moment. "Why are you out here?"

"Why are *you* out here?" Kull countered.

Liam straightened, making him appear even taller. "If you don't answer, you know what I'll do to you, right?"

Kull's eyes flashed to the forest and then to Liam, as if judging the distance. He blinked once and bolted for the nearest group of trees. Liam reached behind his back and unsheathed a weapon. He whipped his arm forward, releasing a crescent-shaped blade. It sliced through the air until it struck Kull's neck, cutting his head cleanly off his body.

While the dust of Kull's body exploded, Liam turned to

me. His dark eyes regarded me steadily. When he finally spoke, I expected to hear sympathy, maybe an, "Are you all right?" but instead I got, "You need to get back to Lucent."

I opened my mouth to speak, but coughed instead. My throat still ached from being squeezed. Barely louder than a whisper, I said, "Why's that?"

"Auras don't leave the school."

I stood up and cleared my throat. "Who said I was an Aura?"

"Please. You reek of Light," he paused and looked me up and down, "and something else. What's wrong with you?"

I was about to deck him when I realized that my head was spinning, but faintly, like I'd stood up too quickly. "You're a Vyken," I said.

His eyes widened. "Wow. I haven't been called that in a long time."

"Why? Is that too nice of a term?" I lowered into a defensive position in case he attacked, but he was frowning and staring at me funny. "Why are you looking at me like that?" I asked.

He shook his head with a puzzled expression. "There's something wrong with you. I can't quite put my finger on it."

"There's something wrong with me? You're the monster."

"So you say." He glanced behind me. "You need to go. It's not safe."

"Don't you want to kill me, drink my blood so you can suck all the precious Light right out of me?"

"That's what you automatically assume, isn't it?"

"Why wouldn't I? That's what you suckers live for."

For the first time, his calm expression cracked. "If you are so anxious to die, I would be happy to oblige, but right now I have more important things to do than deal with a confused Aura." With one downward sweep of his arm, his whole body twisted, then swirled as if he were turning into a small tornado.

In a burst of wind that ruffled my hair, he was gone.

"I'm not confused!" I called after him. I stood alone in the quiet forest, wondering what I'd just seen. A Vyken who can disappear like wind and pass up the chance to kill an Aura?

I turned around and walked back to the school, keeping my head on a swivel in case any more Vykens appeared. So much for that being a rarity. Someone had lied to Christian, and I couldn't wait to find out who. Not only that, but what Liam had said shook me up. How could he have known I felt confused?

I was almost to the wall when I heard, "What are you doing out here again?" I glanced over. Jackson was jogging toward me.

"Hey," I said and kept walking.

"I can't believe you came out here again after what happened."

"Believe it."

"Could you stop walking for a second?" he asked.

I stopped and turned around.

"Hey? What happened to your face?"

I reached up and felt a swollen cheekbone.

"Like you said, it's not safe out here."

Jackson grabbed my arms. "What happened? Did a Vyken attack you?"

"I attacked it." I started walking again.

"You did what?"

"I attacked it," I said, louder this time.

"What were you thinking? You could have been killed!"

"I'm still breathing."

He stopped following me. "I'm going to have to report this."

This got my attention, and I whirled around. "Please don't say anything. I'll be more careful next time, I promise."

"Why do you keep coming out here anyway?"

Now there's the real question of the day. "I don't know. It just feels so stuffy in there," I nodded my head toward the school. "Know what I mean?"

"But that's where you belong. You're safe and protected there."

"I don't need protection."

He reached up and touched my cheek lightly. "Obviously you do," he said.

I pushed his hand away. "You should see the other guy. What's left of him anyway."

"You killed another Vyken?"

"Um, technically, no, but I distracted him long enough so another Vyken could kill him."

Jackson looked at me skeptically. "What?"

"Twisted, right? But I'm telling the truth. This other Vyken came and killed the one I was fighting. And then he sort of, well, he turned into this crazy wind and disappeared."

Jackson stiffened. "What did you just say?"

"Which part?"

"The Vyken wind part. Actually, just start from the beginning. What exactly happened?"

I told him about my fight with Kull and how Liam had shown up. "After Liam insulted me, he just disappeared, literally."

"That's not possible," Jackson said.

"It's very possible. It happened right before my eyes."

"You mean you *think* you saw it," he said.

I rolled my eyes. "I know what I saw. Christian would believe me," I said like a five-year-old. I glanced down at my watch. Not much longer until we were supposed to meet.

"Of course he would."

"What's that supposed to mean?"

"Let's just say that Christian would say anything to get with a girl, even an Aura."

I stepped toward him. "You don't know him."

"Don't I? I only trained with him for three years. How long have you known him?"

I didn't answer.

"That's what I thought. You can't possibly know what Christian is like. He was one of the biggest screw-offs, caring more for girls than our sacred duty to the Auras."

"I don't believe you. Christian takes his position very seriously."

"Is that why your friend—Tracey, right?—ended up dead and you almost died too?"

I slapped him hard.

Jackson closed his eyes briefly and clenched his jaw. "I guess I deserved that. Look, all I'm trying to say is you don't know Christian well enough to be singing his praise. What happened out in the forest with the Vyken turning to wind just can't happen, even if Christian tells you otherwise."

We stood next to the wall in silence for several moments, me looking toward the forest and him looking at me. Finally Jackson said, "I know you'll probably hate me, but your safety comes first. I have to report this."

"Do what you have to do," I said and walked away. Christian and I would have to meet up another time. I didn't dare risk getting him in trouble too. Besides, I didn't want him to see me this mad.

EIGHT

"ARE YOU ALL RIGHT?" MAY ASKED AT BREAKFAST. SHE SAT next to me along with another girl with dark hair almost matching May's, but it was longer. I'd seen her in some of my classes.

I stopped stirring my scrambled eggs. All I could think about was what had happened with Liam last night. Had I made any of it up? Had I finally lost my mind? "I'm fine. Late night studying is all."

"Again?"

"Yeah."

"Aren't you tired?"

"A little."

"Are you taking your vitamins?" the other girl said, eyeing the little blue pill next to my plate. "Oh, by the way, I'm Kiera. I've seen you around."

"Hey," I said and picked up the vitamin. "A super pill. Wouldn't that be great?" I popped it into my mouth and swallowed it.

"Hey, I forgot to tell you," May said. "I'm in your PE class now. You're in it too, right, Kiera?"

Kiera smiled and nodded.

"Really? How come?" I asked.

"Dr. Han rearranged my schedule. I think he could tell I was getting bored not having kids the same age in any of my classes."

"That was nice of him."

May pointed at my face. "Why is your cheek so red?"

"Is it?" When I'd gotten back last night, my cheek had been swollen a deep purple. I was afraid I would have to make up a story about falling down the stairs or something, but by this morning it had almost healed.

"Hey, Llona," Ashlyn said from the next table over. "Any ghostly visits lately?" Twitters of laughter from the girls around her accompanied her words.

"Hey, Ashlyn," I mocked. "How about cluing me in on your stupid joke?"

"Just ignore her," Kiera said. "She's like that with everyone."

Just then I noticed the room had grown strangely quiet. I looked around to discover the source. *Christian.* My heart somersaulted. He was with Jackson and another Guardian, heading toward the teacher's table. Several of the girls were giggling and looking in their direction. They did stand out, especially Christian. He was taller than the other two, his hair longer, messy just past his ears. He glanced at me, the corners of his mouth threatening a smile.

"Wow," May said, her voice low. "You're all aglow."

I blushed and quickly looked down. Right now my heart was overpowering my mind.

May nudged me. "Maybe you can set me up with one of his friends. They're not so bad either."

"Wish I could have some of that," Kiera said, and May laughed.

I nodded and forced myself to take a bite. *I will not look up. I will not look up*, I said to myself over and over.

"Hello, Llona."

I looked up. Christian was standing next to me.

May giggled.

"You look well," he said, then paused. His eyebrows tightened. "Your cheek. What happened?"

Instinctively, I touched it. "Ran into a wall late last night."

Christian tensed. "That must have been some wall."

"It was. It kept me from going somewhere important."

He reached up, as if to touch me, but stopped himself. "Are you okay?" His eyes, always full of concern, bore into me.

I nodded.

Jackson appeared. He patted Christian on the back. "You ready to go?" Jackson stopped when he saw me. "See any more spooky wind, Llona?" He exaggerated the words with his hands, wiggling his fingers through the air.

Christian looked from Jackson to me. "What are you talking about?"

Jackson laughed. "One day Llona will tell you. Come on. Let's go." He started walking away. Christian turned to me. He looked torn, like he didn't want to go. I decided to help him out since girls were starting to look at us strangely.

I glanced down at my watch. "I better get going too. Those twelve-year-old girls in my history class get mean if I'm late. See you in PE, May." I held my hand out to Christian. "Good seeing you again."

He took hold of it firmly, securely. I wondered if anyone else could feel the heat passing between us. "I'm sure we'll see each other again," he said.

I reluctantly let go and walked away, feeling both happy and sad. Before I stepped out of the dining room, Sophie caught my eye, and I almost stumbled. It was her expression that did it. She was watching me leave and smiling, or smirking, as if she knew something I didn't. I raised my hand to wave, but the second our eyes met, she turned away. I shook my head. I would never understand that woman.

I went straight to Denelle Hall and into my classroom, sitting in the back. If I sat anywhere else, one of the girls would complain that they couldn't see over my freaky head. Their words not mine.

I pushed Christian from my mind and opened my history book to page fifty-nine. I had found something in it over the weekend that didn't make sense, and I wanted to ask Ms. Ravitz about it. As soon as she came in, I raised my hand.

"Yes, Llona?"

"I have a question."

Ms. Ravitz erased the whiteboard from a previous lecture. "What is it?"

"Um, well, I was wondering if there are any other Auran history books?"

"Of course. There are many."

"I mean, any before this one." I held it up. "The earliest date I can find is 1909. What about our history before that?"

"They're in storage to keep them safe."

"Can I see them?"

Ms. Ravitz tilted her head and smiled at me sympathetically. "They are too fragile for your fingers."

The other girls giggled.

Ms. Ravitz waved them silent. "If you really want to, you can see them, but you have to have special permission from Cyrus. We treasure our past, but really all you need to know is our history after P-Day. Can someone tell me when that was?

A girl with a long brown ponytail raised her hand.

"Yes, Emily?"

"P-Day was on April 13, 1939."

I leaned over and whispered to another girl. "What's P-Day?"

"Preservation Day," she whispered back.

"And why is that date important?" Ms. Ravitz asked.

Emily smiled. "Because that's the day the Council decided to preserve the Auran race. They restructured all the Auran schools and organized the Guardian watch program."

"Good, Emily. And it's important to note that our very own Cyrus was a part of that great event."

That name again. It sounded familiar, but I couldn't remember where I'd heard it before. I raised my hand again and said, "Who's Cyrus?"

Ms. Ravitz shook her head. I could tell I was really starting to irk her. "Cyrus is the President of Lucent Academy and the head of the Council," she said.

I nodded, remembering how Sophie had mentioned his name on the first night.

Ms. Ravitz continued, "You haven't met him yet because he's visiting Ellie Academy in Ireland."

I'd heard of Ellie. It was one of the three Auran schools. In addition to Lucent there was also Ruddy Academy in Australia. Three council members resided at each one, making up the traditional nine members. I wondered how often Cyrus visited them. Another thought came to mind. I raised my hand again. Ms. Ravitz sighed and said, "Yes, Llona?"

"If Cyrus was around for P-Day, wouldn't he be like a hundred years old?"

Emily blurted, "How do you not know any of this?"

"Be kind, Emily," Ms. Ravitz said. "Llona wasn't raised like the rest of you. Her parents didn't teach her our history."

I wanted to shout that they had, but it was very different from what I was being taught now. They taught that Auras had fought to rid the world of Vykens not hide from them.

"Llona, Cyrus is a Geo, which means he can manipulate the earth's crust. It's quite a special gift to be able to move boulders, dirt, and trees the way he does. And because his kind was made from the earth, they can live for hundreds of years. Unfortunately, Cyrus is the last of his race. Vykens hunted and destroyed his kind almost two hundred years ago. He was afraid the same would happen to Auras, and that's why he helped establish P-Day."

"Oh," I said.

"Any more questions?"

I shook my head, feeling very stupid. Why hadn't my parents told me any of this?

I kept my mouth shut the rest of class. That is until a Lizen girl opened the classroom door and handed Ms. Ravitz a note. She looked up at me. "Llona? You're needed in Ms. Edevane's office."

"Right now?" I wondered why Sophie would want me in the middle of the day.

Ms. Ravitz looked down and read the note again. "Looks that way."

This can't be good. I gathered my books and left the room.

I took my time crossing campus back to Chadni Hall. After thinking about it, I had a pretty good idea what she was going to talk to me about.

After I took the elevators up to the fourth floor, where all the teachers' offices were, I knocked on Sophie's door. "Come in," I heard her say.

I opened the heavy oak door and was surprised at how dark the room seemed. She must've had the lights turned low. Strange for during the day, but then again, everything Sophie did seemed strange to me. "Hi, Sophie," I said and gave her my best smile. Sophie was dressed all in purple with her brown hair ratted high. She looked like a tulip.

"Have a seat, Llona."

I gulped, sat down, and focused on my shoes.

"I'm not sure what to say to you, Llona," Sophie began. "I am so disappointed."

Keep focusing on the shoe, I told myself. I tried not to get angry, but already my insides were turning hot. Why was I getting so upset?

"What were you thinking leaving the school at night?" Sophie continued. "It's dangerous out there, Llona. You could have been killed! Are you listening to me?"

I raised my chin. "I'm listening."

She slammed her fist down on the desk. "What were you doing outside the walls in the middle of the night?"

"Running."

"Then why not use the track?"

"I'm a wild horse," I said. "I like to run free, not be confined to a corral." Despite it being a lame metaphor, I smiled, but Sophie's stern expression didn't crack. Jake would've liked it.

"I don't care," she said. "You are not to leave these walls, do you understand?"

"I thought you said I could come and go as I please." My fingers rolled into my palms. *Stay calm, Llona.*

"In the daytime, sure, I guess as long as you keep up on your studies. But at nighttime you stay here."

I stayed silent, taking deep breaths through my nose.

"I'm trying to protect you, Llona. Surely you are mature enough to see that."

"I know," I said. So far she hadn't said anything about the Vykens, which made me think Jackson hadn't told her everything. Maybe he wasn't as bad as I thought he was.

Sophie glanced away, her mouth turned down. "Are you happy here?" she said.

I shrugged. "I want to be."

"Is it difficult having Christian here?"

"Christian was my Guardian, nothing more."

Sophie leaned forward. "I hope so. I'd hate to see anything

bad happen to him because he's distracted by you."

I cleared my throat and glanced away. "Nothing is going to happen to him."

She leaned back. "Good. Now please try to be happy, Llona. There is so much good in this school and in these girls."

"I never said there wasn't."

"I know, it's just," she sighed, "there is so much of your mother's spirit in you. She disobeyed the rules too, and look where that got her."

I stood up. "What happened to my mother was not her fault."

Sophie motioned for me to sit down. "In a way it was, dear, and I mean that in the most sensitive way. I loved her too. Don't forget that."

I couldn't stand to hear her profess a love toward a sister she barely spoke to. Sophie hadn't known my mother, not really. "I have to go," I said. I didn't give her the chance to stop me. I was out the door and rushing down the hall before the familiar anger rising inside me did something I'd regret.

NINE

"I don't think I'll ever get used to this," May said.

I could barely hear her over the sound of several pairs of feet pounding on asphalt. "I don't think any normal person could. This is ridiculous!"

A whistle blew signaling the time for us to move to the back. We parted ways, letting the girls behind us move forward, while we slowed up our run until we were behind the pack of running girls. The "pack" consisted of thirty girls running side by side, six rows deep. Every time Ms. Haddy blew the whistle, we were required to rotate forward.

"Tell me why we do this again?" May asked. This was her third day in PE, and every day she asked this same question.

In a mock, high-pitched voice I imitated Ms. Haddy: "We need to be fair and give everyone the opportunity to be first!"

May laughed. A couple of girls running in front of us glanced back at us and glared.

"I don't know how much more I can stand," I said.

The sun was high in the sky, drenching us in its heat. I wiped the sweat from my brow. What I wouldn't give for a little breeze. Maybe it was time I created my own.

"What can you do about it?" May said.

I lowered my voice. "I have a theory, one I plan on testing today."

"Do tell, Sherlock."

"I think the other girls hate this as much as we do. And I think they want to run faster too but are afraid to go against what they've been taught."

"They look pretty content to me," May said.

"Wanna bet?"

She smiled. "You're on. Ten bucks says you can't get any of them to do anything different."

The whistle blew again.

"Deal." Instead of moving up to the next row, I stepped outside the uniformed lines and picked up my pace.

"Miss Reese?" I heard Ms. Haddy call.

I kept running. I passed by Kiera, who eyed me suspiciously. Ms. Haddy yelled again. "Miss Reese! Get back in line!"

When I reached the front of the line, I said, "Bet none of you can beat me!" I took off running, not waiting for a response. I knew it would take a moment for them to process what I was doing.

I paced myself about fifty feet in front of them. Behind the girls, Ms. Haddy jogged after us, her normally white face growing redder and redder as she called my name. Her scarlet cheeks stood out against her white shirt and short skirt. Ms. Haddy looked like she was in excellent shape. I bet if she tried, she'd easily outrun me.

After almost thirty seconds of running by myself, I was ready to admit defeat to May, but then I heard footsteps fall out of sync with the others. I glanced over my shoulder to see a grinning Kiera gaining on me. I picked up my pace to keep in front of her. Soon there were more hurried footsteps until, finally, all of the girls were attempting to pass me.

But I wouldn't let them.

I pushed them hard, to the point where I knew Light would fill their entirety. The girls ran fast, faster than a normal human, and with purpose, like horses returning home after a long journey. The air was electrically charged with power, and I hoped they felt it too.

Ms. Haddy, who had given up trying to catch us from behind, had changed directions and now ran toward us, blue eyes blazing. Her once perfectly long and straight blonde hair was now wildly in disarray.

She froze in the middle of the track and held her hand out in a stopping gesture. As we drew closer, she closed her eyes tight as if she were afraid we might trample her to death.

I stopped just in front of her and turned around. The girls also stopped, their faces filled with both wonder and awe at what had just occurred. We looked at each other in silence, our eyes passing from one to another. And in those brief seconds, we knew with every fiber of our beings the true power of Light.

The moment was ruined when Ms. Haddy grabbed me roughly by the arm and dragged me away. "You are in so much trouble, Miss Reese!" Her voice was shrill, and I turned my head away to protect my ears.

Back to May, I called, "You owe me!"

* * * * *

"Sit there," Ms. Haddy said.

I obeyed.

She sat across from me behind her desk, typing into a computer—pounding it was more like it. "Of all the most horrible, most wretched things," she muttered. "Never have I seen anything so disgusting."

I ignored her quiet rant. Nothing she could say right now could bring me down. A major breakthrough had occurred, and for the first time I felt happy being at Lucent.

Ms. Haddy continued to hammer the keyboard. "Your father will hear of your behavior!"

"My father?"

"Yes. I'm going to call him right now, and don't you beg me not to."

Obviously she didn't know who I was. "Excuse me, Ms. Haddy, but my father is dead."

She stopped typing and looked up at me. "Then I'm calling your mother. Now where is your file?"

I cleared my throat. "My mother's dead too."

She looked at me again. I could see the conflict in her eyes as she tried to decide whether or not to show me mercy. She didn't.

"Then I am calling your—" she looked at the computer monitor—"uncle."

"He's at work right now."

"Then we will interrupt him like you interrupted our class today. I feel sorry for you, Miss Reese." She picked up the phone and dialed a number. "May I speak to a Mr. Jake Reese?"

Silence.

She kept her eyes on me, no doubt searching for any panic in my expression. I gave her nothing.

"Hello, Mr. Reese. My name is Ms. Haddy. I'm a PE instructor at Lucent Academy and"—a brief pause—"No, Llona is just fine. I'm calling to tell you of a most disturbing event that just took place."

As she proceeded to give a very dramatic account of what had happened, I tried to imagine Jake's reaction. I would be surprised if he was even listening.

Ms. Haddy paused. "Of course you can speak with her. She's right here." Smirking, she handed me the telephone.

I pressed the receiver to my ear. "Hi, Jake."

At first I couldn't hear anything, and then all of a sudden

he burst into laughter. I tried to keep a serious face, nodding my head every so often so Ms. Haddy would think I was getting an earful.

"Jake," I finally said, somewhat forcibly.

Through what sounded like choked-on tears of laughter, he said, "That has got to be the funniest thing I have ever heard. I can't wait to tell Heidi."

"Yes," I said, keeping a straight face. His girlfriend would appreciate it just as much as he did. Those two were cut from the same cloth.

"Good for you for running faster than everyone else. I'm proud of you!"

"Is that all?"

"Um, keep up the good work? Oh and call me later so we can talk more. I miss you, Tink."

My heart warmed at the mention of my nickname. He'd been calling me that ever since I was little and had an obsession with Tinkerbell. "Ditto. Tell Heidi hello."

"You got it."

I handed the phone back to Ms. Haddy.

"Thank you, Mr. Reese. Llona has . . . hello? Hello? Are you there?" She pulled the phone away from her ear and looked at it. "He hung up."

I stifled a laugh.

"No matter. I'm sure he gave you a good talking to."

I nodded. "Yes, ma'am."

"As for your punishment, for the next week during class you will copy the student manual. Is that clear?"

"Yes, ma'am."

"You must also apologize to the class for your disruptive behavior. And if you ever do something like that again, you will face a much more severe punishment."

I assured her that copying the manual was severe enough.

* * * * *

After Ms. Haddy let me go, I headed to the dining room in search of May. I found her sitting with Kiera; they looked deep in conversation. Neither of them noticed me until I pulled up a chair and sat down next to them.

"Where's my ten dollars?" I grinned and looked at Kiera. "Hi, Kiera."

May pulled out her wallet and handed me two fives. "You earned it."

"What made you do it?" Kiera asked me.

I took a bite from the sandwich in front of me. "I had to know I wasn't the only one who thinks running like that is dumb. Besides, I knew they had it in them."

"You think you changed any of those girls?" she asked. She leaned forward, elbows on table.

"What do you mean?"

"Look around. Those girls have already denied what they felt."

I glanced around. Sure enough many of the girls were looking in my direction. And they weren't friendly looks either. I set my sandwich down. "But why? I know they felt what I did."

"Because then they would have to do something about it. Their lives are easy here. They're protected; they have all that they want or need. If they go against what is being taught, then they will lose it all, and that terrifies them."

"What makes you so different?" May asked Kiera.

"Like you," she looked at me, "I haven't spent much time here. My parents are divorced, and although my mother believes in the Auran way of life, my father helped me see a different point of view. He visits me every Sunday."

"This school teaches some good, doesn't it?" May asked.

"Of course. It's just that the teachers are so out of touch

with the real world. They want us to be all the same. It drives me insane." Kiera swept her long brown hair to one shoulder.

"I know the feeling." I stared down at the food in front of me. I had been so happy earlier when I thought something big had happened, but reality set in. Did I really think I could change things from one sixty-second run? "What do we do now?" I asked.

"Keep trying to change their minds. Look for opportunities for them to feel Light's power." She turned to May. "You're the lucky one."

"Why's that?" May finished up the last of her hamburger.

"You're a Fury. You don't have to deal with all this stuff. Dr. Han pushes Furies hard."

"That's not necessarily a good thing. The other day he was yelling at me because I couldn't snap my fingers to create fire. The other kids were laughing hysterically."

"How far back does the history of Furies go?" I asked.

May thought. "Um, we haven't gone too much into the history, but just flipping through a book I did see a section that talked about some war the Furies and Auras were in back in the 1700s."

Kiera looked surprised. "Really?"

"How far back do your books go?" May asked.

I crumbled up my napkin. "It should go back for thousands of years, but the books mostly show only the history after 1939." I stood up.

"That's weird," May said, joining me.

"Why do think that is?" Kiera asked.

"I don't know yet, but I think it was deliberate. You guys want to discuss it sometime? Maybe after the dance this weekend?"

Kiera groaned. "The dance! My mom was supposed to send me a dress, but I still haven't gotten it."

"I have a bunch. I bet they'd fit you," May said, and the two began making plans.

I let them walk in front of me. They didn't seem as concerned as I was about the inconsistency. Maybe I was being paranoid. I sighed. At least there was the dance to take my mind off things.

But then I remembered.

At my last dance, my friend had been murdered.

TEN

"Are you ready?" I heard May say just outside my door. Beyond her voice were many others, all filled with excitement for the dance.

I looked in the mirror. My long hair was down and straight as always. I wish I could've worn it up, as it would've made the flattering neckline of May's red dress more noticeable, but I didn't dare risk my bite marks being seen. I did, however, slide a gold headband just past my forehead. It would have to do.

"I'm ready," I said.

May opened the door and gasped. "That dress looks amazing on you! Consider it yours."

I laughed. "Thanks, but I'm sure it looks better on you. Is that outfit new?" May was wearing a tea-length, black lacy dress.

"It is. My mom sent it to me just for this occasion."

"It's beautiful. You're going to break some hearts tonight."

May looked in the mirror and smiled. "That's the plan." Her eyes met mine. "Are you going to be okay with Christian coming and all?"

I glanced away. "It will be hard, but I have to keep my distance." The moment I found out Guardians were going to be at the dance, I felt sick. Christian and I had shared a very special moment dancing, and I didn't want to be reminded of how great we really were together.

"You mean you can't be together while you're at Lucent, right?"

I shrugged.

May came to me and placed her hand on my arm. "I know what Sophie said really scared you, but that doesn't mean you two are going to share the same fate as your parents. You guys are different."

No, I'm *different*, I thought.

"Why do you look so sad?" May asked.

"Sometimes I wonder is all." I walked to the door and forced a smile. "Come on. Let's go rock some guys' worlds. After you." I motioned my arm forward.

Getting downstairs proved harder than I anticipated. The halls were packed with girls, all laughing, fixing hair, and admiring dresses. From the conversations I was hearing, it had been almost a year since their last dance.

"What do you know about these boys?" I asked, leaning into May to avoid a chatty group of girls clogging the hallway.

"They are from a super rich private school in New York City. The school's known for spitting out high-profile lawyers, doctors, and politicians." May glanced around to see if anyone was listening while we walked into the elevator. "I even heard some of the girls say they hope to find their future husbands from this group. Crazy, right?" She pushed the button going down.

I leaned against the elevator railing, nodding. "Do you think these guys know who we really are?"

"According to Valerie, there's a long-time rumor at their school of what we are, but none of them know whether or not to believe it."

I thought about this all the way to the bottom. When the doors opened, I stopped just outside the elevator. The lobby was packed with teenage boys, but some looked older—early twenties, maybe. They were all dressed in suits, clean shaven, with hair combed back. And by their expressions, they were just as happy to be here as the girls.

"Let's go into the dining room," May said, pulling me along, weaving in and out of girls and boys, all of whom were preening and strutting around like prized dogs at a dog show.

Both May and I gasped at the sight of the dining room, which had been transformed into a ballroom. The chandeliers were lit by what looked like real fire, but I didn't know how that was possible. On the outer parts of the room, long, silk-looking white curtains layered into each other and fell from the ceiling, making the room feel like we were in the clouds. The room smelled like lilacs, but even stronger was the smell of cider and pastries against the wall.

In front of the room, on the slightly raised platform where Sophie usually spoke from, an orchestra played classical music. I didn't recognize the tune, but it sounded like Bach.

May scooted me to the side of the doorway so students could get by us. "This is so beautiful! I'm shocked," she said.

"Who knew?" I agreed.

Within minutes the dining room was packed. Several students had already begun dancing, and by the looks of it, the Auras and the private school boys were well trained in the art. "You know how to dance?" I asked May.

She shook her head. "But I'm more than willing to learn. See those guys over there?" May pointed to two boys not far from us.

"The ones with the blond hair?" I asked.

She nodded. "I'm going to ask them to teach us to dance." May grabbed my arm. "And you're coming with me."

"Wait, no!" I said, but it was useless. She was pulling me forward with a death-like grip.

"You are going to have fun tonight if it kills me," May said over her shoulder. She stopped in front of the boys. "Hey, guys. Are you two having fun?"

The blond one with green eyes said, "We might be soon. What're your names?" He looked us up and down, along with his friend who was blonder, but with brown eyes.

"I'm May and this is Llona. And you guys are?"

Brown eyes said, "I'm Tyler. And this is Corey."

May smiled. "Nice to meet you boys, but you see, we," she motioned at me and her, "have a problem."

"Oh yeah?" Corey said. "What's that?"

It was about this time that I noticed a steady line of about twelve guys come through the door, also dressed in black tuxedos. But they carried themselves differently from the private school boys. They were stiffer, more alert. And then I saw Christian.

May tugged on me to get me to face forward, toward Tyler and Corey. "We can't dance," she said, "and we were hoping you could teach us how."

Tyler bowed and extended his hand toward me. "We'd be honored."

I glanced over again toward the doors. The Guardians had spread out and positioned themselves around the room. They looked like club bouncers, with their hands clasped together and their stern expressions.

"Go ahead, Llona," May encouraged.

I turned back to Tyler and took his hand. He guided me onto the dance floor, glancing back at me several times to make sure I didn't get tangled into other dancers.

Halfway there I felt Christian's eyes on me. *Don't look over*, I told myself. *Stare straight ahead*. Maybe Christian would get angry at me for dancing with someone else. That would sure make things easy if he was the one who ended our relationship.

But as Tyler placed his hand around my waist, I knew that would never happen. I'd have to really mess things up to make him do that.

"Do you really not know how to dance," Tyler asked, "or was your friend just saying that?"

I glanced over at May not far away with Corey. She was moving with him as if she'd invented ballroom dancing. "Apparently *she* was just saying that, but I honestly can't dance." I made a mental note to scold May later.

"It's easy," Tyler said. "I hold your hand like this," he raised his left hand, which was holding mine, "and then you put your left hand on my shoulder and rest your arm on mine. Easy, right?"

"Sure, but what about my feet?"

"Just follow me," he said and grinned. He pressed me to his chest and practically lifted me as he spun me around the room. The way he was doing it made dancing easy. It almost felt like I was floating.

"So, where are you from?" he asked.

"I moved here from Utah not long ago."

"Utah, huh? I've been skiing there. I loved it. You ever been?"

I laughed. "I tried once. My little car wouldn't make it up the mountain, and I had to go back." Just then—it was an accident, I swear it was—my eyes met Christian's. He gave a tight smile and nodded formally, making me lose my balance, and I stumbled.

Tyler's grip tightened. "You okay?

I nodded. "Klutzy, I guess." I turned my head the other direction, away from Christian.

Tyler and I continued to talk. He seemed like a normal guy with high ambitions. Already he was interning at the mayor's office in New York City. Under any other circumstance I might've been interested in him, but all I could think about was Christian, despite my best efforts not to.

When the orchestra finished, Tyler asked, "Can I get you something to drink?"

"I'd love something."

"Wait here then," he raised my hand and kissed the top of it gently. I stared after him, wondering what that would've felt like if I wasn't in love with someone else.

I stayed where I was, swaying slightly to the violins that had just started up again. I glanced over when I heard May laugh again. Corey was dipping her. She looked like she was having a great time.

"You look beautiful," a familiar voice said.

I turned around. Christian was standing directly in front of me, only a few inches of air between us. The nearness made my heart race. I lowered my eyes. "Thank you. You look good too."

"I want to dance with you," he said, breathing deeply.

I looked up, glancing around nervously. "You can't. You know that."

He closed the small space between us until I was forced to step back. "I don't care." He moved toward me again.

My cheeks flushed, and I made the mistake of looking into his eyes; they burned with passion, and the lights above reflected in them, making them even more intense. He reminded me of a hungry wolf. I stepped back again. "We can't."

He moved forward. After me. I continued backing up to keep our bodies from touching, but he wouldn't stop.

I glanced behind me. Christian was guiding me into the long, white curtains hanging from the ceiling. "We can't do this, Christian. You have to stop."

"Stop me, then," he said. He kept pursuing, and I kept moving.

I felt the soft material part as I stepped backward into it; the silkiness of it against my back was like a hand caressing my skin. I sucked in air and continued to move into the white layers until they hid us completely.

Christian said nothing. His gaze left my eyes and traveled to my mouth, considering it like it was something he wanted to conquer. My lips parted in anticipation of what was to come. His fingers found mine, and he tugged my hand forward, pulling my body next to his. His other arm tightened against my back until I was pressed against him.

Christian's lips fell onto my neck. Very gently, he kissed my skin. His mouth continued to trail up my neck until he found my lips. The kiss started out soft, but all of a sudden my arms were around his neck, trying to get him even closer.

"Um, you guys might want to stop."

I immediately stepped back, my breathing coming in great gasps.

May was a few feet away, parting the curtains. "Sophie's looking for you, Christian. And she's mad."

I looked back at Christian. He was staring at me, breathing just as hard and cheeks flushed. He smiled. "I better go."

I nodded.

Christian remained where he was, still looking at me like he wasn't finished. I didn't dare move either. I didn't want to.

"Oh, come on!" May said. She pushed Christian away. "And straighten your tie!"

Christian looked over his shoulder at me and winked before he disappeared.

"That looked pretty hot," May said.

With Christian gone, the realization of what had just happened hit me hard. "What did I just do?"

May laughed. "Kissed your boyfriend. What's the big deal?"

"We need to stay away from each other, remember? At

least until I figure out what the future holds for us."

"Does he know that?"

I paused. May had a point. I shook my head. "I really need to grow a pair of ovaries and just talk to him."

May smiled. "You'll figure it out." She put her arm around me and ushered me forward, parting the curtains along the way. "Tyler's looking for you."

I groaned. "I think I'll sneak outside. He's nice, but I don't feel like dancing anymore."

"I'll come with you for a minute. I could use some fresh air too."

"Is Corey cool?" I asked her when we were almost to the doors.

May nodded. "He's just super formal."

"Which equals boring."

May smiled. "Maybe."

"Hey, guys, wait!"

I turned around. Kiera was hurrying toward us, lifting up her green gown so she didn't trip. "Where are you going?"

"Outside," May said.

"We'll be back though," I added.

Her shoulders slumped. "Can I come? I just endured a ten-minute lecture on US relations with the Middle East."

I laughed and pushed open the door. "Sounds like we could all use a break."

We were only a few steps into the hall when two Guardians appeared. Jackson being one of them. Other than them, the hall was empty.

"Hello, Llona," he said, nodding his head. "You look lovely tonight, as do your friends."

May and Kiera turned to me, probably expecting an introduction, but I didn't have time before the other Guardian said, "Where do you three think you're going?"

"Lay off, Spencer," Jackson said. "They probably are just going to powder their noses. Isn't that right?"

May laughed. "Do we look like the type of girls who powder our noses?"

Spencer sneered. "Then you must be trying to go outside to meet up with some boys, isn't that right?" He flipped his head to the side, to get his long brown hair out of his eyes.

"No," I said and my gaze met Jackson's. "It's like he said. We're going to the restroom."

Jackson smiled.

"Let's go, girls." I began to walk, but Spencer stuck out his arm, making me run into it. And it was this unwelcomed contact that sent a surge of anger, igniting that dark thing inside me I didn't understand.

"I don't believe you," Spencer said. "You said your name's Llona?" He looked at Jackson, who gave him a warning look. "As in, Llona Reese?"

I turned to him slowly, my breathing quickening. *Stay calm*. "Is there a problem?"

"I've heard about you. You're a troublemaker."

Jackson straightened. "That's enough, Spence. Let them go."

"What he said," May said. She pulled on my arm to get me back by her and Kiera.

I should've gone with her, but all my nerves were burning with energy, and not the kind that made me want to run. The kind that made me want to fight. I thought of all the ways I could hurt him, and the sound his bones might make when I broke them, and the blood I might see. My expression must've been showing my thoughts, because Jackson gave me a firm nudge. "Go. Get out of here."

My mind broke through some of the anger, and I took a deep breath. Spencer was staring me down, and it took every ounce of strength I had to turn away. "Come on," I said to May and Kiera.

We were halfway down the hall when May asked, "What was that all about?"

I just shook my head, but then I heard Spencer's voice say, "That girl is a certifiable nut job. Did you see the way she was looking at me?"

Whatever restraint I had been maintaining shattered. I whirled around and walked back to Spencer.

Jackson was shaking his head. "What now?" he said.

Spencer pointed a long finger at me. "You better stop right there."

I cocked my fist and propelled it forward like a rock from a slingshot. It smashed into Spencer's nose. The sound of cartilage and bone grinding against each other sent a shot of adrenalin throughout my body. But it was the blood spraying from his nose that excited me the most. As Spencer was falling back, I jumped on top of him, my dress ripping up the side, and continued to smash my knuckles into Spencer's blood-covered face.

I landed three blows before Jackson was tearing me off. May was right there, telling me to calm down. Behind her, Kiera's eyes were big. I saw and heard them all, but all I felt was the storm raging inside me. I struggled against Jackson, thrashing my head and legs at him in an attempt to free myself so I could get back at Spencer.

"Chill out, Llona!" Jackson shouted.

May stepped in front of me and placed her hands on my arm. I cried out when they began to burn my arm. The pain of it was enough to bring me back. I looked at May.

"I'm sorry, Llona," May said, her eyes tearing.

I glanced at Spencer. He was lying on the ground, holding his face and moaning.

"Are you finished?" Jackson asked.

I relaxed in his arms. He let me go, and I stumbled forward, away from them. I looked back just once. They were all staring at me with horror, but their shock and disgust were nothing compared to the way I felt about myself.

"I'm sorry," I whispered, just before I turned and ran down the hall and out the doors.

ELEVEN

Nighttime had arrived, but it still wasn't dark enough for me. The full moon cast light in every direction, making it difficult for me to hide. I found a place, behind Risen Auditorium, where it was quiet and dark. I leaned against the building, breathing heavily. Adrenalin, along with that other thing, still coursed through me, and it took several minutes until I was able to relax fully.

I sunk to the ground, May's dress already ruined, and buried my head into my hands. The air cooled the back of my neck, and it was a welcome relief to the heat I'd felt earlier. I remained like this for some time, and only when I heard the last of the vehicles drive away from Lucent did I finally move.

Peeking around the side of the building, I saw that the grounds were empty and quiet. A few lights remained on inside Chadni Hall; probably the Lizen woman cleaning up after the dance. But after another thirty minutes, the lights shut off and a breeze blew as if Chadni had given one last breath before it fell asleep.

I didn't return to my room. Instead I left my shoes next to the brick wall and headed toward the shed near the outer wall. The grass was damp under my bare feet, and its coolness spurred me on. I picked up my pace, wanting to get as far away from Lucent as possible. Within feet of the shed, I leapt up to the roof and over to the stone wall. I paused, the forest only a short run away.

So much had happened tonight. I glanced back at Lucent, wind blowing the dress around my legs. What if Christian had seen me earlier? Would he have been as disgusted as the others? Maybe I should be more concerned with trying to protect him from me than anything else.

I stared out into the forest, thinking of Christian, and swallowed hard. What would I have to do to push him away? He meant everything to me, but I couldn't bear if any harm were to befall him. I loved my mother, but how could she risk the life of the man she loved, especially if she'd been warned ahead of time?

As much as I wanted to go into the forest, I stayed, knowing that I shouldn't give in so easily to these new desires inside me. Whatever they were couldn't be good. Not wanting to think of what had happened anymore, I sighed and laid back on the top of the wall, my legs crossed. I stared into the black sky and began to count the stars.

I was on seventy-two when a sound made me sit up. I looked toward the forest, my skin exploding into a cold chill. There it was again. A low, throaty growl near the tree line maybe fifty feet away. The forest was an impermeable wall of darkness. A tree moved, more like bent forward, branches snapping and wood breaking, as if someone incredibly strong had pushed against it.

I stood up—more like jumped up. A figure stepped out of the forest; moonlight bathed his bare, muscular chest, and when he lifted his head, his eyes glowed an eerie yellow. His mouth opened, like a tiger yawning, and blood dripped from his teeth.

I stumbled back at the sight of the Vyken, almost falling

from the wall, but the momentum of my arms kept me in place. The Vyken's eyes focused on me. I glanced around, frantically looking for a Guardian.

The Vyken began moving. Toward me. My breathing quickened. *What is he doing?* His pace increased until he was sprinting. I quickly jumped off of the wall, inside Lucent Academy, and backed up.

I'm safe. Lucent is safe, I told myself, breathing hard. I kept my eyes on the wall, all the while stepping back slowly. But all that changed when the Vyken's tensed body appeared over the wall as if he were flying. He landed on the ground in a crouched position, and his head snapped up in my direction.

I stopped breathing and turned to run, my hair tangling around my face. I ran as fast as I could, my bare feet kicking up grass and earth. Behind me, I heard footsteps pounding. And they were gaining on me.

I looked around, trying to decide which direction to go. The dorms at Chadni were too far away. To my left was Denelle Hall, which was probably locked, but straight ahead was the clock tower, a steel door at its base. I'd only been in it once before, and as far as I knew, it shouldn't be locked.

I ran harder, but it wasn't much faster because I was already sprinting. Every time I took a breath, my lungs felt like they were being shredded. I glanced behind me. The Vyken was only twenty feet behind, blood smearing the lower half of his face. The distance between us wouldn't give me enough time to open and close the door. I needed to move faster.

Focusing all my energy, I went beyond the Light, to where the dark parts of my mind were, the parts I'd felt earlier tonight. There I found pieces of Mr. Steele, his strength, his speed.

I willed it into me despite my earlier horror. I needed strong power and fast. A burst of strength, far surpassing anything I'd ever experienced, shot through me like a bolt of lightning.

I sprang forward, putting a greater distance between me and the Vyken, and just in time too. I reached the clock tower and shoved my shoulder into the old, metal door. It opened with a great groan, and as soon as I was in, I slammed it shut.

Now to lock it.

I frantically looked around for something to use, but there was nothing. Only a dusty concrete floor and a circular staircase going up. Reacting quickly, I used my new strength to break the metal handle. I only hoped that would be enough.

I backed up and stepped upon the first stair. A crashing sound, like the Vyken had just run into the door, echoed throughout the circular tower. So far the door was holding. I took another step up.

Only a sliver of moonlight had found its way to the bottom of the tower, casting shadows in every direction. They seemed to shudder when the Vyken pounded on the door. Dust billowed up from the floor and spun in the gray light like dancing dead fairies. The door wouldn't hold much longer. Where were all the Guardians?

I wiped sweat from my forehead with the back of my hand and hurried up the stairs. Below me, the door burst open, and a great wind rushed up to greet me. Behind the thundering noise, I heard my name being called. Far away.

I paused midway up the stairs and glanced out one of the tower's few windows. Christian was sprinting toward us, shouting my name. I glanced around at the buildings, expecting to see lights turn on, but no one heard his cries.

I continued up the stairs, creating balls of Light as I went. Some of the dark power I'd been given dissipated, and I stumbled on the last step. My leg was stretched out, dangling over the stairs, and the Vyken grabbed it. I jerked my leg free, but cried out when his nails tore through my skin. I continued forward, scampering into the lone room at the top of the tower and to the other side. I pressed my back against the stone walls, my hand shaking beneath several glowing lights hovering just above them.

As soon as the Vyken appeared in the doorway, I tossed a ball hard. He dodged it by jumping up along the side of the wall, his nails and bare toes somehow finding a hold in the thin cracks of the wall. I threw another one, but he was already moving, scrambling alongside the stones like a spider. He was grinning.

I rolled away from the wall until I was in the middle of the room. I lost sight of him for just a fraction of a second, but that was enough. The Vyken was gone, or, I should say, hiding. He was still here. I could feel him. I looked up toward the rafters of the tower roof. It was pitch black.

At the bottom of the tower, I heard Christian begin to ascend the stairs. "I'm coming, Llona!" he yelled.

Still staring up, I created Light again in the palm of my hand and willed it to rise. The closer it got to the rafters the faster my heart beat. Sweat rolled down the small of my back.

Light began to fill dark spaces, exposing that which wished to remain hidden. My Vyken was there, but he wasn't alone. Another sat crouched on a beam. Where his left eye should've been there was an empty hole.

I screamed when my Vyken dropped from the ceiling, extinguishing the light. He fell onto my stomach, pushing my shoulders into the floor. I tried to create Light, but it was as if he knew what I was going to do because his hands slipped up and pinned my wrists together. He bent forward and inhaled my skin. The warmth of his breath steamed my ear when he said, "I'm going to eat every part of you."

Just then Christian burst into the room, breathing hard and eyes burning with a rage I'd never seen in him. Panic tore through me. He was too emotional, too upset. He wouldn't sense the other Vyken until it was too late.

"Christian," I cried, but the Vyken on top of me shoved his hairy forearm into my throat, cutting off not only my warning, but air too.

Christian rushed forward, failing to see and hear the Vyken falling from the beam behind him. He was almost to me when the Vyken behind him raised his hand. Moonlight shined off the blade he carried.

I struggled, trying to do something to warn him, but something else stopped him before I could. Before the blade sliced into Christian, a thin strip of a shadow, shaped like an arm, swept out from the darkness, catching the Vyken's leg. The Vyken fell forward and stumbled into Christian. Christian turned around and stared in shock. He looked back at me, and I knew he realized his blunder.

Before he turned to fight his Vyken, he quickly kicked at mine, knocking him partially off me. I squirmed the rest of the way out while Christian scooped up the knife from the floor and moved backward toward me. The two Vykens also paired up and stared in our direction, hunched over and fists ready.

"You okay?" Christian said, his eyes darting around the room.

"Fine. You?"

"Never better."

The Vyken with the missing eye lunged first. Christian swung the knife but missed. The Vyken caught him in the back with his foot, sending him across the room and away from me.

The other Vyken, the one who had smelled me, rushed forward. I dove out of the way at the last second. We did this a couple of more times before I realized I was actually enjoying this cat and mouse game. Maybe it was because I didn't feel like a mouse anymore.

I smiled, and once again searched inwardly for the darkness that gave me the addicting power. I found it, a little too quickly, and embraced it. Just like before, new strength filled my being, and this time when the Vyken lunged, I didn't move. I let him crash into me. We fell to the ground, punching and shoving, but I managed to position myself on top of him this time.

I should've used Light right then, but instead I wanted hand-to-hand combat to see what I could do. I swung hard, he caught my fist and twisted it back. If it wasn't for my new strength, I probably would've cried out and rolled into a ball from the pain. But not now.

"Use your Light!" Christian yelled. He had his Vyken pinned up against the wall. Both of them were fighting for control of the knife.

I ignored his advice. What I was feeling now was far more powerful than anything I thought Light could do.

With my arm pinned behind my back, I threw my body forward and head-butted him. Dazed, he let go of my arm, which was already cocked and ready to go. I swung it at his cheekbone; it shattered under the force.

The Vyken looked at me, in both pain and surprise, but his expression quickly turned to anger, and he bucked me from him. I somersaulted away and stood up, grinning.

"Who are you?" he said as he circled around me. I kept up the game, letting him move.

"What are you doing?" Christian shouted. He had his Vyken pinned to the ground.

Having fun, I thought. I charged the Vyken and leapt into the air, legs forward. My feet connected with his chest, sending him several feet back into the wall. He bounced off it and fell forward, face first. Dust billowed up around him, and when he looked up, his fangs were bared and eyes glowing.

I nodded my head. "Let's go, creeper."

Snorting, he rushed forward. I dove out of the way but

wasn't fast enough. His clawed hand raked the back of my head, and I felt his nails slice into my flesh. I dropped to the ground on all fours, blood dripping from my neck and turning my hair red. It was the first time my hair had ever been another color.

I stood slowly, trying to shake away the pain. By the time I was up, the Vyken had his arms around my chest and was tightening. I glanced at Christian. Somehow in his scuffle the knife had been knocked from him. He still had the upper hand, straddling the Vyken, raining blows on his head, but without the knife he wouldn't be able to do much more.

The grip tightened on my chest, but it didn't hurt as much as it should've. With blood running down my gown and Christian needing help, I acted fast. Taking advantage of my shorter height, I bent forward fast, flipping the Vyken over me. He landed on his back, gasping.

Before he could do anything else, I picked up his head—the feel of his matted hair and hard skull felt like a rotten melon. I twisted hard and actually laughed when I heard one "pop" after another as his vertebrae snapped. The Vyken let out an agonizing cry of anguish and pain. While he writhed on the floor, I walked to the knife and picked it up. I felt Christian's eyes on me, but I didn't look over.

Raising the knife above my head, I said, "Ashes to ashes," and slashed the knife down into the Vyken's neck. The blade slid into his pale skin and stopped only when it hit the wooden floor. His head burst first; the ashes stuck to my blood-soaked hair. I inhaled deeply and closed my eyes, feeling like I could conquer the world.

"Knife!" Christian yelled. I turned to him. He was breathing heavy and had sweat dripping off his forehead. But it was the way he was looking at me, like he didn't know who I was, that made me look down. I hurried over to him and gave him the knife. The Vyken beneath him was still struggling, but his one good eye was such a mess that he couldn't see out of it to properly get at Christian.

With one swipe of his hand, Christian beheaded the Vyken. Before it had even turned to dust, he was coming toward me. "Let me see that wound," he said.

"It's fine," I said, brushing his hand away. I still didn't look at him. I was afraid of what he'd see in my eyes.

"Llona—"

"Where are the other Guardians?" I asked. "How come you're the only one out here?" I went to the window and looked out. All of Lucent was asleep, unaware of the danger. Christian came up behind me. I felt him lift my hair to examine the wound. I was careful to keep the bite marks on the opposite side of him.

"There was a miscommunication," he said. "Spencer and Jackson were supposed to be out here, but apparently Spencer's nose got broken, and he failed to find anyone to replace him. This looks bad, Llona." I heard a rustling of material and then felt something warm press against the back of my head.

"It will heal," I said. I reached up and replaced his hand on the material, which I realized was his shirt, and continued to press it to my head. I turned around. "About Spencer—"

"That's why I came out here. I was hoping to find Jackson, or even better, you, to see if it was true. That's when I saw the Vyken chasing you." He looked at me, but, again, I averted my eyes. "Did you really punch Spencer?"

"Yes."

Christian was quiet for a moment before he said, "I'm sure he deserved it."

"Maybe."

Christian stepped by me and looked out the window, searching left and right. "One thing I don't get is where Jackson is. He should've heard you screaming or me yelling. I don't get it."

"Maybe he was fighting his own Vyken out there."

"Maybe."

I turned to him, meeting his eyes, but I was careful to step to the side of the window, where shadows covered my face. "Why are there so many?" I asked.

Christian shook his head. "I don't know. Something's wrong here. I felt it the moment I first arrived at Lucent." He took hold of my hand. Moonlight covered him, illuminating his blue eyes and accentuating the muscles on his bare chest. I, however, remained in the darkness.

"You could've died tonight," I said.

He smiled. "Lucky the Vyken tripped then, eh?"

It was then I remembered what really happened: a thin shadow slicing forward, catching the Vyken's leg. But that was impossible, right? Maybe I'd imagined it.

Christian squeezed my hand. "You okay?"

I lowered his shirt from the back of my head. "You were careless. You rushed in when you shouldn't have."

"I thought he was going to kill you."

"It's me, Christian. If I had been anyone else, you would've noted your surroundings first. Listened closer. You probably would've been able to see him with that Guardian eyesight of yours."

"You don't know that."

I sighed.

"I get where you're going with this," he said. "Really, I do. You think that I'm only thinking of your safety, and guess what? I am. But that's what boyfriends do. Forget about me being a Guardian for a minute. If I was just a regular dude, I would've done the same thing."

"But you're not regular. You're special, and because of me

you're not using your gifts, which is going to get you killed."

Christian pulled me into the moonlight with him and wrapped his arms around me. The skin on his chest was warm. "You worry too much. At least about the wrong things. We need to figure out what's going on around here."

I nodded. He was partially right.

"I'm going to see you back to your room, and then I'm going to talk to some of the other Guardians." He turned me around. "Let me see that wound again."

I stepped away from him. Already it was feeling better, and I didn't want him to see how fast I was healing. "I'm fine. Really." I held out his shirt. "Do you want me to throw this away?"

His expression pained. "Yes. I don't ever want to see that much blood outside of you again."

I lowered the shirt. "Let's get out of here."

Christian said nothing to me the rest of the way back to Chadni, and I didn't speak either. I was still too stunned by what had happened, specifically with me. I was hoping it had escaped Christian's notice, but when we stopped just beneath my window, he said, "I have to ask, Llona," he paused as if searching for the right words. "What happened back there? Why didn't you use Light to kill the Vyken? And how come you were so strong?"

I looked beyond him, past Lucent and to the forest beyond. What could I say? I hardly knew the answer myself, other than Mr. Steele's bite had left something inside me, and I . . . what? Sort of liked it now? How disgusting was that?

TWELVE

MORNING FINALLY CAME, BUT YOU WOULDN'T KNOW IT BY looking outside. The sky was a deep gray, promising rain. I'd been listening to the wind howl all night. It started up just after I said good-bye to Christian. I hadn't been able to give him a good reason why I was able to fight the Vyken the way that I did, but, gratefully, he didn't push the issue. He seemed to have bigger things to worry about.

Because I had no appetite, I decided to skip breakfast and take my time getting ready. Whether I would admit it or not, I really didn't want to face May and Kiera. Or Christian, if he showed up.

My door opened. Tessa stood in the doorway holding an armful of towels, looking surprised. "I'm sorry," she stuttered. "I thought you'd be at breakfast."

"No problem. Come on in."

She disappeared into my bathroom.

"You know I can get my own towels, right?" I said loud enough for her to hear. Ever since I had asked Tessa about the smell in my room, upsetting her, I'd made it a point to be as friendly as I could. I figured we'd become friends eventually, and then she'd tell me the truth. But now I didn't want to wait. While she was still in the bathroom, I darted across the room and shut the door.

Tessa walked out of the bathroom and said, "You are not required to—" She saw me blocking the closed door. "What are you doing?"

"I want answers."

"I don't know what you mean," she stammered.

"My room. I asked you once before about the funny smell and you bolted. You know something. Tell me, please?"

"How can you even smell it?" she said, her voice low.

"So I'm not crazy! What happened in here?"

"We're not supposed to talk about it."

"If anyone has a right to know, it's me. I'm the one who has to live here."

Tessa sat down on the bed, facing the window. She looked small and helpless with her hands resting gently on her lap. "A girl named Britt lived in this room before you. I was her servant for over three years. She was beautiful and kind, loved by everyone. But something happened. She stopped smiling. She stopped talking. Eventually she even stopped going to classes. The teachers tried to talk to her, but she would get angry. I remember finding holes in her walls where she had punched them. I had never seen an Aura get that angry before; none of us had. One day I came in here and found her crying. She kept saying, "I can't control it anymore," over and over. I tried to comfort her, but she wouldn't be consoled. The next day I found her. There was blood everywhere." Tessa stood up. "Right there. That's where she did it." She pointed to a spot across from the bed.

"Did what?"

"Killed herself."

The air in the room turned thick, and it caught in my throat. Tessa was pale, and I felt my own head begin to spin. I dropped to the bed next to her. "Why?"

Tessa shook her head. "I don't know. Nobody does. It's the first case of an Aura suicide. Ever." She stared at the floor.

"So that's why the other girls keep giving me a hard time about my room."

"The other girls don't know it was suicide."

"What do you mean?"

"The teachers told them she died of unknown causes."

"And they bought that?"

"Could you see any of the girls here questioning them?"

"No, I guess not."

"They didn't let anyone in here for several weeks while Lizens remodeled the room. I scrubbed the floor for hours, but there was still a stain so we had to put in carpet." For the first time her voice cracked.

I put my arm around her. "I'm so sorry."

"Sophie told me not to tell, said there would be consequences." Her bottom lip began to quiver.

"It's okay. I promise I won't say anything."

"I hate keeping this secret. And I hate this place and what it does to people." She began to sob, her shoulders shaking violently. "So many lies."

I held on to her—rather, she clung to me. I rubbed her back. "It will be okay. We'll fix it, I promise." I continued to say soothing words until she stopped crying.

When the bells chimed, she pulled away. "I'm sorry. You're going to be late." She dried her eyes with a tissue from my nightstand.

"I don't care. Some things are more important."

She smiled at me. "Thank you."

"Have you always lived here?" I asked.

She nodded. "This is our home."

"Are there other Lizens outside of Lucent?"

"There are more colonies, but at the other Auran schools in Ireland and Australia."

"How come there aren't more of you?"

She swallowed. "We have a difficult time having children. Something in our genetics."

"I'm sorry. Maybe there's something medically that can be fixed?"

She shrugged, her eyes sad.

"Has your kind always served Auras?"

"I don't know. We don't keep a history."

"That's weird. There's got to be something. I'll look around in our library."

"But why? It won't change anything."

"Knowing the past can be very powerful. You never know. The Lizens could have once been a powerful society where Auras served them."

"I doubt that," she said. There was a hint of bitterness in her voice.

"Do you hate it?"

She looked at me. "It doesn't matter. I have no other choice." She stood up and went to the door. "I really should be going."

"Um, okay. Do you want to hang out some time?"

"I don't think that would be proper, but thanks." She reached into her pocket. "Oh, and this is for you." She tossed me a folded up note.

After she left, I opened the letter. As I suspected, it was a note from Christian. It didn't say much, but his words gave me comfort. "I'm here for you," it said. I dropped to my bed and curled into a ball, thinking of him, Tessa, . . . and the girl who had killed herself.

THIRTEEN

It was a beautiful Sunday morning. At least, that's what I told myself. I was determined not to let the events of the dance ruin the last of my weekend. It was going to be great, despite the fact that the gray sky and pregnant clouds screamed rain. Again.

I needed to do something fun today, something normal. I quickly dressed and walked down the hall to May's room. It took her a moment to open the door.

"What's up?" she said through a big yawn.

"Do you want to do something today? Go to town, shop a little?"

She frowned. "What time is it?"

"It's nine."

She turned around while smoothing back her dark hair, which she had been growing out, and looked at a clock on her wall. "I would love to, but I have to meet with Dr. Han at noon."

"On a Sunday?"

"I know, boring. He's having my class meet with another Fury, and this was the only time the person could come." She shrugged. "We're discussing what it's like for Furies on the 'outside.' Maybe Kiera could go with you."

"Doesn't she hang out with her dad on Sundays?"

"That's right. She does." May played with her hair. "I wish I didn't have this thing. I could really use some shopping time." Here eyes narrowed. "How are you going to get there?"

"Sophie said I could borrow her car sometime. In a minute I'm going to find out if she meant it."

"So you're going by yourself?"

"Probably, unless—" A thought occurred to me. "I have to go, but I'll see you tonight."

I skipped the elevator and took the stairs to the fourth floor, where all the teacher's offices were. My guess was Sophie was still here despite it being the weekend. She never spoke of going anywhere else.

My hunch was right, but Sophie was in her office with Abigail going over paperwork. I stuck my head into the doorway. "Hey, Sophie," I whispered.

Sophie looked up. "Good morning, Llona. Do you need something?"

"Can I borrow your car? I'd like to do some shopping in Cold Spring."

Sophie's face scrunched, and it looked like she was about to say no, but Abigail interrupted her. "What a wonderful idea! You should do lunch while you're there too. There's the cutest restaurant right on Main Street."

Sophie looked at her. Abigail was smiling big. When Sophie turned to me, I gave her my most eager face. She exhaled. "Fine, but be back before dark."

I gave her a quick kiss on her powdered cheek. "Thanks, Sophie." Before leaving I winked at Abigail. She winked back.

I left the building and walked across campus to Lambert House, where the Lizens lived. The building looked just as nice as the others on the outside, but the inside definitely needed some work. Rugs on the wood floor were frayed, and black scuffmarks scratched the pale white walls.

I crossed the small lobby to an older woman sitting on a worn, cornmeal-colored couch. Her leathered face and hunched over frame were evidence of a long, and probably not easy, life. Her right arm was completely covered in dark green scales, and her eyes, slightly covered by a few stray strands of gray hair, stared down at something on her lap.

"Excuse me?" I said.

Her head remained down, but her eyes slowly met mine. The motion creeped me out, and I shivered. "Hi, um, I'm looking for Tessa?"

"Are you lost, Aura?"

"I'm looking for Tessa," I said again.

"Did she forget to do something for you?"

"No. I just want to talk to her. Please, do you know where she is?"

Her tired gray eyes drifted upstairs. "351."

I went up the stairs to the third floor. The poorly lit hallway helped hide the outdated wallpaper and the holes in the carpet. I found this out the hard way by tripping over a large section that had come unglued and was curling up on its end. Why was this place in such ruins? The whole place reminded me of a poorly made horror film.

I relaxed when the door to 351 opened. Behind it, a petite woman's green eyes widened. Definitely Tessa's mother. She had the same dark hair and patch of brilliant scales on the side of her face.

"Hi, I'm looking for Tessa?" I said.

"Is something wrong?" she asked, with a hint of panic in her voice.

"No, not at all. I just wanted to hang out with her. Is she here?"

Her mother tilted her head, eyeing me up and down. I must have passed inspection because her face brightened. "Tessa is in her room. Come in, come in. I'm so glad you came to visit. I'm her mother, Lilly. And you are?"

"My name's, Llona. Llona Reese." I stepped into the room. Two great mirrors on opposite ends made the small living room appear much larger. An old floral sofa looked out of place next to a circular cherry coffee table. On its top, flowers in full bloom filled an antique-looking vase. With little to work with, Lilly had done a beautiful job creating a warm and inviting environment.

Lilly turned toward a hallway and called, "Tessa! You have a visitor." She looked back at me. "I thought I knew all the Auras, but I don't think I've seen you before."

"I'm new."

"Did you transfer from one of the other schools? In Ireland perhaps?"

I shook my head. "No. I lived in Utah and went to a public school before I moved here."

Her eyebrows lifted. "How is that possible?"

Gratefully I didn't have to answer. Tessa walked in, giving me the same expression her mother had just given me. "Llona, what are you doing here?" she asked.

"Just wanted to hang out, is that okay?"

She glanced over at her mother and then back at me. "I guess. Come on back."

I followed her down the hallway to her bedroom.

"You two have fun," her mother called after us.

"Wow! Cool pictures," I said as soon as Tessa closed the door. Superheroes, painted or drawn on canvas, hung on her walls. "Did you do all these?"

"Yeah. I know, nerdy."

"No way! I love superheroes. These are incredible."

"Really?"

I nodded and continued to admire the paintings. Tessa

had taken her time with each one, sparing nothing on details. "These are good." I looked back at her. She was sitting on her bed, tugging at a loose thread on her bedspread. "Seriously, you should work for Marvel or something."

"With this face?" She broke the string with her fingers. "No, my only job will be serving Auras, no offense."

"None taken." I sat on a chair in the corner of the room. "I don't get it."

"Get what?"

"What's the big deal? So you have some scales on your face? I think they're pretty. It makes you look . . . retro."

She snorted. "Right."

"I'll prove it to you."

"How?"

"Come with me."

"Where?"

"Let's go do lunch, wander around Cold Spring. I've heard it's a really cute town."

She practically wilted. "No way."

"Just this once. Come with me. I bet you'll be surprised how accepting people can be."

She shook her head. "I can't."

I let out an exaggerated sigh. "Sure you can."

"No, really. I don't think I can even if I wanted to."

"Are you saying they keep you prisoner here?"

"Of course not. It's my kind, the Lizens. They don't want any attention drawn to us. I think they're afraid we'll be shipped off and studied in some underground lab."

"For having a few scales? I've seen far stranger-looking people than you guys, believe me."

She shifted nervously. "I don't know."

I was wearing her down. "Come with me, please? We'll only be gone for a couple of hours."

"What will I tell my mom?"

"I'll tell her we're going hiking or something." I couldn't believe I just said I'd lie. Surprisingly, it didn't bother me like I thought it should. Something to think about later.

She glanced up at a picture of Wonder Woman on her wall and studied it. "Okay, I think I will."

I threw my arms around her. "Awesome!"

Twenty minutes later, we were driving toward Cold Spring, the closest town to Lucent Academy. Tessa gripped the side of the car. Her knuckles were so white I thought I might be looking at bone. I placed my hand on her arm to transfer Light, but for some reason decided not to. The thought of using it like that made me feel uncomfortable. Instead, I said, "It will be okay. I promise, you'll have fun." She agreed, but she still looked tense.

Our short trip to Cold Spring turned out to be beneficial for both of us. It was just the break I needed. We ate inside an old, colonial-style house that had been converted into a restaurant. Black and white photos of people, probably the town's founders, hung on the walls. They looked happy. I noticed Tessa studying them closely and wondered what she was thinking.

Halfway through lunch, I began to grow anxious. I tapped my fingers on the wooden dining table and bounced my knee up and down. My energy was off the charts for some reason. What I needed was to go running, and soon.

As for Tessa, her whole countenance seemed to have gotten brighter, especially after the waitress complimented her cool "tattoos." She relaxed after that and opened up, telling me of her challenges as a Lizen. She admitted she wanted to go to college, like actually go and not get an online education like many of the other Lizens. I admired her bravery and told her so.

* * * * *

"Can I tell you something?" Tessa asked me when we returned to Lucent.

The lobby of Chadni Hall was empty, but I could hear girls playing in the recreation room not far away. I thought about joining them, maybe beating someone at a game. I wouldn't mind beating something. "Sure," I said, looking past her.

"I don't want you to take this the wrong way, but you remind me of her."

"Who?"

"Britt."

I looked at her, eyes narrowing. "The girl who killed herself?"

She nodded.

"Talk about a mood buster," I said. "I've been compared to a lot of things, but never a suicidal freak."

"There you go again. That's what I mean."

"What?"

"Sometimes you say horrible things. Things an Aura, or even a normal person for that matter, would never say."

I rolled my eyes. "I'm just kidding."

"No, you're not, and even if you were, there are other things too. Britt was short-tempered and moody, like you, especially at the end. She lied too."

"So what are you saying?"

"Something's going on with you, and I just don't want to see what happened to her, happen to you. You're not being yourself, and it worries me."

I stepped closer to her, heat burning my gut. "How would you know? You don't know me."

"Maybe not, but I do know Auras, and you are not acting like one."

Every nerve ending vibrated within my body. "And you're not acting like a Lizen. Shouldn't you be making a bed or something?"

She stared at me for a moment, then blinked as if holding back tears. "Right. See you."

After she left, I stormed up to my room and slammed the door. Why did everyone think I had to be such a goodie-goodie just because I was an Aura? Did being at Lucent mean I couldn't have any fun? I took a deep breath. The smell of my room, a rich, metallic blood odor, no longer made my stomach roll. It made my mouth water.

I slumped against the wall and slid to the floor. I stared at the window, waiting for the inevitable night to come. Hours passed. I was practically willing the light from my room. I was so transfixed that I didn't answer when I heard May knock on the door and call my name. And then, slowly, as the sun set, darkness crept toward me. I smiled.

The moment my room was entirely black and I could hear no movement from within the school, I opened the window. The faint sound of hundreds of heartbeats rose from the forest. They seemed to be calling me. The creatures of the night.

I leapt from my window and hit the ground running. I kept to the shadows, avoiding light at all costs. After jumping over the rock wall in one bound, I tore through the forest, searching for the one thing my body seemed to want. The desire was so strong, it overrode the voice screaming warnings in my head. I thought of Christian, but I couldn't stop.

A strong heartbeat lured me to the left. I stopped and listened. The rhythmic beat betrayed a large animal hidden within a nearby clump of trees. I stealthily made my way to its secret spot. Within ten feet a deer bolted, but I was faster, spurred on by the new and powerful force within me. I tackled it to the ground, my knee on its gut, my hand pressing its head to the ground.

I stared at its struggling body beneath me in both awe and horror. I had taken it down. I had the power to destroy its life.

The vein in the animal's neck pulsed. I wanted to stop that pulse.

I closed my eyes tight. *I don't want this*, I tried to convince myself. *This isn't me*. But . . . if it wasn't, then why did every part of me want to destroy the life in my hands?

My eyes opened. *What did it matter anymore?* With both hands I lifted the deer's head and prepared to twist.

FOURTEEN

I SCREAMED A TERRIBLE CRY TO PREVENT MYSELF FROM HEARING the sound of the deer's bones breaking, but my scream was cut short when something slammed into me, knocking me to the ground. I tried to get out from under it, but whatever had pushed me off the deer was much stronger. I swung my legs up to try and kick at it.

"Hey!" a deep voice said.

I continued to fight much like the deer had beneath my grip moments ago.

"What's wrong with you?" the voice said.

I continued to struggle until I felt the entire weight of my attacker cover my whole body. His strength felt like a concrete wall bearing down on me. In my ear, I heard, "Stop fighting. I'm trying to help you."

I gasped for air. If I stopped moving, then I'd have to face what I'd almost just done. "Please just kill me," I whispered.

My attacker sat up, legs straddling my waist. His arms pinned my hands to the ground. "What did you say?" he asked.

I opened my eyes. Liam, the Vyken who'd turned into wind, stared at me in shock. I turned my head away. "What do you want?"

"I was stopping you from doing something stupid. What is wrong with you?"

Tears stung my eyes. "I don't know."

He moved off my body and sat next to me, still staring. "What's your name?"

Before I could stop myself, I whispered, "Llona."

Liam waited a few seconds before he said, "From the moment I met you, Llona, I felt there was something different about you."

That was the last thing I wanted to hear, especially from a Vyken. "I have to go."

"No way. We need to figure out what's going on."

"What does it matter?"

"You're not a full Aura, are you?"

"Of course I am." How could I admit that I might be something else?

Liam frowned. "It's not possible. A Vyken wouldn't dare."

"Dare what?"

"Come here." He reached for me.

"No."

"Quit being difficult. Come here."

"Don't tell me what to do!" The anger, always at the surface, bubbled over. I turned to leave, but suddenly Liam was behind me, his arm around my chest, and with the other he was trying to force my neck to the side.

"No! Please! Don't bite me," I yelled. I couldn't move from his crushing grip.

"I'm not going to bite you, fool. Just hold still."

Because I couldn't do much of anything else, I did as he asked. His grip relaxed. With his free hand he swept my hair back and drew in a breath. "I'm so sorry, Llona."

The way he said it, all sincere-like, made me sick. No one was going to feel sorry for me.

"We have to talk," he said. "You need help. You're turning into a Vyken, but you can beat it if you let me help you." His eyes were big, and he looked frantic.

"I will never need the help of a Vyken." My hands balled tight.

"Its poison is in your blood. It's changing you."

I fixed my hair back over my neck. "You're lying."

"Am I? You're in denial, Llona. You can feel the evil destroying you, making you do things you wouldn't normally do, say things you wouldn't normally say."

I stared at the ground, not wanting to believe.

His voice lowered. "I've been where you are. It's a dark and lonely place."

I looked up at him. "I won't listen to your lies." I turned and ran away.

His voice carried into the forest behind me, "I'll be here!"

I don't know how long I ran, but I didn't stop until my legs gave out. I fell hard; my knee smashed into a rock hidden within the tall grass. I gritted my teeth and immersed myself in the pain. It was a welcome distraction from an even greater torment. But after several minutes, the pain subsided, and all I had left were Liam's words. I rolled over and tried to throw up, but nothing came out.

I dropped onto my back and stared into the night sky. As much as I didn't want to believe Liam, he was right. I may not have known that I was turning into a Vyken, but I knew there was something inside me, taking hold. A dark and dirty seed had been planted, and its roots had begun to grow.

* * * * *

I lost track of time, lying on the cold ground, when the sound of a snapping twig made me sit up. The forest was quiet, except for . . . I listened closely. The soft rustling of leaves and grass. Something was coming my way. I scrambled over behind a nearby tree and waited.

After a minute I peeked around the trunk. Not far away a form moved in and out of the shadows. I couldn't sense if the thing was Vyken or human, but the moment it stepped into the light of the full moon, and I saw its face, I knew it was a Vyken. And by its slender form, I guessed a woman, but I couldn't tell by the face, which was missing half of its leathered skin. The other half was a rotted skull with a green, moss-like substance clinging to the cheekbone. The bone was a dirty yellow, the same color as her two rows of broken teeth.

She looked around and sniffed like she was searching for something. Her eyes jerked to the tree I was hiding behind. I ducked farther behind it and held my breath, my heart pounding and sweat breaking on my brow. Any other day I would've jumped at the chance to fight, but I was still too afraid of what Liam had told me and of what I already knew. Was I seeing my future?

"I smell you, Aura," the woman said. Her voice was deep and raspy.

I left my hiding spot and ran as fast as I could, crashing through the forest, arms outstretched. I pushed my already exhausted legs hard as I hurdled over, under, and around what felt like an Amazon jungle.

The Vyken chased after me, making a strange sound with her throat, almost like a pig grunting. I looked back at her and saw that the sound was from the wind moving between exposed cords on her neck where there was no skin. The sight and sound of her made me find a second wind, and I sped up.

Bursting through a tall bush, I moved to take a step but found nothing but air. I fell, more like bounced, end over end down a steep hill. I didn't stop moving until I landed in cold water. I sucked in air and quickly stood up. In front of me was a lake the size of a football field. Moonlight stretched across it like a lit-up road. I looked around. Other than a steep incline around the water's edge, most of which was covered in trees and bushes, there was no easy way around it.

I thought about climbing back up the hill, but even as I thought it, I heard the female Vyken coming closer. Having no other choice, I moved farther into the cold water until, once again, my foot found no ground beneath me. A sharp drop-off plunged me into the water. I gasped at the shock of it and swam backward to keep my eyes on the top of the ridge.

Just then the hunched-over female appeared. I took a deep breath and dipped beneath the water's surface. A few feet away I spotted a branch attached to a fallen tree lying at the bottom of the lake. I swam over and took hold of it to keep me from floating up.

Through the clear water, I could just barely make out the Vyken's form as she made her way down the incline. When she reached the water's edge, she paused and scanned the surface. After a moment, she turned and began to move back up the hill. Just in time too because my lungs were burning.

I was about to push up when all of a sudden she stopped and turned back around. I bit the insides of my cheek to keep from instinctively taking in a breath.

She returned to the water's edge, and what she did next had me frantically looking around for an escape. Her black boot slid onto the water's surface, and as soon as it touched it, the water beneath her foot turned to ice. Another step. More ice. An ice bridge was being created wherever she moved. Ten more steps and she'd be standing directly above me.

Although I was terrified, my lungs no longer cared. I let go of the tree branch and began to float up, but just as I was about to break the surface and gasp for air, something took hold of my ankle and pulled me down.

FIFTEEN

I FOUGHT AGAINST THE TIGHT GRIP AROUND MY ANKLE SINCE all I could think about was getting air, but when my feet touched ground, and I felt arms spin me around, I was surprised to see Tessa, her hair swirling in the water around her. She signaled for me to relax. I signaled back that I was going to pass out if I didn't have air. She shook her head and rolled her eyes.

What did that mean?

Tessa patted my chest and gave me the thumbs up sign. I looked down at my almost non-existent breasts and raised my arms as if to say, *huh?*

She laughed and tried again. Pretending to breathe, she patted my chest and gave me a thumbs up again. I think I was starting to catch on. I was so busy trying to communicate with her that I didn't notice I no longer needed air . . . as long as she was touching me. It was like she was transferring air into my lungs. I smiled big.

Tessa's smile disappeared, and she pulled me close, pointing upward. Up above the Vyken's icy footsteps passed overhead until we could no longer see her. We waited several minutes before Tessa began to move to the other side of the lake, pulling me with her. The bottom was squishy and threatened to suck us in with every step. Because of this we moved quickly.

This far down, the water was surprisingly clear, giving me a spectacular view of this strange underworld. Schools of fish swam by us, some large, some small, but each of them beautiful in their own way. They reminded me of people. Tessa looked at me knowingly. This deep in the water her scales seemed to be glowing, and I wondered if she was more comfortable down here than up above.

As soon as we surfaced, I sucked in air. "What was that?" I asked right away.

"Which part?"

"All of it. You, what the Vyken did, the breathing. I feel like I've just entered the Bermuda Triangle." I followed her to shore and, like her, began to ring out my clothes. A slight breeze made me much colder than I'd been under the water.

"I've never seen a Vyken do that before," Tessa said. "Maybe she was some sort of water creature that got turned into a Vyken. Pretty scary, though."

"Terrifying." I flipped my hair upside down, careful to keep my bite marks on the opposite of Tessa, and squeezed the water from it. "So what was that cool trick you did in the water?"

"All Lizens and anyone they touch can breathe underwater, but please don't tell the Auras."

"Why?" I rubbed my arms to try and get warm.

"We've given them so much already, but there are some things we want to keep to ourselves." Moonlight shimmered against her green scales.

"I get that. Your secret is safe with me."

Tessa began to walk, half pull, herself up the steep incline toward the forest. "So what were you doing out here anyway?"

"I was—" I shook my head, realizing that something else had to be said first. I hurried after her. "I owe you a huge apology. We had such an amazing afternoon, and then I blew it. You were right about what you said earlier. Something is going on with me, but I'll figure it out and make it up to you somehow."

"Will you take me out again? Maybe to see a movie?"

"Easy enough. I'd love to."

"Then you're forgiven." She smiled and started walking again. "So, seriously, what were you doing out here?"

I thought of Liam. "Running."

"You shouldn't be out here."

"Should you?"

She stopped moving and turned to me. "No, but my life is not as valuable as yours."

I scoffed. "That's the dumbest thing I've ever heard."

"The Auras' numbers are dwindling."

"And from what you've told me, so are the Lizens'."

"But we don't affect the world like Auras do. Even if it's from a distance, you guys do so much good."

I stared at her, aghast. "Who's teaching this crap? Any person can make a difference in the world."

"But you have Light in you!"

"And you have the ability to breathe underwater and who knows what else. Everyone has something unique about them, but that doesn't make them special. It's what they do with their gifts that makes them special. Light means nothing if I don't do something with it." I swallowed. "The way I've been acting lately, maybe I'm turning into a Vyken." I waited for her reaction.

Tessa laughed and kept walking. "Now that's the dumbest thing I've ever heard."

Since Tessa seemed to know where she was going, I followed. After a few minutes of silence, I asked, "Do you think all Vykens are evil?"

Tessa thought a minute before saying. "Well, if I go off the same rationale you just gave me, it would depend upon the Vyken's actions. Does a person just become an evil Vyken, or is it their actions that make them so? I'm sure somewhere along the line, though, there's a point of no return."

"I get where you're going with this, but let's say there's a Vyken that hasn't done anything wrong and is actually nice. How do I know he's not tricking me, waiting for me to become vulnerable?"

"Are you talking about someone specific?"

"Maybe." I snapped off a thin tree branch in passing and proceeded to break it into pieces.

"Spill."

"I don't know that much about him as I've only met him a couple of times. But he's fast and does this cool thing with the wind—"

"Liam?"

I stopped her. "You know him?"

"I've met him a few times over the years, but lately he's been coming around a lot more, asking me all sorts of questions about some of the Guardians and who else I've seen out here. But, wait. Liam isn't a Vyken."

"Um, yes, he is."

"No he's not. He's an Enlil."

"What's an Enlil?"

"He controls wind. Liam's a good guy, Llona. And he's here trying to help the Auras, not harm them." Tessa turned onto a worn trail. The dark silhouette of Lucent Academy came into view.

"I knew Lizens were simple, but I didn't know they were naive."

Tessa whirled around. "You're doing it again."

I closed my eyes tight. "Right. I'm sorry. I didn't mean it."

"What's going on with you?"

The painful memory of the night's events and what I'd almost done to the deer rushed back. "I'm not sure yet, but I'll figure it out."

She touched my arm. "Do you need help?"

"I don't think anyone can help me." I started walking again, picking up my pace.

"You're not alone, you know," Tessa said from behind me.

I reached the wall and looked up, pretending I hadn't heard her. "So how do you get over?" I could easily jump it, but didn't dare in front of her.

"Over here." Tessa walked to the wall and, at eyelevel, lifted what looked like a stone. Beneath it was a keypad. She pushed a series of numbers, and a section of the wall opened like a door. If I wasn't feeling so depressed, I would've commented how James Bond this all was, but instead I went quietly through the door.

Before we split ways, I said, "I'm sorry again, about before."

"It's okay."

I nodded and walked away. "I'll see you."

"Liam's a good person. So are you," she called after me.

I raised my hand to signal good-bye, but kept walking forward.

Back in my room, I left the lights off, collapsed into bed, and touched the necklace Christian had given me last year, which I had worn ever since. "Endure to the end," it said. Could I endure, and to what end?

I need Christian, I thought and rolled onto my side. If it was possible for someone to be a half-Vyken, he was the only person at Lucent I dare ask, but his answer terrified me.

SIXTEEN

Because I'd barely slept, it took some convincing, but eventually I rolled out of bed and went into the closet to pick my clothes out for the day. This proved difficult. All I could think about was how my life might never be the same. If what Liam had said was true and I really was becoming a Vyken, then Christian had been trained to kill me. I sat down and kicked the closet door shut, trapping me in the small closet.

I stayed there, willing myself to get up, when I heard the chimes. I wiped at my eyes and stared at the back of the door. *Time to get up and pretend everything's okay.*

As I was rising, I caught a glimmer of blue near the hinge of the door. A brick was dislodged just enough for me to notice. I reached for it and wiggled it around. With a little more effort, I removed it from the wall and peered inside. A book, no bigger than my hand, lay hidden inside. I took it out of its hiding spot and brushed the dust off its cover.

Opening to the first page, I read: "This diary belongs to Britt Myers." I jumped when I heard a knock at my door.

"Llona? You in there?" May called.

I opened the closet door. "I'm just getting ready."

"Are you coming to breakfast?" she asked.

"Yeah, I'll be right there."

"Okay, see you." I heard her footsteps move away from the door.

I stared down at the diary in shock, wishing I could skip classes, but that was a lot harder to do when you actually lived at school. Dressing quickly, I applied more makeup than usual to hide my red eyes and then stuffed the diary into my bag.

In the dining room, I dropped into a seat next to May and Kiera. "How's it going?"

Kiera set down a glass of milk. "Good."

"Did you have fun with your dad?" I asked her.

"Yeah, it was awesome. He took me to see a Broadway play. Have you guys ever been?"

"Once," May said, "My mom took me . . ."

Just then Tessa reached over my shoulder and set down my breakfast plate and blue vitamin. "Get any sleep?" she asked quietly while Kiera and May continued to talk.

"Sort of."

Tessa patted me on the back and walked away. I watched her and the other Lizens serve the rest of us while I rolled the pill between my fingers. So bizarre. I wondered when Auras first started having servants. I took a bite from a toasted bagel.

"Llona?" May asked.

I looked at her. "I'm here. Sorry. What's up?"

"Kiera asked you what you did yesterday."

Almost snapped a deer's neck, ran from a water-freezing Vyken, and walked underwater without breathing. "Nothing," I said and popped the pill in my mouth.

Across the room I watched Tessa clear Ashlyn and clan's table. They didn't notice her efforts. Well, one girl did. She pointed at a glass that Tessa had forgotten to clear. I took another bite, my mind wandering to the diary inside the backpack at my feet.

"Did you get any studying done?" Kiera asked, but I didn't

answer. I wanted to do something else. Even though I wasn't finished with my food, I stood up, threw the backpack over my shoulders, and began stacking my dishes.

"What are you doing?" Kiera asked.

"Clearing the table." I gathered my silverware and put it onto my plate.

Kiera's eyes widened. "That's the Lizens' job!"

"I can clean up my own crap." I lifted my dishes. Several heads turned in my direction.

"Wait," May said, quickly gathering her dishes too. "I'm coming."

She stood and followed me toward the kitchen. The room was silent. I glanced at Tessa briefly; she was shaking her head at me in horror. At the same time Sophie stood up. She rushed over to me as if I had fire coming out of my head and blocked the way to the kitchen doors. Through a forced smile she said, "What are you doing, dear?"

"Cleaning up."

"We have people for that."

"Do you pay them?"

She laughed. "Of course not. They enjoy doing it."

"Since when do others love picking up the half-eaten crumbs of spoiled brats?"

She gasped, along with all those within earshot.

I brushed past her into a hot kitchen. Two Lizen women were scrubbing a steaming grill. They looked up at me and froze.

"Where do we wash our dishes?" May asked before I could. I loved May.

The women continued to stare, but a familiar face rushed forward. "Llona?"

"Hi, Lilly. May, this is Tessa's mom. Can we wash our dishes real quick?"

"No, no, no!" She took the dishes from our arms. "You mustn't do things like this. It is the Lizens' job."

"Says who?" I asked.

"Please, Llona. We like to serve Auras."

"Llona!" Sophie's sharp voice made me spin around.

"What?"

"I want you in my office, now." The several yards of shimmering material around her waist billowed outward as she spun quickly on her heel.

I took a deep breath and exhaled. "Fine."

Sophie turned to May. "And I want to see you after."

"Why?" I said. "She didn't do anything but follow me."

"Actually," May interrupted, "Llona was copying me. She's always doing that." She looked over at me, and together we burst into giggles.

Sophie's face burned red. "Both of you, follow me now." She turned around and walked back through the dining room that was full of whispers and glares. May and I lagged behind her, while under my breath I hummed Darth Vader's theme song.

* * * * *

Sophie closed her office door behind me. "I'm getting tired of these visits, Llona."

I dropped into my usual chair. "Me too."

"Don't get smart with me," she snapped.

"Is being smart a crime too?"

Her shoulders sagged as she lowered herself into a chair. "I don't know what to do with you," she said more to herself than me.

"Can you tell me what I did wrong? I honestly thought I was being helpful."

"It wasn't necessarily wrong, it's just that you're taking away from others."

"You mean the Lizens?"

"Of course. Serving us is their identity. It makes them feel important in the world. Before us their race had almost become extinct. We saved them."

"So in return, they are in our servitude?"

"We didn't ask them to do this; they chose it."

"They may have centuries ago, but has anyone asked them lately if they enjoy waiting on us?"

"I haven't heard any of them complain."

"Why do they need to? Look at their faces! They look miserable."

She shook her head. "I truly doubt that, Llona."

"Seriously? Open your eyes. Or are you afraid that if you do, you and all your precious Auras might actually have to lift a finger around here?"

Sophie leaned back in her chair, looking amused. "So that's why you think we've gathered every young Aura we can find—to pamper them? You are a naive, ignorant child."

"And you are a stubborn, closed-minded adult."

A tense few seconds passed. I was about to apologize, but my aunt smiled.

"You are so much like your mother," she said. "I'm surprised how much I've missed this banter." She stood up and came around in front of me. She leaned against her desk and said, "I really messed things up with your mother, and I don't want to do that with you. How about a truce?"

"Like what?"

"How about I try to be more aware and open minded and you try to understand what we're trying to do here. Our safety is everything."

"Fine. I'll try."

"Good. Can I get a hug?"

I stood. "Of course." Her arms came around me. I was surprised to discover how much her touch reminded me of my mother's. I resisted the urge to cling to her.

Finally, Sophie let go and looked at me. "You have so much potential, Llona. I can't wait to see what you do with your future."

* * * * *

Feeling better about my relationship with Sophie, I crossed campus to return to class. We might not have had a lot in common, but we were family. With so few family members left, I resolved to try harder.

My etiquette class had already begun, so I slipped in quietly and took the nearest seat. I tried to pay attention to what Ms. Williams was saying, but I couldn't stop thinking about Britt's diary. I was itching to read it. I glanced around for a fire alarm but found none.

A girl next to me raised her hand in response to a question I hadn't heard.

"Auras are always polite and kind," she said and looked at me. I glared back.

"Exactly," Ms. Williams said. "Well done, Kim. What about public outbursts? Is that an appropriate behavior for an Aura?"

I glanced around. What was this? A lesson directed at me? *I don't think so.* I raised my hand.

Ms. Williams seemed surprised to see my arm occupying air space. "Llona?"

"I think there is a time and place to stand up for what you believe in, no matter who's around or what's going on."

She pursed her lips. "Actually, Llona, an Aura should always be respectful, and if she has a disagreement with someone it should be handled in private." Ms. Williams turned to pick up a lesson book, and even though the air was thick with tension, I raised my hand again.

Ms. Williams looked up; her right eye twitched. "Yes, Llona?"

"I disagree." A couple of girls snickered, but I continued. "Sometimes it takes just one person to stand up and voice their opinion. Just one person to make a difference, to make things better."

"What are you saying?" Kim asked. "You think you're in an oppressed society?"

"Maybe I am."

"That's enough!" Ms. Williams said. "Llona, I think you've caused enough of a disruption for today. I'm excusing you for the rest of class."

"Really?" I didn't mean to sound so excited.

"Yes. I want you to go straight to the library and read over the lesson, and when class is over, you and I will have a little chat."

I grabbed my backpack and stood up. "Deal." To the rest of the class, I couldn't help but say, "Have fun being brainwashed."

I found a quiet spot in the back of the library and sat down. I placed the diary in front of me and stared at its worn blue cover. In a way I felt wrong about what I was doing. This journal didn't belong to me. It belonged to Britt's family. They should be the one to read her last words.

But.

What if it said something horrible? Maybe it was best that they remember her how she was, before she died. I thought about it for a few more minutes before I chose to read it. I opened the book and scanned the first pages. Britt seemed like a normal girl. She had friends. She did well in school. She even had a crush on one of the Lizen boys. Interesting.

Britt talked a lot about wanting to be a good Aura. She had

plans of marrying a politician, even to go as far as planning his campaign. After that she wanted to use her influence to help impoverished children in other countries. Britt clearly enjoyed life and had a promising future, but then I stumbled across an entry where everything changed:

October 5

I had a horrible dream last night. You know the kind that seems so real it haunts you the rest of the day? I haven't felt the same since.

In my dream I was in the woods. Not sure how I got there. I was wandering around trying to find the school, and I was freezing cuz I was only in my gown. But then I saw the big wall and I felt better. Circle it until I get to the gates. That's what I told myself.

I was about there when a man walked toward me and asked if I was lost. I thought maybe he was a new Guardian, but when I saw he had a tattoo of a blade on his head, I knew he wasn't. And this is where my dream went south—the tattooed man rushed me and bit into my neck. It hurt something horrible.

In my dream I tried to fight him, but it was like hitting a concrete wall. And then when I thought I was going to die, another person appeared and pulled the man off me.

"That's enough," he said, and his voice was surprisingly pleasant. Anyway, I couldn't see this new person's face, as he was wearing a long robe with a hood over his head.

He didn't say anything else, but he did drag away the man who was acting all crazy and still trying to get at my neck. And then I was alone. With all the blood coming out of me, I thought I'd feel pain, *but I didn't. I just lay there until I fell back asleep. When I woke up, I was back in my bed, feeling fine.*

The dream really scared me, but what was even scarier is when I noticed two red holes in my neck. I must've scratched myself or something, cuz . . . I don't know what else it could have been.

The whole thing was just weird. Hope I can forget about it soon.

Love,

Britt

I stared at the entry, my hands shaking and the book shaking even more. She'd been bitten, like me. My stomach turned over, and my throat quivered. I took several deep breaths to keep from throwing up.

It took a long time for me to calm down, and when I did I turned my attention back to the diary. After Britt's "nightmare," she didn't write in it as much. Her final entries scanned a two-month time period. The entries where short; her handwriting had become erratic, almost illegible.

Britt was angry, and she didn't know why. Everyone bothered her. She was getting into fights. In one entry she wrote:

I wish I could kill them all.

The ink was smeared, then:

What am I saying? What's happening to me? I'm a monster.

She wrote, "I'm a monster" over and over until the page was filled. I turned to the final entry. All it said was:

December. Almost Christmas. Something's wrong with me. I think I'm possessed. If only I could've been a better Aura, but there's no more time. I have to kill a demon.

And that was it. I closed the diary and cried. I hurt for Britt. No one knew what she was going through, not even herself. She must've felt so alone. I also cried for myself. Her death could very well be my future. I'd rather die too than become a selfish, evil monster that preyed on other Auras.

Britt's diary entries only confirmed what Liam had told me. I thought of his offer to help me. If he was telling the truth and there was a way to stop the poison from changing me, I had to try it. And fast.

As for Christian, what would I tell him now? I had my answer. I thought me being an Aura and him a Guardian was bad enough for our relationship, but how about a half-Vyken and a Guardian? I almost laughed. And then I cried again.

I glanced up at the clock. Ten more minutes before Ms. Williams came to give me a piece of her mind. Just enough time for me to regain my composure and pretend like I wasn't turning into a monster.

* * * * *

Ms. Williams's lecture wasn't as bad as I thought it would be. I was confused, she thought, because of my "misguided" childhood. She felt bad for me and wanted to help me through my trying time. If only she knew.

I kept quiet the whole time, thinking only of the diary. When Ms. Williams was finished, she gave me a hug. I let her.

I went to the rest of my classes, the diary weighing heavily on me. I was glad when they were over and returned to my room, where I fell asleep as soon as I collapsed into bed. Too many emotions for one day. But with sleep came more nightmares. Vykens running through the forest, dropping from trees, climbing the walls of Lucent Academy. And on the roof, I was there, waiting to greet them.

I woke up screaming just as the chimes sounded. It took me a second to realize I was in my room. I let out air real slowly and sat up. Only a dream.

I took a few minutes to calm down, then headed downstairs. I was about to go inside the dining room when I felt someone tug on me from behind. I turned around. "Christian." My heart broke.

Christian wasn't smiling. "Are you okay? I've been looking for you."

I shrugged. "I've been around."

"How's your head?" he reached up as if to check it, but I stepped away. "What's wrong?" he asked.

"It's all better. Doesn't even hurt." I was about to say more when it looked like a shadow passed overhead and it got noticeably darker.

I glanced up, but Christian looked to the window. "Sun must've gone behind a cloud," he said and ran his fingers through his hair, tugging on it hard. "Something's got to change, Llona."

I lowered my eyes to his, no longer searching for invisible shadows. "I couldn't agree more."

He sighed, like he was relieved. "Good, because I have to see you more, like every day, even if it means I'm not a Guardian anymore."

I gasped and my knees almost gave out. This wasn't what I was expecting. I shook my head. *Just spit it out, Llona!* "I think we need some time apart. Just for a little while," I said quickly. "I need some time." I couldn't look at him. I clasped my hands together on my chest in hopes they could hold my heart together.

Finally Christian spoke. "I don't understand."

I tried again. "It's not safe for you to like me. I'm not . . . normal."

Christian took hold of my arms, regardless of the girls walking by us. "Whatever this is, Llona. We'll get through it. I love you."

I shook his arms off me. "I'm sorry, Christian. Please." Tears filled my eyes. "Just stay away from me." I turned and rushed down the hallway, away from the dining room and away from Christian.

Instead of returning to my cramped, smelly room, I ran from the school, no longer caring who saw me leave. But who would be watching? No one. The Auras were together beneath the light of fancy chandeliers while I raced toward darkness.

SEVENTEEN

I RAN INTO THE FOREST, DARTING AROUND TREES, UP AND over fallen limbs, and thought of Christian. How could he ever want to be with someone like me? A damaged Aura. What future could we possibly have?

I stopped and gasped for air, my hands on my shaking knees for support. But it wasn't enough. I stumbled to the ground, onto my back, and looked up. Pieces of the night sky twinkled through the cracks in the tree branches.

"What are you doing out here?"

I sat up. Liam was walking toward me. I grunted and fell back into the grass.

"It's a school night," he said.

"And?"

"Shouldn't you be hanging out with friends, studying?"

"'Cause I fit right in."

Several seconds passed before he said, "I meant what I said before. I can help."

"I know." *And I will take it as soon as I work up the courage to ask you.*

"I've been where you're at. I know what it feels like."

I smirked. "To be a teenage Aura who wants to claw her skin off?"

"To wish that you'd never wake up. Because when you're awake all you want to do is destroy everything around you, even yourself. Every breath threatens to suffocate you until you wonder if death would be better."

I swallowed hard.

"You don't have to feel like that," he said.

Two sparkling pieces of sky came together when the wind blew a branch to the side. I sat up again. "How can I trust you?"

Liam looked around. "Is there anyone else trying to help you? Anyone at all who would understand what you're going through?"

I stood. "What do I need to do?"

"Use your most precious gift.

"Light? How?"

"Wow. You're a lot further gone than I thought if you don't know what I'm talking about." He took three steps until he was standing directly in front of me. I resisted the urge to step back from his powerful presence. "When is the last time you used Light?" Liam said.

I thought about it. "A while."

"That's a problem. The Vyken's poison inside you is trying to kill everything that's good about you. And you're letting it."

"I'm not letting it. I'm using Light."

"To harm others."

I scoffed. "Not others. Bad guys. Is there something wrong with that?"

"It can be. It all depends on your motivation to use violence. Is it because you're craving the destruction, or are you trying to help someone, even if it's yourself?"

I knew the answer right away but didn't tell him that. Ever since I'd been bitten, I craved contention and the thrill that came with it.

Liam continued, "The Vyken's poison feeds on chaos and

death. If you continue on this path, it's only a matter of time before you do the unforgivable."

"What's that?"

"Deliberately and knowingly take the life of an innocent soul."

I shrunk back, embarrassed. "That deer the other night . . ."

"Not quite an unforgivable act, but if you would've gone through with it, I don't think you could've come back. Taking a life can make one feel extremely powerful. It's the worst kind of addiction." Liam leaned toward me, as if he were about to reveal a great secret. "But know this, there's more power in saving a life. The Vykens will never know this. It's easy to take lives, but to save them, that's a lot harder, hence the greater reward."

"How do you know I'm not already too far gone?" I looked down at the ground. "It sure feels like it."

Liam tilted my chin back up. His hand was surprisingly warm. "Because you're here, which means you want to change, correct?"

I nodded.

"Good. Let's get started then." He turned around, surveying the area.

"Wait, what? Right now?"

Liam looked back at me. "You have something better to do?"

I straightened. "What do you want me to do?"

"Why don't you show me what you can do? The non-killing stuff, that is."

I held my hand in a closed fist in front of me, turned it over, and opened it. A lighted ball the size of an apple appeared. With a single thought, the Light split into several pieces. I raised them into the air and spun them around.

"Wow," Liam said, sarcastically. "Not impressed."

With a flick of my wrist, I sent the balls flying just over Liam's head. He had to duck to keep from being hit by the last one.

"Those sort of look like weapons to me," Liam said.

I huffed. "Fine." I lit another ball; this one I shaped into a thin spear the size of a needle.

"What's that supposed to be?" he asked.

"I made something just like this the other day to pick the lock to the nurse's office."

Liam sighed. "So you used Light to break into somewhere you weren't supposed to be?"

The way he said it made it sound all wrong. "That's not what . . . I don't know." I threw up my arms. "You're confusing me."

"No, you're confused. You can't tell what's right and wrong anymore." He paced in front of me. "I want you to think back, before you were bitten. What did you use Light for?"

It took me a minute to think. The memories were painful. Tracey.

Liam placed his hand on my arm. "Why is this so hard?"

I jerked away. "Let's just get this over with." I took a deep breath and thought back to the trick Sophie had shown me in the forest back in Utah. Closing my eyes, I focused all my senses. I sought out nearby life, all the creepy crawlies. The process came easily, mainly because a part of me wanted to destroy them all, but I didn't focus on the darker part. I focused instead on their life force. A burning started deep inside me, warming my insides. When I had located all the life around us, I transferred Light to them.

I opened my eyes when Liam whistled. It looked like the stars above had fallen to the earth around us.

"It's beautiful," he whispered, as if the sound of his voice might ruin the celestial moment.

I, on the other hand, struggled to feel it. Liam must've noticed my bored expression because he said, "Focus on the connection you have with the living. On how you can make them stronger, better. You have a gift. Use it."

I moved around the lights, examining them. Bugs scurried up bark, in and out of the grass. Birds rested high in the trees. A twinkling light just in front of me drew my attention. A butterfly perched on a branch beat its wings, yet it couldn't fly. "Its wing is broken," I said to no one. Its life force was waning, making Light flicker within it.

"You can fix it," Liam said over my shoulder.

I continued to stare at the butterfly; Light shined through its blue transparent wings, reminding me of a church's stained glass window. An ancient instinct raised my hand just above the wounded butterfly. Beneath my palm, Light bathed the butterfly. Its wings began to beat—both of them, fast and furious until the butterfly rose from the limb. As it fluttered away, an indescribable feeling washed over me, and for the first time since Tracey's death, I felt peace.

Liam cleared his throat. "Not bad. How do you feel?"

I turned around to face him but had to step back as he was a little too close for comfort. "A little better, actually." My chest felt lighter, and I inhaled deeply. "Can I do that with people too?"

He shook his head. "I doubt it. Besides, it would probably kill you."

"Good to know." I turned around, staring at all of the lights. "There's something I still don't understand," I said and dropped my connection with the forest, extinguishing the light around us. "What's with the blood?"

"Blood?"

"I can smell it, really strong. And sometimes," I paused, "I crave it. It makes me sick."

"It's your Vyken half. You're sensing everything a Vyken senses."

"But they want Light, not blood."

"But where is that Light?"

It dawned on me. "In our blood."

"Exactly. It's the only way a Vyken can tolerate it. The Light has to be filtered somehow, otherwise it's too powerful and will kill them. And Vykens salivate at the smell and sight of blood the way a human does with a candy bar wrapper, because they know what it contains."

This made sense, but I still wasn't sure about something. "So what are you, then?"

Liam turned around, his eyes greener than I remembered. "First, and foremost, I'm an Enlil, despite the Vyken poison inside me. Enlil's can control wind, one of the earth's four elements. We were created to help protect the earth and those living on it."

"Are there more of you?"

A shadow darkened his face, sending a cold shiver up my spine.

"Not that I know of."

"What happened?"

His gaze met mine; the heat of it warmed, more like burned, my insides. "Vykens either killed us or turned us. They've done this to a lot of races. Anything to further their cause."

I thought hard, trying to find some silver lining on the conversation that clearly invoked painful emotions for him. "So if they got turned, that means they're like you, right? Not all evil and wanting to kill Auras?"

He chuckled. "If only. I'm the only one who did it."

"Did what?"

"Resisted."

"I don't understand."

"Yes, you do."

I didn't want to believe it. There had to be others who'd overcome being bitten by a Vyken.

Liam looked up, his eyes searching the trees, and I wondered if he was trying to put the night's puzzle pieces together like I had earlier. "It's just us," he finally said. "That is," he looked back at me, "if you survive. You still have a lot to overcome."

"So, how long?"

Liam walked away. "How long for what?"

I followed him. "For me to get rid of the poison. I want my life to get back to normal."

Liam stopped so abruptly that I almost ran into him. He whirled around. "Poison? Don't you understand? It's a part of you now, and it will always be inside you just waiting for you to succumb to it."

"So you're saying I have to battle these, these," I fumbled to find the right words, "serial killer tendencies the rest of my life?"

He didn't say anything, but the sadness in his eyes was answer enough.

I shook my head. "I can't. I can't do it. How do you stand it?" My voice was growing louder. "How do you keep from peeling the skin off your bones? I can't go through life like this!"

Liam looked away.

"Answer me!" I said. "I don't want to feel like this anymore."

"Then give up," he whispered.

"That's your answer?"

He turned to me. "What do you want me to say? You have three choices: give in to the dark poison and become a full Vyken, die, or deal with it and be somewhere in between. It sucks, I know. It's hard, it's painful, it burns, and every day it's a constant battle."

Seeing the pain on his face and knowing what he had to endure for so many years softened me. "What happened to you?" I asked, my voice gentle.

He stared at me, an inner rage burning, and I swore it made his green eyes glow. "People think the death of a loved one is the hardest thing to overcome, but it isn't. There are far worse things than mourning." His jaw clenched tight, and I knew he wouldn't say more.

Although my desire to transfer Light had been almost nonexistent the last few weeks, I reached out and placed my palm on his arm. It took just a second to transfer Light's calming power.

Liam's whole body reacted as if it were giving a long-awaited sigh of relief. He looked at me, surprised. "What was that?"

I shrugged. "A little comfort, I guess."

He stared at me until I began to squirm. "Why are you looking at me like that?" I said

"Nothing, I . . ." but he didn't finish his sentence. Instead he began walking back toward the school. "You know, maybe there is hope for you."

I caught up to him. "What do you mean?"

"I didn't realize how powerful Light is. Maybe it's enough to stamp out the Vyken's poison. I hope so, because you'd get bored living forever."

EIGHTEEN

My heart skipped a beat. Maybe I heard wrong. "What did you just say?" I asked.

"Live forever. That's what Vykens do, as long as their head is still attached, that is. Surely you knew this." Liam kept moving, his head turning side to side as if he were looking for something. "You've got to get back. It's not safe for you out here."

"Hello? You just dropped a bomb on me. How could I live forever? I'm only half Vyken." Saying that out loud made me feel dirty.

Liam didn't explain. Instead, he grabbed my arm. "Don't you feel it?"

"What?"

Faster than I could blink, he whirled me around and pressed my back to him. "Shhh," he whispered in my ear. "Listen. Concentrate."

I did as he asked even though the warmth of his body against mine was oddly distracting.

"Far away: two Vykens, maybe three, but they're there," he said. "Do you feel it?"

I focused all my senses, especially my hearing. I could hear movement, heavier than the normal beasts of the forest, yet agile and full of grace. Much like I imagined a tiger would sound prowling through the jungle.

"Their numbers are growing," Liam said, letting me go. "We're concerned something big is coming."

I turned and looked at him. "You keep saying *we*. Who is *we,* and, now that I'm thinking about it, why are you always out here?"

Liam glanced around, before he looked back at me.

"What?" I said. "You expect me to trust you, but you won't return the favor?"

"I was sent here."

"By whom?"

"The Deific."

"And they are?"

He thought. "They're a group of people, some graced with unique abilities, who fight the bad in the world, whatever form that comes in. The Deific was formed hundreds of years ago and was a small group at first. You see, along with the Auras, they were able to keep the world in balance, but then the Auras withdrew themselves, first from the Deific and then from the world. Their presence is barely felt now, and it's caused all sorts of problems for the Deific."

"Why did they send you here?"

He paused, eyes searching my face, for what I didn't know, and then said, "In the last three years there's been an increase in Vyken activity."

"How much of an increase?"

"More than we keep track of. Vykens used to keep a low profile and only occasionally attacked an Aura on the outside, but that's not the case anymore."

"What's changed?"

"Vykens are no longer confined to the night. They are able to do things in the day. It's like doubling the amount of time for mayhem."

I shook my head. "But that means—"

"They're ingesting Auran blood," he finished. "And more so than the number of Auras being killed on the outside. That means someone's supplying blood to them. Someone at Lucent is my guess."

I remembered the IV bag Christian had found. "One of the Guardians," I said.

"I've suspected them for a long time, but I don't have any proof. And if one's involved, then there's a good chance others are too. One Guardian can't be doing all this."

"What do you want me to do?"

"I'll worry about the Guardians, you just find out more about the blood. I know they draw an Aura's blood at least once a month. It would be nice to know who implemented the program. You also need to find out where the blood's being kept."

"While I'm at it, why don't I just find out who's giving it to the Vykens?"

"By all means, Ambitious Annie."

"And what exactly will you be doing?"

He looked away. "You probably haven't realized it yet, but I can't get much done during the day."

"Why not?"

His eyebrows lifted. "Vyken blood. Sunlight burns my skin."

I hadn't even thought about that. "Why doesn't it me?"

"Auran blood, remember?"

"Then why don't you get some? I could—"

Liam shook his head. "No. Not my beverage of choice. I don't want the temptation."

"But if it will help you—"

"I said no."

"Fine," I said, surprised by his sudden hostility. "Look, I'll see what I can find out, but stay close. You still have a bunch of questions to answer."

"I'm not going anywhere."

"Good." With Liam helping me, I might just survive.

* * * * *

As soon as sunlight invaded my room, I jumped out of bed. I didn't even know why I bothered lying down after last night; I hadn't slept at all.

The discovery last night had really freaked me out. I was tempted to tell Sophie, but then I remembered why I wouldn't. I could hear what she would say now: "Llona, an Aura's blood is sacred. Why would anyone here want to give it to Vykens?" *Well, guess what, Auntie? This perfect world you've created isn't so perfect.*

I picked up a rubber band and was about to pull my hair back when I saw the bite marks in my reflection of the mirror. I looked at them closer, surprised to see that they didn't seem as red as before. I ran my fingers over the raised bumps. They still hurt. I chose to do nothing with my hair and left it down like always.

Because I still had time to kill before breakfast, I studied Britt's journal again, hoping I'd find a clue to what had been going on at Lucent. I flipped through the pages several times until I thought I'd found something. I didn't think anything of it before, but after last night, I didn't know what to believe.

Three months before Britt died, she had started dating Jackson, and she really liked him. I thought about this. Jackson was always lurking outside the walls at night, but he was a Guardian. A Guardian working with Vykens was almost impossible to believe, despite what Liam said. But then, who else would do something so horrible to the Auras? Just then the chimes sung their song. I closed the diary and tucked it into my bag.

On my way to the dining room I stopped by May's room. When she didn't answer, I skipped the elevator and took the stairs since my body was feeling more energized than usual. *Must be a full moon.* I was pretty much over its pull, but every once in a while I still felt it.

I walked into the crowded dining room, searching for May. The smell of ginger and sliced oranges drifted out from the kitchen, and the aroma perked me up. May was sitting at a table talking to Ashlyn and her friends. I gritted my teeth and prepared for the worst.

"Hey," I said and sat down next to her.

She looked at me surprised. "I didn't think you'd make it to breakfast."

"How come?" I picked up my blue pill and was about to pop it into my mouth but stopped when she said, "I stopped by your room at midnight but you weren't there. Figured you'd had a late night and would sleep in."

I lowered the pill, noticing that Ashlyn was listening closely and watching me even closer. "I couldn't sleep," I said.

"I saw you," Ashlyn said.

I froze. "What are you talking about?"

"With your old Guardian. Christian's his name, right?" She smiled sweetly. Like the devil would right before he dragged your soul to hell.

May must've noticed how I bristled because she said, "What are you getting at, Ashlyn?"

Ashlyn looked around the table, as if to make sure everyone was listening. "You two were speaking, well, like you knew each other *intimately*."

I gritted my teeth. "You don't know what you're talking about."

"Really?" Ashlyn said and smiled again.

"What's your problem?"

Ashlyn leaned forward. "We've all heard about your mother—"

"Don't go there," I warned. I balled up my fists, practically crushing the pill in my hand.

"—and it sounds like you're following in her footsteps. Anyone can tell you're crazy about him."

"Let's go," May said.

But Ashlyn wasn't done. "Hopefully, though, Christian gets as far away from you as he can before you both end up dead."

I jumped up and was about to throw myself across the table to beat the crap out of her, but May stood and stepped in front of me. "Leave," she said. "Now. You don't want to get in trouble again. I'll deal with her."

I looked over her shoulder at Ashlyn's smug smile. "One of these days I'm going to punch the Light right out of her."

"Fine," May said, "but not now. Go cool off."

"Whatever." Before I walked away, I tossed the pill at Ashlyn. She gasped when it hit her in the forehead.

NINETEEN

Great. I'd put May in the middle of me and the other Auras. That's the last thing she needed. She deserved so much better. I headed upstairs, shaking my head. *Later. I'll get her alone and talk about it, but first I need to do some investigating before classes.*

I stopped at Abigail's door and knocked.

"Come in," she said

Abigail was sitting at her desk, staring down at a stack of papers on her desk, pencil in hand. "You couldn't have come at a more perfect time, Llona. These words were beginning to look like hieroglyphics."

I dropped into a nearby chair. "What are you working on?"

"As I'm sure you've heard, Cyrus is back. He wants a full report on how all the girls are doing. He's always worrying about their health." She glanced at a clock on the wall. "Don't you have class soon?"

I opened my mouth to speak but was unsure what to say. "Actually, I had a nightmare last night," I said, recovering quickly.

"What about?"

"Well, I was in a car accident and was rushed to the hospital. I'd lost a lot of blood, and because no one was with me, a nurse gave me normal blood, and it killed me."

Abigail set her pencil down. "That's horrible."

"I know." I leaned forward. "But it got me thinking. What if something did happen to me, and no one was around to give me the right kind of blood?"

Abigail smiled. "You'll be fine. Normal human blood and all. It will just weaken you a bunch and make you feel like you're on drugs. I know, because it's happened to me once."

"But what if I don't want to feel like that?"

"I don't understand."

"Is there a way I can keep a bag of blood with me just in case?"

She tilted her head. "Like in your purse?"

This time I laughed. "No, maybe in my car or something. I just want to know where it's at in case I ever need it."

"Honestly, the best place for it is here. We keep it under lock and key and as long as you stay in contact with us, we'll respond quickly to an emergency. And when you leave Lucent, your assigned Guardian will have some on hand too."

"Do the Guardians over at Waverly have access to our blood?"

She pursed her lips. "There's no need."

"But what if one of them really needed it. You know, in case we're hit by terrorists or something."

Abigail squirmed in her seat. "First, nothing is going to happen to us, and second, if for any reason a Guardian needs blood, he'd only have to get the key from myself or Cyrus."

"You two are the only ones with keys?"

"Yes. Sometimes the other faculty members will ask to borrow it, but it's always returned."

I thought about this. Maybe someone had made a copy of the key. They'd be able to do it easily enough.

Abigail rested her elbows on the desk. "What's this all about, Llona?"

I looked up. "There was something else in my dream. A Vyken was taking my blood, and it wasn't just him. There was a whole line of them, just waiting."

"Are you having a lot of nightmares?"

"No. Just these two, but they freaked me out. What if a bunch of Vykens got access to our blood?"

Her eyes grew big, glassy, and blue. "That would be really bad indeed. They could destroy the Auras." She began to fan herself with her hand. "Now you're giving me nightmares!"

I stood up. "Well it was just a dream, right?"

"Thank goodness."

I opened the door, but before I left, I asked, "One last question, where is the blood room?"

"It's in Denelle Hall. At the rear of the building."

"Thanks. And have fun with all your paperwork."

I headed straight for Denelle, passing several girls on their way to class, books in hand. School would have to wait. I wanted to see this blood room.

I hid at the rear of Denelle where I wouldn't be seen and waited until all the girls were in class. After several minutes, I opened the glass door and looked inside. The hallway was empty. I quietly snuck to the last room and placed my hand on the doorknob.

"What are you doing?"

I froze, but when I realized I recognized the voice, I exhaled and turned around. "Hey, Tessa."

She was standing at the opposite end of the hall in an open doorway. She came toward me. "What do you need in that room?"

It took me two seconds to decide to trust her. Besides, she seemed to know more about the school than anyone. "Can you keep a secret?" I asked.

She pointed to her head. "You'd die if you knew the secrets this vault contains."

"Well here's one more for you. Last night I went outside again—"

"That was stupid."

"Liam was there. I got him to tell me why he's hanging outside the walls all of the time." I quickly told her about the blood and the Vykens getting access to it.

"That's messed up. So what are you guys planning?"

I turned the doorknob, but it was locked. "I need to get in here and look around." I produced Light in my palm and held it up to the lock so I could see its inner workings. It was just like Abigail's. *Nice.*

"What are you doing?" Tessa asked.

I shaped the Light in my hand like I'd done before. "You'll see." In less than a minute the door opened.

"Cool trick," Tessa said. "Who knew Auras would make great thieves?"

I smirked and went inside. When Tessa reached to turn the light on, I stopped her. "Leave the lights off. Just in case."

"But I can't see anything."

I produced more Light and sent it across the room, giving us just enough to see what we were doing.

Tessa looked around and gave a low whistle. "Creepy," she said.

The room was much bigger than I had thought and cold too, like we'd walked into a giant refrigerator. My body physically reacted to the overpowering smell of blood, but I forced the desire away, even more repulsed with myself.

I continued surveying the room. At the rear of the room were two desks, papers scattered over the top of one of them and an older-looking computer on the other.

Moving down the aisles, I checked the names of students

and the dates written on the bags. "Who have you noticed come in here?" I asked Tessa, who was following behind me. The dates on the bags were recent, all within the last few months.

"Abigail comes in here a lot. And I've seen Ms. Haddy and Ms. Crawford."

"Can you think of any other reason a teacher would come here other than for blood?"

"Maybe they keep their own here?" Tessa suggested. "Or they could be making a delivery."

"Maybe." I continued down the aisle and raised my hand, letting my fingers trail across the plastic bags holding the blood. "I feel like I'm missing something."

"Like what?"

"I don't—" Just then I felt a faint but familiar feeling. "Whoa," I said and stumbled back.

Tessa put her hand on my arm to steady me. "What's wrong?"

"I can't believe it. I can't believe they'd do it."

"Do what?"

I carefully reached toward the bag of blood I'd just touched. When my fingers were within an inch of it, my hand began to tingle like it had fallen asleep. I wondered why the sensation wasn't stronger. "It's a Vyken's," I whispered.

"Vyken?" Tessa looked around. "Where?"

I pointed at the bag with a girl's name written on it. "There."

Tessa's eyes grew, mirroring my own horror. "In the bags? All of them?"

I shook my head and began to walk up and down the aisles again, my hands stretched out. "I don't think so. These," I touched several bags while I walked, "are Auran." I returned to where Tessa was. "And these," I trailed down the row, both hands touching blood on each side, "are all Vyken." My skin began to itch as if spiders were crawling up and down my arms and legs.

I stopped moving. The rabbit hole was a lot bigger than I expected. "What is going on here?" I said. "This is the one place everyone told me I'd be safe. What am I supposed to do now?"

Tessa came to me, her eyes sad. "It will be okay. You can leave, go somewhere far away. I'll understand."

"Huh?"

She patted me on the arm. "You have every right to be frightened, after everything you've been through."

"Frightened? I'm freaking angry!" I walked by her. "I just spent a year dealing with Vyken crap. Out there." I pointed far away.

"So are you going to leave?"

"Not in a million years. Lucent Academy is the one place Auras are supposed to be safe. Someone's going to pay."

"But what can we do?"

I looked back at the Vyken blood. "We'll destroy it all. Starting with the Vykens'." I started to walk back to it, but Tessa stopped me.

"You can't."

"Why?"

"Because then they'll know we're on to them. We need to figure out who's doing this, then we can destroy them."

"Screw that," I said and knocked her arm away, but she grabbed me again.

"This is not the time to be impulsive, Llona. Think for a minute. There's something a lot bigger going on here than just someone selling Auran blood to Vykens."

This stopped me. "Like what?"

"Why was the blood replaced?"

"So no one would know blood's missing."

"But why with Vyken blood? Why not with a human's? Wouldn't that have been easier?"

Tessa had a point. She continued, "What would happen to an Aura if her blood was transfused with a Vyken's?"

My head snapped up.

"It would probably kill them," she said.

I shook my head. "No. It would turn them. The poison." My hand went to my neck. "Like a bite."

"Turn them into a Vyken? But how do you know?"

I met her gaze. Could I tell her? Before I could answer my own question, the sound of the outside door opening made me extinguish the glowing Light on the other side of the room.

"Llona?" Tessa whispered.

I reached for her in the darkness until I found her arm. "This way," I said.

We moved quietly to the opposite wall while heavy footsteps grew louder. I stopped when I reached the desk I'd noticed earlier. "Quick! Hide behind this."

I slipped next to her just as the door swung open.

TWENTY

The light flipped on. Both of us sunk farther to the floor. As long as whoever had just come in here didn't look toward the desk, we would go unnoticed.

Tessa tightened her grip on my hand, and when I saw her face I was afraid she was going to scream. I squeezed her hand and even transferred Light to her. She visibly relaxed and began to breathe normally again. I gave her a reassuring smile.

As soon as I felt she wasn't going to freak out, I signaled her to be quiet, then slowly inched my way over to where I could see around the desk. Standing three rows over was a man, his back to me. He was reading the labels on the bags of blood. After a moment he lifted a bag off its hook and placed it inside a briefcase.

He turned to the side, and I saw who it was. I quickly covered my mouth and slid closer to Tessa. For several seconds nobody moved. I was afraid he'd hear my heart pounding and discover us hiding, but then he began walking. The door opened, the lights turned off, and the door closed.

Both Tessa and I sighed at the same time.

"That was close," Tessa said. "Who was it?"

Light appeared in my palm. I raised it in front of us. "Dr. Han."

"The Fury?"

"Uh-huh. And he took some blood." I walked to the rack he'd been looking at.

Tessa followed. "What would he want with Auran blood?"

"Good question." I looked at the name on the rack. "Not an Aura. Another Fury."

"Who?"

I met her gaze. "May."

"Why would May's blood be in here?"

"Probably the same reason they have ours." I followed Tessa out of the room.

"Let's just get out of here," she said. "We'll figure it out later."

I locked the door and closed it. "I feel sick."

"Look," Tessa said when we reached the front door.

I peered out the glass door. Dr. Han was walking toward Chadni Hall. "Let's follow him," I said.

As soon as he turned the corner, we opened the door and jogged to catch up.

"I don't think this is a good idea," Tessa said. "The last person I'd want to mess with is a Fury."

I peeked around the building just in time to see him open and close the front door. "Come on," I said.

Tessa made it to the front door then stopped. "I'm not supposed to go in this entrance."

"Oh brother, come on." I opened the door.

"Serious. I can't. You better hurry. He's getting away."

I glanced inside and then back at Tessa. "I'll see you soon," I said and ducked inside.

Dr. Han was getting inside the elevator. I waited until I saw which floor he stopped on and then headed for the stairs, racing up them until I reached the fourth floor. I opened the door just in time to see a door at the end of the hallway closing. It had to be him.

I walked quickly, yet casually, down the hallway, passing by Sophie's office. So far the offices were empty. All the teachers must be in class.

When I reached the door Dr. Han had gone through, I paused. What now? Bust down the door all gangster-like and say, "Give me back my best friend's blood?" I so needed spy lessons. I turned around and headed back the way I came, feeling stupid for even coming this far. I needed a plan.

Just as I walked by the elevator doors, they opened. "Llona?"

I froze.

"What are you doing?"

I whirled around and thought quickly. "Hi, Sophie. I was looking for Ms. Crawford. I wanted to talk to her about my grade."

Sophie placed her hand on my shoulder. "What are you talking about? We don't give grades here."

Of course you don't. "Right. I mean I just wanted to see how I'm doing in class. I don't feel like I'm grasping everything."

Sophie studied my face. Finally she moved away. "Ms. Crawford's in class. You should know that because that's where you should be."

"Right. I know, I'll just—" I tried to get away, but she stopped me.

"While you're here, Llona, why don't you come with me?"

"Where?"

"I was just on my way to visit with Cyrus and welcome him back. He's finishing up a meeting."

"Um, that's okay. "

She moved me forward. "I insist, Llona. It will only take a few minutes."

I forced a grin. "Would love to." But when Sophie knocked on the same door Dr. Han had gone through, my smile became real. This couldn't be any more perfect.

Sophie opened the door. Cyrus's office was really more of a library. There were a couple of huge mahogany desks sitting opposite each other, and every wall was lined with wooden shelves. The books within looked very old. I would've loved to explore them, but I just then realized I wasn't alone.

Standing next to the desk on my right was an extremely handsome man who looked to be in his fifties with a streak of gray in his dark hair. A navy blue suit fit him well, but it might've just looked that way because the man standing next to him looked completely out of place. He was shorter than the first and was wearing a tan polo shirt and wrinkled black pants.

On the other side of the room was Dr. Han, and next to him stood Christian. He smiled, but there was sadness in his eyes. I had hurt him.

"Welcome back, Cyrus," Sophie said. She walked forward and hugged the tall, handsome man. This surprised me. I expected Lucent's president to look much older. Sophie turned to the man next to him; he startled a little under her gaze. "And you too, Jameson. We're all very glad you've both returned safely."

"It's good to be back," Cyrus said.

Sophie looked back at me, and I thought she was going to introduce me, but a knock at the door interrupted her. We all turned around. Jackson was standing in the doorway with Spencer.

"You wanted to see me, Sir?" He was addressing Cyrus, but at the last second he looked at me and winked. I looked away and at Christian, who no longer looked sad but confused and a little angry.

"Hello, Jackson, Spencer. Yes, I wanted to see you. Can you give me a minute first? We have a visitor." Cyrus's dark eyes settled on mine, and I had a difficult time looking away.

"Cyrus, this is my niece I told you about, Llona," Sophie said. "She was Laura's daughter."

Cyrus stepped forward at the same time Jackson closed the door. "I was very fond of your mother," he said. "I was sorry for her passing."

I nodded but just barely. The air in the room had turned thick like smoke. I looked around, but no one else seemed to notice the change.

"Are you enjoying Lucent Academy?" Cyrus asked.

"Um, yes. It's—" The room was getting hot. I took a step toward Christian and my eyes flashed to his. His whole body tensed as if he knew something wasn't right with me. Next to him, Dr. Han frowned as he looked to me and then at Christian.

Cyrus moved closer. Jameson moved with him, and I sensed Jackson and Spencer coming up behind me.

"It's what, Llona?" Cyrus said.

The suffocating sensation grew, and my head began to spin. *No, not here, please.* I met the eyes of everyone in the room. Now Dr. Han was coming toward me. Who? Who was it? Although I knew there was a Vyken in the room, I couldn't pinpoint who it was. Why were my senses so dull?

When I stumbled, Christian caught me. "What's going on, Llona?" he said it as if we were the only ones in the room.

"A Vyken," I gasped.

"Here?"

"What's the matter?" Cyrus said.

"Llona?" Sophie asked.

The room began to teeter as everyone closed in on me. A Vyken was only feet away. *Focus! Who was it?* "Christian?"

And that's when Cyrus reached for me.

I yelled, "It's him! He's a Vyken!"

Christian didn't question. He reacted so quickly that I didn't even notice where he'd come up with the knife in his hand. He slashed downward on Cyrus's arm and was about to strike again when the knife's handle turned a fire red, thanks to Dr. Han.

Christian cried out and dropped the blade. As soon as it hit the floor, Jackson tackled him to the ground.

"What in the world is going on?" Sophie said.

I looked around the room. Jameson was attending to Cyrus's arm, Jackson was sitting on top of Christian, who only looked at me with concern in his eyes, while Dr. Han was staring down at me like he wanted to turn me as red as he had the knife. I would've said something, but the room was still spinning, and I couldn't get my legs to move.

"Get her out of here!" Cyrus said through a clenched jaw. He was bent over and holding his hand over his arm.

Sophie took hold of my arm and literally dragged me from the room, and shoved me into the nearest empty office. "What was that, Llona?" she said after she closed the door.

With every breath my head began to clear. "I, I don't know," I stammered. "There was a Vyken."

"A Vyken?"

I nodded. "In the room. I think it was Cyrus."

Sophie laughed. "That's absurd! He's been our headmaster for decades. Don't you think we would've known?"

"Someone in that room is a Vyken," I mumbled. But what if there wasn't? What if the Vyken side of me was throwing off all of my senses?

"Do you have any idea what you've done? You'll be lucky if Cyrus lets you stay at Lucent, but Christian, he was already on probation."

My head snapped up. "Probation? Why?"

Sophie clicked her tongue. "I don't have time for this. You go back to your room, missy, and we'll finish this chat later. I need to tend to Cyrus."

I dropped into the nearest chair, going over the events

again. Had I really sensed a Vyken? And if I hadn't, then that meant Christian just knifed the most important person at Lucent Academy. I was really screwing up his life.

A door slammed in the hall. I looked up just in time to see Christian walk by.

"Christian!" I said.

He whirled around and looked from me to Cyrus's closed door. Very quickly, he pulled me farther into the empty office and closed the door.

The suddenness of it surprised me, and I said, "Christian, I—"

"Are you okay?" he said, breathing heavily through his nose, his brows drawn together.

"Me? How can you ask that?"

"I can't believe it. Cyrus a Vyken?" He was staring at me with such trust, such loyalty, that I felt even sadder. There wasn't a thing in this world he wouldn't do for me.

I glanced away from him and shook my head. "You shouldn't have done that, Christian. It was too impulsive."

"But you said he was a Vyken. Is he or isn't he?"

I closed my eyes and breathed in. "I'm not sure. Everything just started spinning."

Christian took my hand. "Are you ill?"

I jerked it away. "Listen to yourself! Do you realize what you've done? You may never be a Guardian again. Ever!"

Christian's face grew red as he responded to my own anger. "I don't care about that anymore! Don't you get that?" His jaw muscles bulged, and he rolled his shoulders like he was trying to relax. In a much gentler voice he said, "What's going on, Llona? I know there's something you're not telling me."

I pursed my lips and stared at the ground.

Christian reached up and pressed his palm to my cheek. "Please, Llona. Whatever it is, we'll get through it. Just talk to me."

I leaned into his hand; his touch calmed my nerves. The world felt right here, like I was normal, like nothing had ever changed me.

Christian dropped his hand to my shoulder, then trailed it down to my hand, where he held it. "What you said before, about us needing time apart. You didn't really mean it," he paused, "did you?"

I looked him in the eyes. "I need some time. Please, that's all I can say right now."

"Are you in some kind of danger?"

I shook my head. "I need to go."

His hand tightened on mine. "Talk to me, Llona."

"Let go, Christian."

He stared at me for what seemed like a very long time. Finally he let go. "I'm here for you. Always."

"I know." I went to the door and opened it. "I'm so sorry, Christian." As I walked away from him, down the long hallway to the elevator, I resolved to make things right, to expel the demon from me once and for all.

TWENTY-ONE

I STAYED IN MY ROOM THE REST OF THE DAY, TRYING TO figure out what had happened in Cyrus's office. I kept going over the events in my head, tried to slow them down, hoping to find an answer. The more I thought about it, the more I knew there had been a Vyken in that room. But was it really Cyrus?

A knock at the door made me sit up. I went to it and opened it just barely. My heart lifted a little when I saw May. "Hey, come on in," I said.

May walked in, holding a lunch bag, and closed the door. "You look like crap," she said.

I puffed my cheeks and blew out air. "Rough day, for sure."

"Maybe this will help." She handed me the bag. It smelled like a turkey sandwich.

"Thanks," I said.

"So about earlier, with Ashlyn. Sorry she was so rude. I let her have it after you left."

"You didn't need to do that."

"Of course I did. You're my best friend, Llona."

I looked at her, thinking. Enough was enough. She needed to know what was going on, most of it anyway.

"What?" she said.

"We need to talk." I paused "And not just you. Let's get Kiera and Tessa too."

"Like a meeting?"

"Yes, an important one. The one I talked about before the dance."

She nodded as if she'd been waiting for this. "I'll go find Kiera, and I just saw Tessa downstairs."

"Cool. I have something to show you guys."

Ten minutes later all four of us were in my bedroom. I closed the curtains to give us more privacy even though we were several stories up.

"This is a little weird," Kiera said, looking around suspiciously.

"Just wait," I said. "It's about to get weirder. Have a seat."

Tessa sat on the floor, joining the others. "Does this have anything to do with what happened earlier today?"

"Yes, and there's more."

"What are you guys talking about?" May asked.

I sighed. "There's something going on at this school."

"Like what?" Kiera asked.

I reached into my backpack and pulled out Britt's diary. "It starts with this."

"What is it?" May said, taking it from my hands.

"It's a diary. I found it hidden behind a brick in the closet."

"Whose?" May and Kiera said at the same time.

I looked at Tessa. "Britt's."

Tessa shook her head. "I don't think you should be reading that."

"Maybe I shouldn't have, but I'm glad I did."

"Wait," May said, "who's Britt?"

I glanced at Kiera. She looked pale. "I knew her a little," she said. "Britt used to be in Llona's room." Kiera brought her knees to her chest, her arms wrapped tightly around them.

"Where is she now?" May asked.

Kiera looked beyond me. "She died."

May gasped. "How?"

Again I waited for Kiera to answer.

"Nobody knows. They found her in her room."

"In this room?" May clarified.

"Yes."

May turned to me. "That explains all the ghost jokes then."

"Did you know her very well?" I asked Kiera.

"No, not really. I mean, she was nice and all, but toward the end she started getting in trouble a lot, even causing fights. I thought we would be great friends because of her rebellious streak, but she wasn't interested in friendship or anyone. It was really sad. She died alone."

The room was quiet for a few seconds before May said, "What's it say?"

I took a deep breath and told them the truth about Britt's death, including how she had been attacked by a Vyken.

"So it made her more aggressive," May said after looking up from reading an entry. I avoided her stare.

"Exactly," I said. "She started feeling angry all the time and wanted to hurt others."

"I remember," Tessa whispered.

Kiera's eyes were big. "So what happened?"

"It became too much for her. She couldn't stand the way she was feeling, and she couldn't control it either. She finally killed herself."

"Did they find the Vyken who did this to her?" Kiera asked.

"She never told anyone, but she writes in her journal that two men were involved. One of them had a tattoo of a dagger on his head."

Tessa brought her knees to her chest. "I wonder why Britt didn't tell anyone."

I glanced away. "She was ashamed."

"She must've felt all alone," May said, but by the way she was looking at me, I couldn't tell if she was talking about me or Britt.

"But that's not all," I said. "It's just the beginning." I proceeded to tell them all about Liam (May wasn't at all surprised to learn I'd been sneaking out at night) and the blood being given to Vykens. I spoke of the fight at the tower, and I even told them about being trapped in the blood room with Tessa and seeing Dr. Han. And finally, I told them about what had happened with Christian."

"I can't believe it," Kiera said when I finished.

"Crazy, huh?" I said.

"No, I mean I really can't believe it. It's just not possible! Vykens in the school, especially someone high up? And our blood being sold to them?"

"It's true," Tessa said. "At least the blood part."

I looked at her. "It's all true."

"I believe you," May said. I couldn't help but smile. I loved my best friend. "So what now," May asked. "What can we do about it?"

"We have to find out who's behind it," I said.

"Who does Liam think it is?" Tessa asked.

"Some Guardians, but he doesn't know who yet."

"What about the Vyken in Cyrus's office?" Kiera said.

I shook my head. "I don't know, but I know it was one of them."

"Are you sure?" Kiera asked. "I mean, I've never heard of an Aura who could sense a Vyken."

"That's what's odd. We should all be able to sense the evil in them. What good is our Light if we can't?"

"Go over who was in the room again," Tessa said.

I thought out loud. "Jackson and Spencer were behind me.

Sophie was on my left. Cyrus and Jameson were in front of me, and Christian and Dr. Han were on my right."

"We can rule out Sophie," Tessa said. "And Christian."

I nodded. "And probably Jackson and Spencer too. I never sensed anything when I was near them before."

"And it can't be Dr. Han," May said.

The room grew quiet.

"What?" May said. "It's not him. I've been training with him for weeks now. He's not some evil being."

"But you've never met him up close before, right Llona?" Tessa asked.

"I haven't, but if May says it's not him, then I trust her." It was May's turn to smile.

"Then why did he take her blood?" Tessa said.

"I don't know," May said, "but I'll find out."

"Okay then," I said, leaning forward. "May's on Dr. Han—"

"And I'll watch Cyrus," Tessa said. "See if he does anything suspicious."

"Perfect," I said. "And if Christian will speak to me after today, I'll ask him to check out Jackson and the other Guardians."

"I guess that leaves me with Mr. Jameson," Kiera said, frowning. "Whom we know nothing about, other than he's Cyrus's assistant."

"I'll help," I said. "Tonight I'll find Liam and tell him our plan."

We all stood up. I took the diary back from May and tucked it into my backpack.

"Are you sure you can trust him?" Kiera said. "He sounds kind of spooky."

"I can trust him," I said. Of course I had left out the part about him having Vyken blood inside him just like me. I wasn't ready to explain how a half-Vyken could be trusted; in reality, being part Vyken myself, I wasn't sure anyone should trust us.

"Sounds like operation 'Save Lucent Academy' is in full force," May said.

Kiera opened the door. "Can we have spy names?"

I smiled. "Totally."

"Cool. I'm going to rock my name."

"Me too," Tessa said and followed Kiera out while they exchanged ideas.

I walked May to the door. "There's something else you didn't tell us," May said. She turned around.

"What's that?"

May stared at me for several seconds. "Secrets are like weights, Llona. Let someone help carry the burden."

I knew exactly what she was talking about. "I'm not ready," is all I could say.

She nodded and squeezed my hand. "I'm here for you."

I gave her a hug. "I can't imagine going through all this without you."

She squeezed me back. "We've been through worse, right?"

I nodded and pulled back.

"I'll see you later." Before she left, she added, "Christian loves you, Llona. I don't think he'd care about some silly dream. You need to talk to him." I nodded and closed the door, wishing it was just the dreams keeping us apart.

I sat near the window and waited for nightfall. With every passing second I grew more excited. I told myself it was because of my lessons with Liam, but that was a lie. I couldn't wait to get into the forest, to run through the darkness and feel its coolness against my skin.

A thought crept in before I could stop it: maybe there'd be a Vyken out there. And maybe I'd kill it.

TWENTY-TWO

As soon as the sun set, I escaped through my window. Liam had told me to meet him again in the same clearing where I showed him the lights. I just hoped he was there this early so I wouldn't have to wait in a forest lurking with Vykens. One Vyken might be okay . . .

"You're early," Liam said as soon as I entered the clearing.

I turned around. Liam was leaning against a tree in a black leather jacket.

"You don't waste any time, do you? What, do you bury yourself in leaves, and when the sun sets you rise?"

Liam stepped away from the tree. "What did you find out today?"

"Tessa and I found our way into the blood room. They keep six months of our blood in stock. I think they throw it away after that."

"How is that helpful?"

"Be patient. Some of the blood has been replaced with Vyken blood."

His stone expression cracked. "How do you know it was Vyken blood?"

"I could sense it, just like I knew you were a Vyken, or half-Vyken, I should say." I paused. "But honestly I really only sensed it when I first met you. Since then, I think my senses have been shut off, except for today of course. I don't get it."

Liam began to pace. "This is bad. Real bad."

"What are you thinking?"

"The Vykens must be planning an attack on Lucent. And when Auras are hurt, their blood will be replaced with the poisonous stuff." He removed a cell phone from his pocket. "I have to alert the Deific."

"Wait a second," I said. "That's not all. There's a Vyken in the school."

He froze and looked at me. "Tell me."

"My aunt took me to meet the president."

"Cyrus?"

I nodded. "A Vyken was in the room with us."

"Who was it?"

I tugged at my hair. "I don't know."

"What do you mean 'you don't know'?"

I threw up my arms. "It's like I was saying. My senses are all screwed up. For some reason I couldn't pinpoint who it was. I just had this general overwhelming feeling that a Vyken was in that room."

"Who else was in the room with you?"

I looked at him. "You believe me?"

"Why wouldn't I?"

"It's just that," I shook my head, "the president. The other people in the room. Everyone thinks it's impossible that one of the higher-ups could be a Vyken."

Liam met my gaze. "I'm not everyone, and if you say there was a Vyken, then I believe you. So who else was there?"

I told him.

"Interesting. And you couldn't tell who it was?"

"I'm sorry."

"What about me? We're standing ten feet apart. Do you sense my Vyken blood?"

I focused hard. "I don't. Nothing."

He took a big step toward me. "Now?"

I shook my head.

Another step.

"Nope."

Closer. "And now?"

This time I did sense something. I was starting to feel light-headed, like I stood up too quickly.

He took one final step so he was standing only an inch from me. He looked down at me. "How do you feel now?"

"Dizzy."

"Close your eyes."

I did as he asked.

"Can you still sense me?"

I nodded.

"Where am I?"

"In front of me."

"No, I'm not."

I opened my eyes. Liam wasn't there.

"Turn around."

I whirled around, coming face to face with Liam again, except I stumbled on account of being so dizzy.

He caught me. "Your senses are definitely off. How come you weren't this dizzy the other night?"

I thought back. We had stood close when he was showing me the butterfly. Briefly, but still. I didn't remember feeling all crazy-headed. "I don't know."

"What did you do today that you didn't do yesterday, or vice versa?"

"Get the president knifed?"

He chuckled. "So this Guardian—"

"Christian."

"Christian. He must really like you if he cut the most important person at Lucent in order to protect you."

"Yeah, well, because of me, they'll probably strip him of his title."

"Is that a big deal?"

"It's what he's worked for his whole life."

Liam looked right at me. "Some things are more important than a title."

I glanced away. "What kind of training do you have in store for me tonight?"

"Can you give us some light?"

"No problem." A ball of Light burst from my palm. I mentally stretched it until it was two feet in diameter. I raised it above us.

"It's like the moon," Liam said, staring up at it.

I rolled my shoulders back. "You ready or what?" I needed some real action, something to burn off my energy.

He dropped his gaze. "Tonight I just want you to create, like this moon."

"Psh . . . serious? Can't you give me something more challenging? Like a giant spear or something?"

"I want you to create something beautiful, not a weapon, Llona."

I exhaled. "Right. Stand back then. I'm going to need some room," I said, already picturing what I wanted.

I closed my eyes and focused. When I felt like I knew what direction to take to complete the masterpiece in my mind, I swung my arms over my head, sending Light to different parts of the clearing. Still with eyes closed, I spun and twisted, feeling Light flow from me in all directions. A burning, warm and intense, filled my entirety until I could no longer feel evil pressing against my insides.

I continued my ethereal dance through the forest, feeling as if I was in a different realm. I'd never felt so pure, like I was five again, picnicking with my parents without a care in the world. How had everything gone so terribly wrong? I thought of my parents. Their lives and their deaths. I thought of the Vyken who'd tricked us all. Darkness, full of anger and revenge, returned. I fell to the ground gasping for air.

Liam was at my side. "What's wrong?"

I opened my eyes. Tiny twinkling lights filled the air like drops of rain. I extinguished them. "I can't do this," I said. "Too much has happened."

"But you did do it," he said, placing his hand on my back. "And I could tell that for just a moment you felt it. You were at peace with yourself, with your life."

I looked up at him. "How do you know?"

"Because I felt it too, and I haven't felt at peace for decades." He straightened. "You just have to keep practicing. It will come." He reached to help me up. I took hold of his hand.

"Get back!" a voice shouted.

Liam and I looked over. Christian was running toward us at full speed. Liam's eyes widened just as Christian tackled him to the ground.

"Christian!" I said.

"You stay away from her," Christian said. He managed to smash his fist into Liam's face two times before Liam caught it and twisted Christian's arm, forcing Christian from him.

"Hit me one more time and you'll regret it," Liam said.

Christian lunged for him again, but this time I was ready. I stepped in between them and took Christian by the shoulders. "Stop it, Christian," I said. He looked at me for the first time. I saw the confusion in his eyes. "Stop," I said, a little quieter. "He won't hurt me."

Christian shoved my arms away and stepped back. "What

is going on? First you freak out because of a Vyken and now you're hanging out with one?"

"I'm not a Vyken," Liam said.

I shushed Liam with my hand while I kept my focus on Christian.

"You lie," Christian said. "Jackson told me all about you."

Liam snorted. "I don't think you should be trusting anything a Guardian says."

"Watch your mouth, Vyken," Christian said. Every part of him was tensed, and it took all my strength just to hold him back.

"Christian," I said. "He's an Enlil, and only has the Vyken's poison inside him, but he hasn't let it change him. He's good."

Christian looked unconvinced. "Not possible."

"It is. He fought back the darkness and won."

Christian looked at me, and his expression softened like he was feeling sorry for me. "What's happened to you?"

I couldn't stand the look in his eyes. "What are you doing here?" I asked.

"May said I could find you out here, but she didn't tell me you were on a date," Christian said, glaring at Liam.

I shoved him. "Are you going to let me explain or do you want to keep acting like you know everything?"

"Fine. Explain."

I took a deep breath. "Christian, have I ever lied to you?"

He didn't answer, but his jaw tightened.

"Have I?"

"No, but you *are* keeping things from me."

I nodded. "You're right. I have, but for good reason. I'm trying to protect you."

"Protect me?" He laughed. "From what?"

I realized the conversation was not taking the direction I wanted it to just yet, so I said, "Just listen to me when I say there's something big going on at Lucent, and I'm trying to get to the bottom of it before a lot of Auras are killed. And Liam, although obnoxious at times—"

"Hey," Liam said.

"—is on our side. He can help."

Christian searched my eyes. Finally his posture relaxed, and he stepped back. "I'll trust you, but never him." He nodded his head toward Liam.

"Fine. For now," I said. "But will you at least listen to him?"

Liam shook his head. "This isn't going to work. He's part of them, brainwashed. He'll never believe."

I turned to him. "He might surprise you."

Liam looked from me to Christian. "How do I know he won't run to his friends and tell them everything?"

I sighed really loud. "Will you trust me, please?"

Liam stepped back. "Whatever, but I don't want to be around for this reunion. Why don't you catch him up? I've got some things to do." He was staring off into the distance.

"Um, okay," I said, confused. Liam didn't look back at me when he disappeared into the forest. I shrugged and turned around to face Christian. He was staring at me intently with his lips pressed tight. What I wouldn't give for mind-reading powers. "What?" I finally said.

"Before you tell me what's going on, I have to tell you something." He swallowed. "This time we've been apart, only seeing each other for brief moments, has been the hardest thing I've ever done." I opened my mouth to speak, but he stopped me. "Please don't say anything. Just give me a second." He stepped toward me. "My father encouraged me to go into Guardian training at an early age. It was hard and fun at the same time, but I wasn't sure I wanted to devote my whole life to it. But then I became your Guardian, and it was like I finally believed in myself. I was excited for the future and for the chance to be the best Guardian I could be." He smiled. "I know that sounds cheesy, but I felt whole. And then we were separated. And," he shook his head, "I don't know, everything just fell apart. I lost those feelings, and at first I thought it was because I was faced with no longer being a Guardian. I was a mess. But then I realized something. When I'm around you, Miss Llona Reese, I'm not a mess. You make my world right, not being a Guardian. It's you I want in my life, and I'd give up everything to make that happen."

I lowered my head to Christian's chest. His arms came around me. "Please tell me what's going on," he said.

I looked up at him. "You being with me is dangerous. You saw what almost happened at the tower. What everyone says, about Guardians and Auras being together, I get it now. And I don't want anything to ever happen to you because of our relationship. You mean too much to me."

Christian chuckled and tucked my hair behind my ear. "Is that all that's bugging you?"

I almost said more, the real truth, but he continued speaking.

"You need to know something, Llona. If I were to die tomorrow, or in ten days, or in ten years, all of this, you and me, would have been worth it. I would rather live a short life with you in it than a long one where you and I are not together."

It was then that I understood how my father convinced my mom to marry him. But before I could hear any more declarations of love, Christian had to know the truth. "You can't make that decision yet," I said and swallowed hard.

"And why's that?"

"Because you don't know the whole truth."

TWENTY-THREE

It took me almost an hour to tell Christian everything about what we had discovered to be going on at Lucent because he kept asking questions. When I finally finished, he was sitting on the ground looking pale.

"Are you going to throw up?" I asked.

He gave me a weak smile. "This is so much bigger than I thought."

"What did you think was going on?"

"That maybe a Guardian had turned rogue and was selling blood to Vykens."

I chuckled. "You were half right."

Christian's eyes were full of sadness. "I'm so sorry, Llona. It's like you've gone from bad to worse."

I shrugged. "I'm just glad I found the diary and met Liam."

"Liam," Christian said and twisted his mouth like the name was sour-tasting. "That's one thing I don't get. What were you doing with him out here?"

"He's helping me."

"With what?"

I looked away, a lump growing in my throat threatening to choke me. "There's something else, Christian. Something I didn't know how to tell you before."

Christian stood up next to me. "What is it?"

I searched his eyes. "Just promise you'll still look at me the same."

"Llona—"

"Promise me."

"I promise."

I moved my hair to the side, exposing the bite marks. Christian reached up and touched them lightly with his fingers. "What is this?"

"You know what it is," I whispered.

He continued to stare at my neck. "When?"

I hesitated. "That night on the stage. Mr. Steele bit me just before I killed him."

Christian stepped back. Away from me.

"Say something," I said.

"He bit you?"

"Something else, please."

Christian began to breathe heavily.

"Christian?"

Finally his eyes met mine. "What does this mean?"

"Vyken poison is inside me," I said. It hurt to say it out loud. "The darkness is always here," I patted my chest, "and every second of every day it's trying to swallow me. I don't want to become a monster." A single tear spilled over and ran down my cheek.

Christian took me into his arms and held me tight. "It will be okay. We'll figure this out together." He smiled and looked down at me, giving me no room to ever doubt his love for me.

I nodded and blinked the tears away; they ran onto his shoulder for him to carry. For several moments he stroked my back until he pulled away and said, "I want to help. What can I do?"

"I'm not really sure. Liam's been helping. He's teaching me

to use Light the way it was intended, to comfort, beautify, and, well, you know the speech. I guess I've been using it too much the other way, and it's been feeding the darkness. Liam says it's a fine balance, but if he did it then I can too, right?"

He smiled. "Of course you can, and I'll be right here helping you every step of the way."

I squeezed his hand and smiled back. "We need to have a meeting with Tessa and May. And Kiera should probably come too. Something big and bad is coming, and we need to make sure we're ready."

"Fine. When?"

"Tomorrow," I said. "After breakfast. Meet at the track."

"Don't you guys have class?"

"Not tomorrow. It's career day, which means we're supposed to take the day to research what we want to do with the rest of our lives." I wanted to say more, but the words stuck in my throat. What Liam had said, about living forever. My whole life had changed, but was it really a life worth living if all I ever did was fight against myself?

"You okay?"

I nodded and forced a smile. "Just thinking."

I started walking. Christian came with me, taking my hand in his. I was about to say something when goose bumps broke on my flesh. They were followed by a cold chill crawling up my spine. I stopped and looked around.

"What's wrong?" Christian said.

I didn't see or hear anything. "Do you ever feel like you're being watched?"

He chuckled. "Sometimes." He turned around and scanned the forest with me. "I don't see or hear anything."

"I guess I'm just freaked out." I started walking again, feeling stupid for saying anything. We reached the stone wall. "This is my stop," I said.

"Liam's right, you know," Christian said.

"About what?"

"Your ability to sense Vykens. Something's changed, and you need to figure out what. Pay attention to everything you do, or everyone and everything you're around. Something's messing with your spidey senses."

"Spidey senses?"

"You know what I mean." He gave me a quick kiss. "Stay safe, and I'll see you tomorrow."

* * * * *

Sitting in the dining room, I rubbed my eyes, trying to push sleepiness and a headache away. I was hoping the motion would do just that, but no such luck.

"You look terrible," Tessa said in my ear as she set a plate of pancakes in front of me.

"Thanks," I said. "For the pancakes."

She smiled. "Are we still on for later today?"

Next to me, Kiera said, "Operation Save Lucent Academy is in full force."

All of us shushed her.

"Could you be any louder?" May said.

Kiera flinched "Right. Sorry."

I ate quickly, taking in as much food as I could, while Kiera whispered excitedly about all the spy tricks she thought she knew. It made me worry. She'd never faced a Vyken before and had no idea how bad things could get. I glanced over at May, who looked like she was thinking the same thing. She was silently agreeing with Kiera, but her eyes were sad as if she was remembering what Mr. Steele had done to her.

And Tracey.

I stood up. "I have to get some things out of my room.

Do you guys want to meet me at the track?"

"Sure," May said.

I turned to leave, but Kiera stopped me. "Wait! You forgot your pill." She snatched if off the table and held it out to me. "You're going to want to feel as good as possible."

"Thanks," I said, taking it. "See you in a bit."

I left the dining room and headed toward the elevator while I tossed the pill into the air and caught it again. Up ahead was a drinking fountain. I stopped in front of it and opened my palm. The "A" etched into the pill's center stared at me. I wondered again why my father had never made me take the vitamins, like my mother and the rest of the Auras.

I frowned. And then it hit me like a garbage truck. A super stinky, rotten one.

I looked up and toward the dining room. *Kiera!* I took off running and burst through the doors of the almost empty dining room, even May was gone. Kiera was picking up the pill and moving it to her mouth.

No! I ran faster, trying to maneuver my way through the tables and chairs. I reached Kiera just in time and smacked her hand; the pill went flying across the room.

"Hey!" Kiera said. She whirled around. "What in the world, Llona?"

I glanced over. The few remaining people were teachers, and they were staring. I faked a laugh. "Got you! Just wanted to give you a scare."

"Mission accomplished," Kiera said, "but you made me lose my pill."

When she stood up to find it, I whispered in her ear, "It's the pills. They're stopping Auras from sensing Vykens."

Kiera reared back. "What? How?"

"Look, just don't take it. We'll talk about it when we meet, okay?"

"Okay," she said, still looking confused.

I returned to my room and grabbed the backpack containing Britt's diary. I wanted Christian to go through it to see if he could find something I might've missed.

I was the first one on the track. The whole time my mind was reeling with my discovery. It had to be the pills. It was the only thing that had changed. Moments later, May and Kiera showed up. Tessa was a few minutes after.

"Christian will be here too," I announced to the group.

May smiled. "So you guys worked things out?"

I nodded.

Kiera scrunched her nose. "Worked things out? What are you talking about?"

Tessa and May both looked at me, waiting for me to answer.

"We're dating," I said, and it felt good to say it.

Kiera's eyes grew big. "You're joking, right?" She turned to May and Tessa. "Tell me she's joking."

They both smiled.

"This is huge! You are so crazy, Llona!" Kiera grinned with the others. "I like that about you."

"So tell us about the pills," May said. "Kiera said you freaked out this morning."

I looked at them with a conspiring eye. "You know how I told you guys I could sense Vykens, but the other day in Cyrus's office I couldn't quite pinpoint it? The feeling was hazy, and the same when I saw Liam later. But then I remembered the night before that, I hadn't sensed anything with Liam. He was just a regular guy."

"So what are you thinking?" May said.

"I've been trying to figure out how I could go from sensing a Vyken across the room, to not even knowing I'm touching one, and then to just sort of sensing one. I never took the Auran vitamins before, but when I got here I took them every day like a good Aura, except for yesterday." My eyes flashed to May's. "I'm sure you remember. I was mad and threw my pill at Ashlyn."

"So you think the pills have shut off something inside you, and when you didn't take the pill, your senses started to come back," Tessa said.

I nodded. "Where do the pills come from?" May asked.

Tessa answered. "They come to us in boxes every Tuesday night, and then we take them to Abigail, the nurse. She's the one who disperses them to us, and we set them out in the morning."

"Who brings the boxes?" I asked.

Tessa thought for a minute. "I'm not sure. I've never been there when they come."

"Then we need to find out who's dropping them off," I said. "Do you know what time the deliveries are made?"

She shook her head. "A bunch are made all night long, food and stuff."

"So tonight," I said.

Tessa nodded.

"Okay. I'll stay up and see who comes."

"How do you do it?" Tessa said.

I looked at her. "What?"

"It seems like you never sleep."

Out of the corner of my eye, I saw May studying me closely. "I'm just a night owl. If it gets too late, I'll have Christian take over."

As if sensing his name, Christian appeared. "Sorry I'm late, guys." He sat down next to me and kissed me on the cheek. I looked at him surprised. I guess our relationship was out in the open for the whole world to see.

"Okay, that is too weird," Kiera said.

"Christian, this is Kiera and Tessa."

He held out his hand. “Nice to meet you.” After shaking their hands, he turned to May who was sitting on his other side. “And May,” he embraced her tightly. “So what are we talking about?” Christian asked.

“I found out what the change was,” I said.

Christian’s eyebrows raised. “What?”

“It’s the pills.”

“Pills?”

I explained everything to him. When I finished, Christian said, “I’ll wait with you tonight. Should be interesting.” He took hold of my hand.

Kiera giggled. “I can’t believe an Aura and a Guardian are dating.”

Christian looked at her. “Technically I’m not a Guardian anymore. They stripped me of the title this morning. That’s why I was late.”

I squeezed his hand. “I’m sorry.”

“I’m not. This is what I want. To be with you.”

“So what can we do to help?” May asked.

“I’ve been thinking about that,” I said. “Kiera, I’d like you to talk to Abigail. Ask her about the pills, when in history Auras started taking them, and find out exactly when we started donating our blood.”

“Got it,” Kiera said.

“And Christian,” I said, “you’ve got to get something out of Jackson. The Guardians all seem to listen to him. Be his best friend if you have to.”

Christian nodded.

“What about me?” May asked.

I turned to her. “You’ve got to find out why Dr. Han took your blood. And see if you can get him to talk about the past and his relationship with Cyrus. “

“Done.”

"I can't believe we're doing this," Kiera said, smiling. "Is anyone else as excited as I am?"

Tessa agreed, but Christian, May, and I all looked at each other, knowing there was nothing exciting about it.

TWENTY-FOUR

Before I met with Christian to watch for the night deliveries, I snuck out early to see if I could find Liam to get in another quick lesson. Christian's presence had helped calm some of the darkness inside me, but it was still there just below the surface, whispering inside me, telling me to return to the forest, to seek out life and destroy it.

I was barely into the forest when I heard scuffling noises, followed by a series of grunts and moans. I resisted the urge to race toward the obvious sounds of a fight, and instead remembered to keep my cool like Christian had shown me back in Utah.

In the distance I saw two figures standing next to each other. Their backs were to me, and they seemed to be looking down at something, or someone, I noticed when I got close enough. Because of the distance between us, and because of my recent Vyken confusion, I couldn't tell if I was looking at men or Vykens. Obviously I still had something from the pills inside me. By their appearance, though, I guessed Vykens. Both had black hair, one was spiked high, and the other's was long, just past his shoulders. Spike-head also had a thing for tattoos. Blue ink covered the majority of his exposed skin.

Needing a better look without being seen, I leapt to a branch just above me and swung my legs up until I was able to stand on the thick limb. I began to climb higher and to the other side of the tree. From this view I was able to look down and see who was lying on the ground looking very dead. My heart stopped. *Liam.* I focused my hearing. In addition to voices, I could just make out Liam's shallow breathing.

"That's not what we're supposed to do," Spike-head said.

"But if we finish him off, the Deific will just send more men," the other said.

"And when that time comes, we'll be ready. Right now he's in the way. He's already spoken to the girl."

Long-hair nudged Liam's leg with his boot. "Whatever. Just get it over with."

I leapt from the tree and to the ground just behind them. Light exploded in my palms. Finally I was going to get the chance to fight! This thought gave me pause, and I tried to remember what Liam had taught me, but when Spike-head unsheathed a dagger and raised it above his head, I reacted. Before he could bring it down, I blasted him in the back with a steady stream of Light. His body flew forward and crashed into a tree.

It took just a second for the other Vyken to realize what had happened. And when he did, he rushed toward me, eyes burning with a familiar rage. I recognized it because I felt it inside myself. I dove away from him and rolled on the ground. When I came up, I shot him with more Light from my hand.

Like most of the Vykens I had encountered, I expected him to be surprised to be fighting an Aura, but he looked almost as if he had been expecting it. He dodged the Light and continued toward me. This could be a problem. I bolted to the other side of the clearing where Long-hair was struggling to get up. I kicked him in the face as I passed. He fell backward again.

"I was hoping we'd meet," Spike-head said. "I've heard so much about you."

"Wish I could say the same," I said. I glanced at Liam, who still looked dead. *Get up!* I thought, willing him to move.

"You're prettier than I expected, though. The way others talk about you, I thought you'd have a couple of horns coming out of your head or something."

"Sorry to disappoint."

He shrugged. "It makes no difference to me. I enjoy killing both the ugly and the pretty."

I spotted a fallen branch nearby. Its tip was pointed. "No respecter of persons, that's good," I said, moving toward the branch while Spike-head circled around me.

"I know. I try not to be judgmental. Everyone's equal in my eyes."

"You're a Saint," I agreed. Just then I noticed Long-hair had gotten to his feet and was starting in my direction.

I glanced at Liam for just a second, wishing he'd get up and fight already. Spike-head lunged for me, and I dove for the stick. As soon as my light-filled hand touched it, the whole stick lit up like some kind of Jedi light saber. I rolled onto my back and shoved it hard at the approaching Vyken. I could tell by his expression that he was just as surprised as I was to see my stick of Light, especially when I embedded it deep into his gut.

Knowing a Vyken could easily recover from such a wound, I forced more Light into the limb. It spread inside him, lighting up every vein until his body began to crack. Light burst from the seams until he ultimately exploded, spraying Light and Vyken ash in every direction. I didn't have time to congratulate myself of the awesomeness of it because the long-haired Vyken was almost upon me.

I stood up quickly, the light stick still in hand, and swung low, knocking his feet out from under him. He fell onto his back, and I stabbed at him, but he rolled away. I swung down again, but by the time it hit the ground, the Vyken was gone. *Where did he go?*

My question was answered when a cold arm snaked around my neck from behind. The stick fell from my hand. I attempted to turn around, but his other hand, a big beefy fist, came up hard, hitting me square in the jaw. My teeth rattled and stars exploded before my eyes. I fell limp against him, which turned out to be perfect timing, because all of a sudden Liam was standing in front of me, and when I lowered, he punched the Vyken in the face.

I slouched to the ground while Liam finished him off. It took Liam all of ten seconds to remove the head from his body. The next thing I knew Liam was trying to sit me up. "Llona?"

I touched my head.

"Are you hurt?" he asked.

"My brain feels like it's been through a blender." Slowly, my vision began to clear. Liam was kneeling in front of me, sporting a swollen eye and a cut on his head. "Messing with the big boys again?" I asked.

He smiled. "What, this? This is nothing. You should've seen the three I killed before you got here."

My face grew serious. "There were five of them? This close to Lucent?"

Liam nodded and helped me up. "Let's get you out of here."

I clutched his hand, fear gripping my insides more than I was gripping Liam. "It's happening sooner than we thought, isn't it?"

He motioned his head to the stick lying at my feet. "At least you've got some killer moves."

"You saw that? The whole Jedi sword trick?"

He laughed. "One of the coolest things I've seen in a long time."

"Right?" I laughed with him, keeping the mood light.

Neither one of us wanted to talk about the fact that both of us had almost died.

Liam didn't say anything until we were back by the wall. "So, what were you doing out here?" he said.

"I thought I could have another lesson."

He removed a cell phone from his pocket and began typing into it. With his attention on it, he said, "Your boyfriend can finish up the lessons. He knows more about Light than I do."

"Um, okay." I pretended not to be hurt. I thought we were becoming friends.

"You find out anything new?" he said, still working on his phone.

I told him about the pills. "I'll know more tonight. A shipment's dropped off every Tuesday. We're going to see who does it."

"You and Christian?"

"Uh-huh."

"Good. I'm glad you won't be alone."

Before I could comment, he handed me the cell phone. "I want you to take this. My number's programmed into it."

"We're not supposed to have cell phones on campus grounds."

He looked at me, a single eyebrow raised. "Think you can break that rule?"

I took the phone.

"I have somewhere else I have to be tonight," he said, "but I want you to call me when you discover who's dropping off the pills. And maybe, if it's not too dangerous, get your hands on one of them. I want some of my guys to research what's in them."

"You have guys? I keep picturing just you and some nerd holed up in a basement somewhere, trying to fight crime."

Liam didn't smile. "Just text me. I gotta go." He took two

steps backward, burst into a swirling wind, and disappeared into the forest.

"I was just kidding!" I called after him, but he was long gone.

The forest was quiet. I leapt to the top of the wall and looked out. The moon was partially full, but there wasn't enough light to penetrate the forest's dark ceiling. What was Liam's deal? I got that things were serious, but why couldn't he talk to me like a normal person? *Whatever.* I jumped down and hurried over to the kitchen dock to wait for Christian.

Christian came early. He gave me a quick kiss and jumped next to me on a wooden crate. It was just around the corner from the dock where we wouldn't be seen when the deliveries started to come.

"Have you been waiting long?" Christian said.

"Not really. I got here about forty-five minutes ago."

"Why were you so early?"

"Nothing else to do."

He entwined his fingers through mine. "Grass stain."

"Huh?"

"On your knee. Both of them, actually."

I glanced down at the dark, muddy stains. I could feel a bruise beneath one of them.

"And you have twigs in your hair," he said. "And this." He touched me lightly on the jaw. I winced and turned away.

"What happened?"

"The short of it is I went to see Liam for another lesson, but when I found him, two Vykens were in the process of killing him. I jumped in, we fought. I managed to kill one with this cool light-saber thing I made out of a stick, but then the other one almost killed me. Luckily Liam woke up and wasted him." I took a breath and looked at Christian. His face was contorting into a bunch of emotions but finally settled on relief.

"I'm glad you're okay," he said, "but I wish you'd let me know when you go out on things like that."

"It's not like I'd planned a Vyken-killing field trip. I just went to see Liam."

At that, he looked away. "*I* can help you, you know."

"I know. That's what Liam said too."

Christian looked at me. "He did?"

"Yeah. He said you'd do a better job teaching me about Light, seeing how you know all about Auras and stuff."

"I don't know about that, but I do know you."

I kissed him. "And for that, I'm grateful."

I snuggled up against him, enjoying the warmth of his body against mine. This was where the world felt right.

Christian looked around. "We need a better hiding spot. We're not going to see much from here." He jumped down and rounded the corner to the front of the loading dock. I went after him. "What about up there?" he said.

I followed his gaze. Just above the loading dock was a metal overhang.

"Think it could hold us?" I asked.

"It should, but . . ." he paused and frowned.

"What is it?"

"I'm not sure if you'll be able to make it up there."

I smiled. "Care to make a bet?"

"I'm not a gambling man, but I'll give you everything I own if you beat me."

I shook my head, real sad like. "You're going to make one pathetic poor man."

"On three?"

I said, "One."

He said, "Two."

We smiled. "Three!"

Christian darted to the side of the dock where I knew he'd

use a crate to leap from, but I also knew that it still wouldn't give him the height he'd need to make it all the way to the top. While I thought this through, Christian had already jumped from the crate. His hands caught the ledge, and he was about to swing himself up. Before he could get any farther, I crouched low and pushed off the ground. I was in the air less than a second before I landed on top of the metal overhang. The sound was like thunder, but it was worth it when I saw Christian's stunned expression.

"How did you do that?" he said as he pulled himself up.

I grinned. "So how much am I worth now?"

"I hate to tell you, but you're not going to be rich. After my dad finds out I've been let go as a Guardian, all I'll have are my clothes and my car."

"I'll take the car."

Christian pulled me close. "Will you give me a ride if I need it?"

"I'll get you a bus pass." I kissed him lightly.

"I have the best girlfriend." Christian leaned in for another kiss, but lights flashed, forcing us apart.

TWENTY-FIVE

HEADLIGHTS MOVED DOWN THE LANE TOWARD LUCENT. Christian and I dropped to our bellies. A big white truck pulled up and parked at the dock in front of the garage door. On its side, it read "Pederson Foods." One of the two drivers jumped out and rang a doorbell at the side of the garage door. From our view we couldn't see who answered it.

"The usual?" the driver asked. Whoever answered must have just nodded because the two men began to unload the truck.

For the next thirty minutes, Christian and I waited. I would've been totally bored, but Christian kept me dizzily entertained by rubbing the underside of my hand. I leaned into him and lowered my head. Christian's breath warmed the back of my neck, sending chills up and down my spine, but that was nothing when I felt his lips press to my skin just below my ear. I gasped and inhaled deeply. Christian's hand tightened on mine.

The truck's engine below us roared to life, startling me. When it pulled away, I turned to Christian to smile at him, but before I could, his mouth was against mine. His arm wrapped around me and pulled me even closer. A wave of pleasure rocked me from head to foot.

I pretended I didn't see a flash of lights wash over us, but Christian didn't. He pulled away and whispered. "We'll continue this later."

We flattened ourselves to the roof and peered out. A small, red sports car drove up the lane. I looked at Christian and could tell by his tight jaw and eyebrows that he recognized the vehicle.

The car parked in the loading bay. There were two people sitting in the front, but only Jackson opened a door and popped his trunk. I leaned out a little farther to try and see what was in it. Jackson picked up an unmarked box and carried it to the back door. He propped the box on his knee and knocked. A moment later the door opened.

"Who are you?" Jackson said.

"Just filling in. Beth is sick," a girl said. I recognized the voice.

Christian looked at me questioningly.

"Tessa," I mouthed.

"As if I care," Jackson said. "Just make sure Abigail gets this."

"Is it the pills?" Tessa asked.

"None of your business. Can you move?"

There was a shuffle of feet.

Tessa's voice drifted out the open door. "Where did it come from?"

There was a brief silence before Jackson said, "Know your place, Lizen."

Christian tensed and moved like he was going to jump from the overhang, but I stopped him. He looked at me, and I shook my head. Christian didn't look happy, but he stayed by my side.

"I'm not trying to be nosey," Tessa said again. "I just think it's weird that a Guardian is dropping off an unmarked box in the middle of the night. Even if it is the pills."

Careful, Tessa, I thought.

"And I think it's weird that you're talking to me," Jackson said.

"Could you be any ruder?" Tessa snapped.

There was a scary silence, and I imagined Jackson staring Tessa down. I was surprised by how rude he was being. I almost nudged Christian to go down and teach Jackson some manners, but then Jackson said, "Watch your back, Lizen." He walked out, slammed his trunk, and sped away. I wished we could've seen who was sitting in the car with him.

Christian and I jumped from the roof. He turned to me. "Why'd you stop me from kicking his—"

"Because I don't want you to blow this! If Jackson is playing for the Big Bad, then we need to figure out who's calling the plays."

Christian still looked mad, but he let it go. For now.

"Hey, guys," Tessa said from the doorway.

"How'd you get here?" I asked.

"I told the truth. Beth really is sick. She asked my mother to take her place tonight, but I convinced my mom to let me do it."

We followed her inside.

"That Guardian sure was a jerk. Are the others like that?" Tessa's eyes flashed to Christian.

Christian looked past her. "Normally I'd say no, but now I don't feel like I know any of them."

"Should we open it?" I said, staring down at the box no bigger than the small television in the rec room.

Tessa and Christian gathered around me.

"Someone will know we've tampered with it," Tessa said.

"But we need to know more," Christian said. "Maybe there's something inside about where they came from."

I looked at Tessa. "What do you think?"

She examined the box, running her fingers over the tape. "Let's do it. I think we can tape it back up so no one notices." She carefully peeled up one end of the translucent tape while Christian began on the opposite end. It was a slow process, but eventually they peeled it off without too much damage to the cardboard.

I blew out the breath I'd been holding. "Not bad, guys."

Christian opened the box, and we all looked inside. Small blue pills were packaged in foil sheets stacked high in several rows. I picked one up and turned it over. Two words were printed on the back: *Bodian Dynamics*.

"You need to tell Liam right away," Tessa said when she read the same words over my shoulder.

Christian, who was carefully digging through the rest of the box, said, "There's got to be something else here. A packing slip, note, something." When he came up empty, he sighed.

I took his hand. "We've got a name."

He shook his head. "It's not enough. Why don't I just beat it out of Jackson?"

"Not yet," I said. "What you need to do is become Jackson's close friend. See if he'll let you in on the action."

"And just how am I supposed to do that?"

"Tell him a sob story. You did just get stripped of your title. Maybe you've gone to the dark side."

"He'll never believe it."

Tessa tugged at her hair thoughtfully. "How do you know he's even bad? He could just be delivering the box for someone."

"How can you say that?" I said. "Especially after the way he talked to you?"

Tessa picked up tape from a nearby counter. "You'd be surprised how common that actually is." She shrugged. "We're used to it."

"Well you shouldn't be." I set the aluminum sheet of pills back in the box.

"Either way, I'll get to the bottom of it," Christian said.

"On second thought," I said, "I think I'll take this." I picked the pills up again.

"You sure that's a good idea?" Tessa said.

"I think it's worth the risk. Liam can take it back to his people to find out exactly what's in them."

"Good idea," Christian said. "Now let's seal the box. We've been here long enough."

Tessa taped the box. Only a careful examination would show that it had been tampered with. When we were finished, Christian and I said good-bye to Tessa and closed the door behind us.

As soon as we were alone, Christian touched me lightly on the arm. "Are you sure you're ready for this? With having to deal with everything else?" His eyes flickered to my neck.

"Honestly? I'm sort of in robot mode. I've got a lot of emotions swirling up here," I pointed to my head, "and if I dwell on any of them for too long, I get a little crazy." I thought back specifically to when Liam had me "paint" the forest.

Christian took hold of my hand. "At some point you're going to have to deal with those emotions."

"Sure. One day." I looked up at the moon's location in the sky. "I better get back. Get some sleep before tomorrow."

"That's right," he said. "You have to go to class."

"Nice summer break, eh?" I tip-toed and gave him a quick kiss, afraid of letting my lips linger. Too much temptation.

I was about to turn away when I caught movement, a long shadow, sliding around the corner of the building. "Did you see that?" I asked.

Christian turned. "Where?"

I pointed. "Over there. I thought . . ." I paused, not knowing what to say because I wasn't sure what I'd seen. Something tugged on the edge of my mind.

"Llona?"

"Nothing. Never mind. I think I'm just tired." And I was. I yawned big.

"Let's get you back then." Christian followed me to my dorm building and watched me climb the entire way to my bedroom window. Before I disappeared, I turned around and waved. Christian formed his hand into the shape of a gun, kissed the tip of his finger, and shot me a kiss. I lamely caught it and brought it to my chest.

* * * * *

The next morning, I hurried to breakfast to find May and Kiera. The dining room was unusually quiet. Either it was a long night for everyone or the girls subconsciously felt something was wrong. I hoped for the former.

I spotted Kiera at a table by herself and sat down next to her. "Where's May?"

She shrugged. "Haven't seen her." Kiera was staring down at her clenched fist, looking serious.

"What's wrong?"

Kiera opened her hand, revealing a tiny blue pill. "It's just so strange. I've taken these all my life. Everyone told me they were good for me. How many more lies have I been told?"

"I don't know." I wished I had something more reassuring to tell her.

"Yeah, well, what about the rest of them?" She motioned her head toward the other girls. "When are we going to tell them?"

"We can't. Not just yet, anyway."

"But they're taking these pills."

She was right. The longer they kept taking them, the more danger they'd be in. "I'm seeing Liam later tonight. We'll figure something out." I spotted Tessa on the other side of the dinning room clearing off a table. She nodded at me, knowingly. "Are you talking to Abigail today?" I asked Kiera.

"Yup. I already have a bunch of questions ready to go."

"Good." I stood up. "I'm going to go find May."

"Aren't you going to eat?"

"I'll get something later. See you!" I left quickly, anxious to find May. I tried her room first, but no one answered. Where could she be? A couple of younger girls I recognized walked by. "Hey, have you guys seen May?"

"The Fury?" a girl with bright eyes asked.

"That's the one."

"I saw her with Dr. Han. Outside."

"Thanks," I said. "And stay safe, okay?"

They looked at me strangely, but I didn't stick around to explain.

I inhaled deeply the moment I stepped outside. The air was warm, and the rising sun promised more heat. I glanced up at the clock tower, already longing for night. Lately, whenever I was outside in the daytime, the light made me feel like I was wearing tight clothes, and it took all my strength just to stay in it. I hurried across campus toward Risen Auditorium, to the section of the building specifically set aside for Furies.

I knocked on the back door, but when no one answered, I turned the knob and peeked in. It was dark, but every few seconds a flash of orange would barely light up what looked like a small lobby. I moved into it, waited for another flash of light, and then looked around. The light was coming from a long corridor to my right.

Walking toward it, I passed by several closed doors with room numbers on the walls. At the end of the corridor was a long glass window, sort of like what I've seen on a racquetball court. The room beyond the glass was dark except for a soft glow, like candlelight, at the end.

I looked in just as another burst of light filled the room. My jaw dropped. It wasn't just light. It was a giant fireball hurdling across a long, gym-like room. The fireball hit a metal plate the size of a kiddy swimming pool and then dissipated. Pieces of ash fell to the floor.

I turned my head to see who was the source of the spectacular power.

TWENTY-SIX

MAY WAS STANDING STRAIGHT, HER ARM STRETCHED OUT. SHE didn't seem at all surprised to have just shot hell's breath from her hand. In fact, she looked rather pleased. I didn't know whether to be freaked out or impressed. I chose the latter. She was my best friend after all.

I knocked on the glass. May looked in my direction and waved. Dr. Han appeared at her side to see whom she was waving at. He didn't smile or wave, just clicked something in his hand. Lights turned on. I found an entrance to my left and made a point to go near Dr. Han, just in case I picked up any Vyken vibes.

"That was the coolest thing I've ever seen," I said to May.

"I've gotten better, huh?" She couldn't stop smiling.

"Better? You're like a superhero!"

"This isn't a comic book, " Dr. Han said, his face stern.

"Right. I know. I was just—"

"She likes to kid around," May said. "This is Llona Reese, Dr. Han."

"I know who she is." His eyes burrowed into mine. It made me feel funny, not in a fuzzy-head sort of way, but in a definite this-dude's-got-power way. I stepped back and took a deep breath. Not a Vyken, but not to be messed with either.

"I missed you at breakfast," I said. No other words came to my head.

"I don't eat breakfast," Dr. Han said.

Was I still looking at him? "I mean, May. I missed May at breakfast." I forced myself to look at her.

May was brushing her hands off, sprinkling the floor with flakes of ash. "Sorry about that. I wanted to get some practice in early."

"You sure work hard," I said.

Dr. Han shifted his weight. Or at least I think he did. I got the distinct impression that he had moved, but when I looked at him he was still standing straight, like someone had shoved a stick up his—

"May is a very talented Fury," Dr. Han said. "She must work endlessly to control her skills."

"Looks like she's doing that."

"No," he said, and May and I looked at him. "It's an ongoing battle. We must always control it or it will control us."

"Is it hard?" I asked, honestly wanting to know. I knew what it felt like to have something inside you wanting to take over.

Dr. Han turned to May. "Is it?"

May blushed. "I'm sort of new to all of this, but so far I haven't had any problems."

Dr. Han leaned forward, bending at the waist until he was almost in May's face. "That's because you haven't been tested yet, but you will. And when the rage comes, you'll understand what I mean."

An intense few seconds passed. I swallowed hard before I said, "Good times, huh? Well, I've got to go. Catch you later, May."

It took her a moment to say, "I'll come with you. I've got to get my books." She slipped her feet into nearby sandals. "Thanks for meeting with me early, Dr. Han, and about answering my questions."

"You girls be careful," he said. "You're treading on dangerous ground."

I looked at May, but she just nodded and said good-bye. I followed her out, but as soon as we were out of earshot, I said, "What was that all about?"

May shushed me and mouthed, "Not now."

I glanced behind me. Dr. Han was watching us through the glass. I shivered.

When we went outside, May took hold of my arm and pulled me to the side of the building.

"What's going on?" I asked. She looked pale—not at all how she looked earlier.

"I asked Dr. Han why my blood's being drawn." She looked around like someone might be watching us.

"And?"

"He said he wanted to test it."

"For what?"

"That's what I asked, but he wouldn't say. He got all weird and was trying to change the subject, but then I asked him where my blood was kept."

"What'd he say?"

"First, he froze like I'd said something I shouldn't have, and I didn't think he was going to answer, but then he told me that he keeps it safe. And I said, 'With the Auras' blood?' and he said, 'No. It's with me. And then I said, 'Why is it separate from theirs?' And then guess what he said?"

I let my brain catch up to everything she'd said before I answered, "What?"

She took a deep breath, like she was trying to keep calm. "He said it's safer that way."

I thought about it. "What do you think that means?"

May leaned against the brick building. "I think he knows something bad is coming, but I still don't think he's switched sides."

I just nodded, thinking. "I'll talk to Liam about him. Maybe he knows something." I hoped Dr. Han was on our side.

"Have you seen Christian today?"

I shook my head.

"How did last night go?" May said.

I told her about the pills and Jackson.

"What do you think about Jackson? Think he's switched sides?"

"It looks that way, but we don't know for sure. Christian's going to keep an eye on him."

"That sucks. I really liked him—his looks anyway." She smiled and moved away from the wall.

* * * * *

Only three hours into classes and I was getting restless. So far I'd learned about Light's relationship with water deities, how Light has helped technology, and how an Aura should behave at political dinners. I was ready to fake being sick when Ms. Smitty, the Auran science teacher, began talking about an Aura's DNA and how it differs from a regular human's. "If you look at an Aura's DNA strand," she said while twirling a pen in her hand, "you'll see that it's actually fractured in places, broken some might say. It's our Light that fills these spaces, making us whole. Now if you'll turn to page—"

I raised my hand.

Ms. Smitty looked at me twice as if she were making sure my hand really was in the air. I had yet to speak in this class. "Yes, Llona?" she said.

"But what does that mean?"

"What does *what* mean?"

"So Light fills those spaces. What does that mean for us? How does that affect Auras?"

"It means that you are partly made of Light, white Light to be exact. And what's neat about that? Anyone?" No one answered, so she continued. "White Light is made up of a spectrum of colors that exhibit the characteristics of a wave, or more specifically, white Light is made up of wavelengths of different colors of light. When white Light passes through a prism, the different colors scatter. Most of you see this when there's a rainbow in the sky."

"Rainbow," I whispered. Something jogged my memory, and I raised my hand again.

"What is it, Llona?"

"You said rainbow, like as in transparent, right?"

"I don't understand."

"A rainbow. Everyone knows you can't actually touch a rainbow. Its just sunlight reflecting off the water in the air, like the prism you mentioned. Even though you can see it, it's transparent, almost invisible, if that makes sense." I was getting excited as I remembered how Mr. Steele had said my mother had turned invisible. "So is it possible?"

"For what, Llona?" Ms. Smitty asked, and I could tell by her tone that she was getting sick of me.

"For an Aura to turn invisible? You know, use her body as a prism and transform the white Light in our DNA, making us transparent."

Most of the students burst into laughter, but Ms. Smitty's expression stayed serious. "What you're talking about is extremely dangerous."

The class quieted down. "So it is possible," I said.

"For a highly advanced Aura, and even then I wouldn't

recommend it. You're talking about splitting your cells. It takes an extreme amount of concentration. Auras have died trying it."

"Who told you that?"

Ms. Smitty crossed her arms to her chest. "Are you questioning me?"

"No, I really want to know. Who said it would kill you?"

Ms. Smitty's face turned red. "I know you're not familiar with Lucent's policies, but I can assure you all the teachers here, including myself, are well versed in everything Aura related. Fall in line and trust that we are the experts." She whipped her long, black braid behind her as she returned to the book on her desk.

Normally a comment like that would make me explode, but I couldn't stop thinking about what I'd just learned. My mother *had* turned invisible. It was possible. Now if only I could figure out how.

Class ended. As soon as we were out in the hall, Ashlyn bumped me as she walked past. "If you want to disappear," she said, "we can make that happen." She tossed her head back and laughed. It was difficult, but I resisted the urge to kick her.

I headed straight to my room to drop off my books before lunch. The first thing I noticed was how dark the light in my room seemed, but I didn't have time to ponder on it long.

"Hey, beautiful," Christian said. He was lying on my bed, reading Britt's journal.

"How'd you get in here?" I asked.

"Snuck in." He stood up. "I missed you."

I looked at him and waited for the real reason for his visit.

"What? I did." He sat up and motioned for me to sit next to him. "And I couldn't stand being with Jackson any longer. Something's seriously wrong with him."

I dropped my bag next to the bed and sat down. "How so?"

"He talks like . . . I don't know. It's just off. Like he's better than everyone."

I took hold of his hand. "He said the same thing about you."

Christian held my gaze. "Do you believe that?"

"Of course not. Is he telling you anything?"

"You mean is he spilling the beans on the whole evil plot? Not just yet." He looked down at the journal. "But it's not just Jackson. Since I've come here, several of the Guardians feel wrong, like they know a secret I don't. And I feel like they're watching me."

"Maybe they're trying to decide if they can trust you."

"I thought of that. That's why I tried to get Jackson to do something with me tonight, but he said he was busy. I'm going to follow him and see exactly what he's up to."

"Want some company?" I said, but I secretly hoped he said no. I had my own things to do.

"That's okay. You should stay here and hang with the girls. Do something fun. You still remember what that is, don't you?" He pulled me close.

I leaned against his shoulder and sighed. *Fun?* How could I tell him the only fun I had anymore was when I was fighting?

"Have you talked to Jake lately?" he asked.

This made me smile. "I tried calling him the other night, but he wasn't home. He's really happy with Heidi, living a normal life, in a normal relationship."

Christian leaned away from me. "You'll have a normal life one day and be in a normal relationship too."

I looked passed him. "I don't think so. I have Vyken poison in me. Who knows what that means?"

"But you've been able to fight it so far. Before you know it, it will be gone, and you'll be you again." He kissed my cheek.

I wanted to agree with him, but I knew I would never be "me" again. The darkness had rooted itself inside me, and even though I might learn to control it, it would always be there, just waiting for me to mess up.

He had to sense it too, deep down, and for the rest of his life he'd probably want to fix me. Christian grabbed the journal off my nightstand and began reading it again.

I stood up. "I'm going to find May and Kiera in the lunch room," I said. "Do you want me to bring you back anything?"

Christian stared at the journal. "That would be great."

I waited a second before leaving, watching him and wondering if he'd find what he was looking for. *There's no cure in there*, I wanted to say, but he never looked up.

Because I couldn't find May and Kiera in the dining room, I walked into the kitchen, ignoring the stares of Lizens, and found Tessa. "How's it going," I said.

She wiped sweat from her forehead with the back of her hand and stacked plates of food up her arms. "Good."

"Have you seen May and Kiera?" I picked up the last three plates on the table and followed her into the dining room. Nobody said anything this time.

"Yeah, they're eating outside."

"Cool. Do you think you can get off or stop working or whatever to eat with us?" When Tessa stopped at a table, I joined her in handing out the plates of food. Both of us ignored the snickering of younger Auras.

"Maybe. Give me a second. Wait here." She set the last of the plates down and walked away.

I backed up against the wall. Across the room I locked eyes with Sophie. She was clearly upset but didn't say anything. Instead, she forced a smile. I forced one back.

Tessa returned a minute later. "Let's go before my mom changes her mind." She grabbed my arm and pulled me out of the room, carrying two lunch bags.

May and Kiera were out front sitting on the steps. "I just told her about Dr. Han," May said. She slid over to make room for Tessa. I sat above her, next to Kiera.

"The plot thickens," Kiera said, still looking a little too happy about all of this.

"How about you, Kiera?" I asked. "Did you get a chance to talk to Abigail?"

"I did." She reached into her bag and pulled out a notebook. She flipped through the pages, reading a bunch of notes that started off being about the vitamins, but then changed into Abigail's youth. My mind began to wander.

"Are you listening?" Kiera said.

"Sorry," I said. "I'm listening."

Kiera glanced down at the notebook. "And then I asked her when the vitamins were first introduced. She said in 1921. So then I asked—"

"1921? Are you sure?" I interrupted.

Kiera looked over her notes. "Yup. 1921. But I guess back then it was a powder that they put into tea. It wasn't put into a pill form until the 1950s. As for our blood, they started storing it fifteen years ago."

This I found really strange. Somehow I expected the timing of the pills to correspond with the timing of when they first started storing our blood.

We continued talking through lunch, but gradually our conversation moved away from dark things to superficial things: boys, shopping, and life outside Lucent. I glanced to the forest beyond, the package of pills burning a hole in my pocket. I was wasting time.

"What are you thinking?" May whispered to me while Kiera and Tessa laughed about something that had happened last year.

"I've got to talk to Liam."

"Then do it. I'll go to your next period and pick up your assignment. Tell them you're sick."

"Really?"

"Sure. There are more important things, right?"

I nodded, grateful she understood. "I've got to use the restroom," I said and stood up. "Be right back."

As soon I was in the bathroom, away from prying eyes, I pulled the cell phone Liam had given me from my pocket. I texted to the only number listed in the phone: *Can you meet?*

A minute later the phone buzzed. I answered it.

"What's going on?" Liam said, his voice full of concern.

"I wanted to give you something." When he didn't say anything, I hurried and said, "Some pills. We were able to sneak a foil of them from the box."

"That was dangerous. Someone might notice it's missing."

"Do you want it or not?"

"Who dropped it off?"

"Jackson." I paused. "So can we meet? I want to know what's in them. Your people can do that right?"

"Sure. As for us meeting, don't you have class?"

"This is a little more important, isn't it? And there's something else I want to talk to you about," I said, without knowing exactly what that was. For some reason I felt I had to see him.

He paused before saying, "Can you get out of the school?"

It would be harder during the day, but I felt confident I could do it. "Yeah."

"You know our usual spot? Head north from there until you hit a dirt road. I'll pick you up there. Listen for the sound of my car."

"You drive?"

"Before this assignment I actually had a life, Llona. I don't live in the woods, you know." I heard the smile in his voice. "See you soon."

I hung up and returned to the girls.

"I hope you don't mind, but I tossed the rest of your lunch," Kiera said. "You looked done."

"No problem. Thanks." I didn't look at her. I was too busy surveying the area, looking for an escape route.

"You leaving?" May said.

I nodded.

"Where you going?" Kiera asked.

I patted my pants pocket where the pills were hiding. "I've got to get this to Liam."

"Isn't Christian in your room?" Tessa asked.

I turned to her. "Yeah, how'd you know?"

"I snuck him in."

"Right. Would you mind telling him where I went and take him some food while you're at it? I'll owe you."

"He'll want to go with you," May said.

"I know, but I'm not sure how long I'll be, and he's meeting with Jackson later."

"I'll tell him," Tessa said. "Come on, let's go. I have to help with dishes."

We parted ways. I made sure no one was watching as I walked around the school and toward the back. I headed straight for the shed, pretending it was my destination. When I reached it, I turned around. No eyes were watching. No one cared where a girl like me was going.

TWENTY-SEVEN

I LEAPT HIGH OVER THE WALL. IT TOOK ME ABOUT TEN MINutes to run through the forest and find the road I thought Liam was talking about. The forest felt different in daylight. I didn't like it.

Standing in the center of the dirt road, I looked both directions. *Listen for him*, Liam had said. I closed my eyes and focused. Not far away I heard an animal, probably a rabbit, moving through grass. I listened to its quiet movements. Calculated. Careful. And then I heard a rhythmic thumping. I whirled around, searching for the sound. I took a few steps forward. Definitely this direction.

It wasn't long before I realized the sound was a bass drum, muffled by the walls of metal. I rounded a bend in the road and spotted the back of a black 1967 Chevy Impala. It was Jake's dream car. All the windows were as black as the paint, and they shook from the bass beating from what sounded like rock music. I approached the passenger door. The music disappeared and the window rolled down.

"You made it," Liam said.

I bent down and peered into the car. As soon as I saw him, I grew lightheaded. *Guess the pills have worn off. Good*. I mentally pushed back the dizziness and said, "Anyone tell you it's summer?" Liam was still wearing his leather jacket.

"Sun allergies," he said. "You getting in or what?"

It took me a second to realize what he meant. I opened the passenger door and jumped in, still trying to get over the dizzy feeling. "So, you really can't be in the sun?"

Liam was facing me, but because he was wearing sunglasses, I couldn't tell if he was looking at me or not. A short moment passed before he said, "I can, but it hurts. Instant sunburn." He turned forward and pressed on the gas.

"I meant what I said before. You can have some of my blood."

His hands tightened on the steering wheel. "No."

"I'm just saying. I bet it would make your job a whole lot easier."

"What do you have for me?"

I reached into my pocket and removed the foil of pills.

Liam took it and drove while he examined the casing. "Bodian Dynamics," he said, his voice low. "Doesn't surprise me."

"Who are they?"

"A huge research corporation that has their dirty fingers in everything. I think they have a facility not far from here." Liam turned the car left down another dirt road.

"Where are we going?"

"I have a place not far."

"So you do live in the woods."

He snorted. "It's just temporary."

"Where do you normally live?"

He adjusted his weight in the seat. "All over."

"Vague much?"

"I have a few homes. Maine. Alaska. Canada."

"But where's home? You know, the place where you have Thanksgiving?"

He didn't answer right away, but when he did I regretted asking the question. "Not much of a family thanksgiving when all your family is dead."

I didn't know what to say.

"I've been around a while," he added.

A minute later, the car slowed. "We're here."

I looked out the tinted windshield. A cabin, more like a shack, was just up ahead. "Nice place," I said.

Liam turned off the car. "See you inside." He opened the car door and bolted, hunched over with his jacket pulled over his head.

I followed behind him but not as fast. The area was well covered by trees; the wood cabin almost looked like part of the forest except for a single window near the front door.

"You mind closing that?" Liam said, when I entered the cabin.

I couldn't see him, but when I closed the door, he stepped out of the shadows and flipped on a light, illuminating one big room. A small kitchen was on the right and a bedroom on the left. No pictures, no personal touches. It felt empty even with both of us standing in it.

"Cozy," I said.

Liam held the pill package to the light, examining it. "It's a roof over my head." He lowered the pills and set them on a small table. Using his cell phone, he took pictures of the front and back of the foil. I waited patiently while he typed a message into his phone. When he was finished, he looked up at me. "What else did you find out?"

"What do you mean?"

"You said you had to talk to me about something else. Besides the pill."

Right. I had said that. Standing alone with him in this cramped cabin, I felt stupid for having said anything at all. I should've just given him the pills and left.

"Llona?"

I tried to focus on something in the room, but there was nothing.

"What's going on?"

His voice was full of concern, making me feel even dumber. "Nothing," I finally said. "I guess I was just wondering," I looked up, down, around, "how long it will take to find out what's in the pills."

"I have to give it to them first." He stood up, his hand resting on the table, eyes focused on me.

"When are you going to do that?"

"As soon as you're gone."

"Right." I went into the kitchen, a whole step to my right. "Do you have anything to drink?"

"Water."

I opened the only cupboard and pulled out one of the two cups in it. "So tell me more about these guys you work with," I said while I held my cup under the tap. "The Deific, was it?"

Liam took the cup from me; water was pouring over its edge. I hadn't even heard him come up behind me. He shut off the faucet and turned me around. "What's going on?"

Words twisted inside my brain, giving me a headache. What was wrong? I reached up and touched the marks on my neck. So much was happening. About to happen. I was almost killed last night even though I felt like I could've destroyed an army. I didn't trust myself, and that frightened me.

"Llona? Talk to me."

My gaze met his. "I'm scared."

He stared at me for what seemed like a very long time before he said. "You should be."

"That wasn't the answer I was expecting."

"I'm not going to tell you everything's going to be okay, because it's not."

"But I'm not ready."

Liam shook his head, and his eyes were sad. "None of you are. You're fish in a bowl, and a shark's about to be released."

I rubbed my temple. "You're really not helping."

"Do you know what's happening? Has anyone at Lucent bothered telling any of you?"

"Tell us what?" I said.

"They're dying. Auras. All over the world. Their Guardians too. I just got the message from the Deific last night."

I wiped my brow.

"They are being hunted and killed," he said. "By packs of Vykens."

I must have turned pale, because Liam pulled over the only chair in the room. I dropped into it. "No one's said a word," I said.

"Why?"

I shook my head.

"Why, Llona?" Liam said. "Put the pieces together."

I thought harder despite my headache. Auras and Guardians dying. Pills to make us blind. Our blood taken. A Vyken in the school. The faces of those who had been in the room with me when I'd first met Cyrus flashed in my mind, specifically that of Cyrus and Jameson. Cyrus was the head of Lucent Academy. Everyone respected him. Everyone did what he said. And then I remembered something Christian had told me months ago.

"What is it, Llona?" Liam pressed.

I looked up at him. "The president. Cyrus. It has to be."

"How do you know?"

"Christian called him when he suspected a Vyken was after me. That was months ago. Cyrus had told him not to worry. That it was nothing. That I was safe." I closed my eyes and shook my head. "But it can't be Cyrus. Christian said he cut him, and he didn't heal." I opened my eyes. Liam was smiling. "What?"

"He's a Geo. Even with Vyken blood, he'd still take a day or two to heal."

"But I heal fast," I said.

"Because that's a side effect of Light too. He doesn't have that. He will heal quickly, but not like a Vyken would."

I sat up straighter in my seat. "But then there's the pills," I said. "Abigail said they've been around since the twenties, and Cyrus didn't become president until the thirties, so he couldn't have created the pills, right?"

"Unless the chemical that suppresses an Aura's senses was added later to the vitamins."

"That makes sense," I said and shifted in the chair. "What do you know of Cyrus?"

"He's old. Before my time, centuries before, in fact. And, like me, he's the last of his kind. But we need to make sure he's the one. Think you can find a reason to meet with him?"

"You want me to meet with a suspected Vyken?"

"He won't hurt you in the school. It would give him away."

"Comforting." I sunk into the seat, thinking dark thoughts. They were like shadows on my mind, always there, haunting me. I sat up straight, finally understanding what was really bothering me.

"What is it?"

I looked up at him. "Did you know him? The Vyken who killed my mother?" Before Liam could answer, I added, "I knew him as Mr. Steele, but my mother knew him as Lander."

His expression softened. "I'm sorry. I didn't."

"It's okay. I didn't really want to talk about him, but more about something he said. Before I killed him he told me about the night my father died. Mr. Steele said that my father almost killed him, but someone stopped him. That person broke my father's neck."

"Who?"

"Mr. Steele called him *the Shadow*. 'The Shadow who always watches but can never be seen.'"

Liam's jaw hardened, and he knelt in front of me. "Are you sure? Are you sure he called it a shadow?"

I'd never seen Liam frantic before. "Yes, why?" Liam stood up and turned his back to me. Every muscle in his body looked tense. "What is it?" I asked.

Liam turned around. His expression grim. "It's something very dangerous that we thought had been destroyed. It's been decades since I heard that name."

"What is it?"

He shook his head, looking almost ill. "A creature without any bodily form. It was made by witches in the thirteenth century and does the will of whoever commands it. The Shadow hurt a lot of people in the 1930s, but an Aura"—his eyes flashed to mine—"gave all of her Light to trap it."

"All her Light?" I frowned. "But wouldn't that kill her?"

Liam nodded. "It did, but her sacrifice wasn't in vain. She saved a lot of lives."

"And now it's back," I whispered, "at Lucent." I shivered.

"At Lucent?" He tensed all over again. "How do you know?"

"I didn't, until just now. Since I first came here, I kept seeing shadows move out of the corner of my eye, rooms seemed darker, and I often felt like I was being watched. And the time Christian and I fought the Vykens in the tower, I saw part of a shadow, almost like an arm, reach out and stop a Vyken from killing him. Because everything was happening so fast, I thought I'd imagined it. I wonder why it saved Christian?"

"Someone doesn't want him dead, and that someone is at Lucent. They'd have to be if they are controlling it." Liam sighed and raked his fingers through his short hair. "One more problem. I'll get the Deific on it right away."

"Who was the Aura?" I asked, but just then Liam's phone buzzed. He looked down at it and frowned. "Everything okay?" I asked.

"A blood drop's happening tonight near Lucent."

"How do you know?"

"We've got a guy who occasionally passes info to us for money, or other questionable items," he said.

I didn't want to know what he meant by *questionable.* "Where?"

Liam looked up from his phone. "You're not going."

I stood up, my blood turning hot. "Of course I am. I can help." *And fight. Please let me fight.*

"You're not ready." He turned away and picked up a bag.

"Are you kidding? You saw what I did the other night. I'm good at fighting."

Liam rummaged through the bag, searching for something. "That's the problem."

I crossed my arms. "What's that supposed to mean?"

Liam removed a sheathed knife. "You're forgetting what's inside you."

The next words out of my mouth were a lie. "I know what's inside me, but I'm controlling it. You think a little Vyken poison is going to change me? I'm still—"

Before I could finish my sentence, Liam had me by both arms. "You're not you. Don't you understand? You're different. You always will be. For the rest of your life you're going to be like a person on the edge of a cliff. The smallest moment can push you over, and there's no coming back."

He must've noticed how my anger had turned to fear, because his features softened and his grip relaxed. "I'm just saying you need to remember," he said. "Don't ever think you can control it, that you're better than it. That's what it wants you to feel. Pride."

I sat back down, feeling defeated. "Any silver lining?"

Liam knelt in front of me. "Of course. You get to live."

I looked around the room. "Is this any way to live?"

"It's better than the alternative." Liam straightened. "Look, I'm not trying to freak you out, but I don't want to see you get overly confident and make a mistake. You are an incredible fighter, but you have to make sure you're fighting for the right reasons and not because you long for the fight."

"Why do you do it?" I asked.

"Do what?"

"All of this. Fight for us. Fight for the Deific."

"Because the second I stop, the darkness will overpower me. If I'm not fighting against them, then I'm becoming one of them. This is my life."

I hesitated, studying his face. "How long have you been doing this?"

He looked at me for a long time, and I could tell he was remembering painful memories. "Too long," he said. "Come on. Let's go."

Ten minutes later I was back on the dirt road. Before Liam dropped me off, he warned me to stay away tonight, but, as I raced toward Lucent, I formed a plan. I would go tonight, I decided. No Vyken poison was going to stop me from helping my friends. They needed me, I convinced myself.

TWENTY-EIGHT

"I'm going with you," May said after I finished telling her and Tessa about my plan.

"Me too," Tessa said.

I picked up Britt's diary off my floor and stuffed it back into my backpack. "I can't ask you guys to do that."

"You didn't ask," May said. "We're in this together."

"But it's not you the Vykens are after. They want the Auras."

"Hello?" May said. "We live in this school too, and they're trying to destroy it. We're just as involved."

I didn't want to, but I couldn't help smiling. I breathed a sigh of relief. "I would love some company."

"Where's Christian going to be?" Tessa asked.

I went to the window and peered out. "He's tailing Jackson. Something tells me he'll end up at the same place as Liam."

"The blood drop," May said, and I turned around. She picked up a picture off my dresser and stared at it. It was a photo of us that Jake had taken at our graduation.

"Should we invite Kiera?" Tessa said.

May and I looked at each other. "Let's not," I said. "She seems a little too excited about all this."

"Agreed," May said. She set the picture down.

Tessa leaned forward on my bed. "You have to remember,

guys, that she's never had anything go wrong in her life. This is probably like a movie to her."

"You've lived your whole life here," May said. "How come you get it?"

"Just because I've lived here doesn't mean I haven't seen what's out there." Tessa stood up to leave with May. "What time do you want to go?"

"Meet us at the shed at eleven?"

She nodded. "I'll see you there."

May and Tessa left me alone. I was so jittery with anticipation that I considered running on the track to try and calm down, but I was too afraid of being seen. Instead, I opened my Auran history book and tried to study. A lot of good that did. All I could think about was how I would be fighting soon. Over and over I replayed the mistakes I'd made the last couple of times I fought Vykens and resolved not to make them again.

Sometime later, I sat up when I heard quiet footsteps moving down the hall. I glanced at the time. *Must be May.* I opened the door before she had a chance to knock.

"Nice hearing," she said.

"Nice outfit," I said, and smiled back. She was dressed all in black. She'd even borrowed one of my black beanies.

"I already snuck downstairs," May said. "There are two Guardians just outside the doors. Is that normal?"

"I don't think so." I tried to recall if I'd ever seen Guardians, besides Jackson, in front of the school. "But I've never gone that way."

"What way do you go?"

I opened the window. "Out here."

May looked down. "Are you kidding?"

"It's not so bad. You just have to make it to that pipe." I pointed to the long drainage pipe about three feet over. "Or, if you're me," I looked at her, "you can just jump."

"But that would kill you," May said, her voice quiet, pondering. I waited for her thoughts to gather, waited for her to verbalize what I knew she already suspected. Her eyes slowly met mine. "You're not like you used to be, are you?"

I shook my head.

"He bit you." She reached up and touched my long hair. "That's why you're always leaving your hair down. And why you've been so angry."

"It's inside me, May," I said, barely hearing my own voice. "I feel it all of the time."

She lowered her hand. "But you're not one of them."

"Not yet. I'm fighting it. Liam's helping me."

"I wondered about that." She squeezed my hand. "You'll do it. I know you will."

"Thanks."

May glanced out the window again. "Is there any way your new abilities can help me down?"

"I can throw you out," I offered.

"I'll take my chances with the pipe." May swung her legs over the windowsill and maneuvered herself onto her belly.

"Now reach your foot over," I said. "You'll find a place for it on the metal clippings holding the pipe in place." I waited until May was safely on the ground before I jumped from the window and landed beside her.

"Too cool," she said.

"It doesn't come without a price. Come on. Tessa's probably waiting."

We kept to the shadows as we snuck across campus. May kept glancing sideways at me, but I didn't dare ask her what she was thinking. We found Tessa leaning against the brick wall of the shed. She looked nervous.

"You sure you want to do this?" I asked.

"Sure. No big deal, right?" She started walking. "We go

into the forest. Remove a few Vyken heads. Easy, right?"

May and I looked at each other. "Tessa," I said. "Seriously. You don't have to come."

Tessa stopped at the secret door and entered a code. She took a deep breath. "No. I'm okay. Just need to wrap my head around things."

When the door opened, May had the same reaction I had. "Amazing," she whispered.

"So how are we supposed to find this meeting?" Tessa asked.

I looked around. "Let's walk this way awhile." I pointed to the right where the forest looked the darkest, and, to me, the most inviting. "And then I'll see if I can hear anything."

We moved into the forest, and the moment darkness enveloped me, I became more invigorated. "This is going to be so awesome," I said.

May looked at me. "What did you say?"

"Oh, nothing. Just mumbling." I opened and closed my fists, every part of me humming with dark energy. To help combat it, I quickly produced Light to lead the way, a soft glowing ball in my hand. Not a weapon. Just Light.

When we had moved some distance into the forest, I stopped. "Everyone quiet for a sec," I said. I focused my hearing, listening beyond the sounds of May and Tessa's breathing and crickets chirping. To my left I heard movement. "This way."

"It's about a ten on the creep-scale out here," May said.

Tessa stepped over a log. "It's not bad if you're used to it."

May looked at her. "How often do you come out here?"

"I used to come all the time, but lately there's been too many Vykens."

I stopped and listened again. Out of the corner of my eye, I thought I saw movement to my right.

"Do other Lizens come out here?" May whispered.

I heard a rustling sound, but it seemed to be behind us. How did that happen? I listened again. Faint sounds of someone walking, but this time to my left.

Tessa nodded. "We used to have parties out here."

I turned around. "Let's go back this way," I said.

May glanced behind us. "Isn't that the way we just came?"

"Yeah, but," I paused, listening again, "there's movement all around. Almost as if we're being—"

"Surrounded," Tessa said. May and I turned and looked at her, and my Light dissipated. Tessa was staring at something in the forest. She raised a shaking finger, and we followed its direction.

Vykens.

TWENTY-NINE

"What do we have here?" one of the Vykens said. Next to him was another male who was grinning wildly.

I was glad they looked normal, even though that meant they'd consumed an Aura's blood. I pulled May and Tessa behind me. "Stay back," I whispered.

Tessa clutched my arm, but May ignited her hand on fire.

The Vykens laughed. One of them had a tattoo of a bloody dagger on the top of his bald head. I gasped as I realized who it was. The Vyken from Britt's journal! It had to be. I glanced over at May. She seemed to be thinking the same thing.

The Vyken next to dagger-head looked his complete opposite, more like the good boy-next-door with short, blond hair and a baby-blue polo shirt. "Look, Blade, a baby Fury, a Lizen, and a"—Baby-blue looked me up and down—"what are you, girlie?"

I swung my wrist, creating a tight ball of Light the size of a tennis ball. "You're about to find out," I said.

The Vyken who Clean-cut had referred to as Blade said, "An Aura? But you've got Vyken blood in you. I can sense it from here."

Tessa's head turned in my direction, but I didn't look at her. This wasn't the time for a confession. "All you need to know is that I'm an Aura who's about to dust you," I said.

Tessa tightened her grip on my arm. "I don't think that's a good idea."

Every part of me screamed otherwise. I'd never wanted to fight so much in my life. In less than a second I imagined all the many ways I could kill them. I smiled, all reasoning gone.

"Say the word," May said, another fireball appearing in her other hand.

I stepped forward, ready to attack, when a cold breeze rushed by. I froze. Not because of the sudden wind, but because of the words they brought with them. A familiar voice had whispered, "Why are you fighting?"

I looked around for Liam but didn't see him. How did he do that?

"What are you waiting for?" Clean-cut said.

I glanced back at May and Tessa. Even though May looked ready to fight, I saw the fear in her eyes. As for Tessa, her eyes couldn't be any wider. As much as I wanted to fight, Liam was right. My reasons for fighting right now appealed to my darker side.

"I'm hungry," Blade said. "Let's get this over with.

The clean-cut Vyken shrugged. "Fine by me."

As soon as I saw their bodies jerk forward, I turned and pushed Tessa and May. "Run!" I said as I shot a stream of Light from my palm, hitting Blade squarely in the chest. He flew back, but I didn't see his body fall. I was too busy trying to outrun Clean-cut.

He was only a few feet behind, when May yelled at me to duck. I did as she said. May shot fire over my head and into the face of the Vyken. He fell to the ground screaming, but jumping over his body was Blade, who looked madder than ever.

"Head toward the lake!" I yelled up at Tessa, who was a surprisingly fast runner. She nodded and veered left, bursting through bushes and jumping over fallen trees. If one of us tripped, Blade would be right on top of us. I had to slow him down somehow. I made several balls of Light and tossed them back. Because I was running, my aim was terrible, and he easily dodged them. Not far behind him raced Clean-cut, half of his face still smoking.

I caught up to May. "We're not going to make it. We need a barrier or something."

"I think I can do that." She spun around and, with both hands extended, produced a wall of fire directly behind us. When the Vykens moved to go around it, she swirled her fingers and the edges of the fire wall expanded until it had entirely circled them.

By this time, Tessa and I had stopped to watch. Tessa was breathing heavily when she said, "I'm so glad you're my friend, May."

I was about to add my own compliments when Blade took a step through the flames. His clothes caught on fire, and despite the fact that his skin was bubbling, he patted the flames out with his bare palms.

"It's not going to hold them," May whispered.

I thought fast. "Do it again, May. More fire."

May raised her hands and expanded the fire until it had once again circled the Vykens. Before either one of them had a chance to get through, I blasted it with Light, increasing the heat ten-fold. The fire changed from a bright orange to an ice-blue color. This time when Blade tried to go through it, he cried out and stepped away from the flames.

"How long will it hold?" May said.

"I don't know, but let's not stick around to find out." We took off running again toward the lake.

"How much farther?" May said, panting heavily.

"It's just up here," Tessa said. "As soon as we get to the lake just dive right in, got it?"

May looked at her. "I'm not a good swimmer."

Tessa side-stepped a log. "Don't worry about that. I'll get you."

"Whatever happens, May," I said, "trust Tessa."

Tessa disappeared down the steep hill to the lake. May stopped suddenly before going down, making me run into the back of her. We both fell and rolled down the steep embankment. Tessa was already in the water when we reached the bottom. Her head broke the surface. "Hurry! Get in!"

I stumbled to my feet and waded into the water, pulling May with me. Not far away, I heard the Vykens approaching. May started whimpering when the water line reached her chest. "I hate water," she said.

I looked her in the eyes. "You will be fine. I promise. Just don't worry about breathing."

"What?" she said just as Tessa jerked us both beneath the surface.

I let her pull me down, but May was fighting so hard I had to grab onto her too, just to keep her from returning to the surface. When we reached the bottom, I stood upright along with Tessa, but May kept kicking her legs. I took a deep breath, held it, and let go of Tessa. With both hands, I cupped May's face. It took a second for her to open her eyes, and I made sure that when she did I had a huge smile on my face. May looked puzzled, but smiled sheepishly back when she realized she no longer needed air.

Now that she was calm, I grabbed Tessa's hand. My lungs relaxed as if air had returned to them, but I wasn't sure if that was really the case or not.

Tessa motioned us forward with her head. We all held hands and began to walk on the murky bottom. We learned not to let go, because the second we did we'd start to float back to the top. Somehow Tessa was keeping us grounded.

Walking was a slow process, but that was fine with me. I wanted to make sure that as soon as we did surface, the Vykens would be gone. We reached the end of the lake and began our ascent. After giving us a signal to hold our breath, Tessa let go of our hands and went up first to look around. When she ducked back under the water she motioned us up.

As soon as we broke the surface, May gasped for air and whispered, "That was the strangest thing I've ever done."

I looked all around the lake to make sure we were alone before I said, "But awesome too."

"How do you do it?" May asked Tessa.

Tessa scrambled to the top of the ravine. I was right behind her. "I'll tell you later," she said.

"Right," I said. "We need to find Liam. I've got a feeling there's going to be a lot more Vykens at this blood drop than he was planning on."

May caught up to us. Tessa removed a rubber band from her pocket and pulled her wet hair back. She offered one to each of us. May accepted, but I didn't.

While they wrung water from their clothes, I listened hard, focusing all of my senses. Most of the forest was full of life, insects scurrying for food, hunters hunting prey, but there was one section of the forest that was unusually quiet. "This way," I said, walking straight ahead.

"Can we run?" May asked. "In case there are more Vykens."

"Good point," I said and picked up my pace.

We ran deeper into the forest and farther from Lucent. The landscape changed; older, thicker trees with knots and twists in their trunks looked almost lifelike, and their arms reached up and out in all directions. We crossed over a dirt road, and I wondered if it was the same one Liam had driven on earlier.

"Slow down. Quiet," the wind whispered to me in Liam's

voice. He must've had have some crazy hearing to have heard us, but I was grateful for the warning.

I slowed and signaled for the others to stop. Not far away voices could be heard. "This way," I said.

I turned left and quietly crept through the forest. May and Tessa followed, just as careful to watch where they stepped. The forest broke into a clearing, far enough away that the Vykens wouldn't have heard us, thanks to Liam.

I sunk down in front of a fallen log and peered over it. My fingers dug into the bark when I saw how many Vykens there were, most of them in their true form. There must've been at least fifteen, including the two we'd run into earlier. And standing in front of them was Jackson.

THIRTY

"That snake," May whispered.

I looked around for Christian. If Jackson was here then Christian should be too. I was about to go look for him, but he found me first, scrambling over to us from a nearby clump of trees. His eyebrows were pulled tightly together. "What are you doing here?" he whispered between his teeth. "There's too many of them. You're going to get hurt."

"We came to help," I snapped.

He took hold of my arm. "You need to leave right now."

I shook it off with just as much force. "You have no idea what I'm capable of," I said, and I wasn't sure which side of me was talking.

A breeze picked up. "Save your spats for later," Liam's voice said. "Get ready to fight."

Christian stiffened and looked around.

"I don't get it either," I said.

"What are we supposed to do?" Tessa said.

"Be extremely careful," Christian said.

I strained to hear what Jackson was saying, but it was difficult because we were so far away.

". . . be given more once I have your commitment," Jackson was saying. "And for those who have already had the pleasure of drinking an Aura's blood, more will only make you that much stronger."

The Vykens looked at each other, but no one said anything.

"I get it," Jackson said, his voice soothing. "You're scared. But things are different now."

"Liam," I whispered, knowing he could somehow hear me.

"What?" the wind blew back.

"How many are with you?"

"Two."

"Is that enough to take them, including myself, Christian, Tessa, and May?"

There was a pause before he said, "It's enough to make them run, but—"

"Good," I said and stood up, dodging Christian's outstretched hand. I couldn't wait to get out there and fight. My insides were quivering with excitement just thinking about it, and there was nothing I could do to stop it.

"It's not like it was before," Jackson was saying as I drew closer. "Auras don't know how to fight, despite what you say." Jackson glanced at Blade's burned face. "You don't have to worry about Auras."

I left the shadows and walked toward them. "I am so sick of people saying that," I said. All heads turned toward me.

Jackson looked surprised, but he recovered quickly. "You shouldn't be here, Llona."

"Should you?" I asked.

"What is this, Jackson?" a tall Vyken said.

"A slight disruption, but," he smiled big, and the cruelty of it actually frightened me, "her timely appearance will actually help what I'm selling. Who'd like a fresh taste to feel just how powerful an Aura's blood can be?" A few of the Vykens actually salivated.

"I'd like to see you try," I said, forming a shifting ball of Light in my hands.

"Anyone touches her and I'll rip you to shreds," Christian said from behind me.

"You are so stupid, C.," Jackson said, shaking his head. "I thought you'd want to die a more noble death."

Christian stood next to me. A couple of the Vykens laughed, but I noticed Blade moving back.

"Get it over with, boys," Jackson said. "I still need to finish my presentation."

Three Vykens moved forward, but stopped when one said, "What is that?"

I turned around. A fireball was racing through the forest. It barely missed Jackson, but it caught a Vyken in his arm. Jackson's smile disappeared. "Kill them all," he said.

"Not so fast," Liam said as he moved out from within the shadows. Behind him were two extremely tall men built like tree trunks. Identical twins, by the looks of them. Both had brown hair and the same crooked noses.

The sight of Liam changed the look in Jackson's eyes. "We will still destroy you," Jackson said, but his voice wavered. "You don't have the numbers."

"No more talking," Liam said. And that's all any of us needed.

The forest became a whirlwind of activity all at once. Christian fought a Vyken and had him beheaded before I landed my third blow into a different Vyken who smelled and looked like he'd just come from working in a fast food restaurant. Before Christian's Vyken had turned to dust, he was fighting Jackson.

"Duck!" I heard May yell.

I bent over just as a fireball flew over me and smashed into the chest of a Vyken who looked like he was in the middle of a deathblow to my head.

"Thanks!" I called back to her. I wasn't sure where she was, but she was doing a great job of keeping a bird's eye view on everyone. Fireballs continued to fly across the clearing.

I sidestepped my Vyken and jumped onto his back. I placed both hands on the side of his head and lit them up. The Vyken struggled against me, but I maintained a tight grip around his waist with my legs. In less than ten seconds, the Vykens head exploded into dust followed by the rest of his body. I fell to the ground, my eyes locking with Christian's for a split second before I moved on to the next Vyken. I felt invincible.

The twins Liam had brought along turned out to be extremely helpful. Any Vyken they got their hands on was broken, twisted, and tossed. The two were stronger than anything I'd ever seen, but their size and strength came with a price. They were slow. On more than one occasion, May saved them by using her highly effective fireballs.

One of the twins had a chance to return the favor when a Vyken appeared behind May. The Vyken bashed the side of her head, knocking her to the ground. I rushed to her despite the fact that I had my own Vyken to contend with. Luckily, Christian had become aware of what was going on and side-plowed into the Vyken chasing after me. Meanwhile, May's Vyken jumped onto her and was grasping for her neck, but May must've heated up her hands because every time she shoved him away he cried out and became even angrier.

I was almost to her when out of nowhere one of the twins came barreling down like a raging bull. He dove into the Vyken, and the two rolled off May.

I wanted to keep watching to see who would win, but through all the sounds of fighting I heard Tessa scream. I looked around but couldn't see her. *She must still be in the forest.* I rushed into the woods and found Tessa up in a tree. She was trying to climb higher, but a Vyken was jumping at an unnatural height to get at her. And by the looks of Tessa's torn pant leg, he almost had her.

"Tessa!" I yelled. I ran faster, unsure of what I was going to do next.

That's when I heard Liam shout my name. I looked back but kept running. "Use this!" he called. He tossed a machete-like weapon; it wind-milled toward me until I caught its handle just as I was jumping up to attack the tall Vyken. I jabbed it into the Vyken, but he maneuvered out of the way and the blade tore into his shoulder. I swung again, but the Vyken caught the gleaming steel with his bare hands. He smiled, like he'd gotten the upper hand. I smiled back and lit up every particle of the weapon with Light. The Vyken screamed and stumbled back. I swung again, but he kicked it from my hands, and followed through with a tight fist to my face, knocking me onto my back. Stars exploded all around me, but I maintained consciousness.

The Vyken lunged for me but stopped when a spray of liquid rained onto him. He screamed and clawed at his face as if he'd been doused with acid. Confused, I looked up. Perched above us on a tree limb was Tessa. She wiped her mouth with the back of her hand. *Super spit?* "Wicked," I said and jumped to my feet. I picked up the blade and approached the Vyken, who was trying to run away but kept stumbling because he couldn't see.

The weapon in my hand lit up. I raised it high and brought it down once. His head fell from his shoulders but turned to dust before it hit the ground.

After making sure Tessa was okay, I returned to the fight, feeling like I could've taken them all on by myself. Two more Vykens died by my hands. It felt good. Only a few Vykens were left, and they were running away. I looked specifically for Blade but didn't see him. Either he was dead or he'd escaped with the others. Part of me wanted to go after them just so I could keep fighting, but then I noticed Liam watching me, and I remembered his words of caution, so I remained where I was.

May came to stand next to me. "That was crazy," she said.

"Where's Tessa?"

"Still in a tree."

"You okay, Tessa?" I called and rubbed my jaw. It ached something fierce from being punched.

"Peachy," she called back.

"How are you doing, May?" I noticed her hands were red.

"Amazing! That felt incredible."

"Really?" I said, surprised by her answer.

"Get off me!" Jackson yelled.

I turned around. Christian had Jackson pinned to the ground and with his free hand was smashing Jackson in his already bloodied face. "Why?" Christian said. "Why did you do this?" Another punch.

Liam jerked Christian to his feet while the twins took hold of Jackson. Jackson tried to break free of their grip but stopped moving after just a minute, probably realizing it was pointless.

"Tell me why!" Christian yelled again. Liam was having a difficult time holding him back.

"You smug, arrogant—" Jackson said, but his words were cut off when one, or both, of the twins tightened their grip. Jackson lowered his voice. "You think this life we live here is perfect? We're given all these abilities for what? To babysit princesses?" He spat the words in my direction. "We were meant for more, Christian. And you'd see it too if you weren't hanging around social rejects."

Christian broke free from Liam, or Liam let him go, and punched Jackson again, this time knocking him unconscious. The twins held up Jackson's limp body by his arms. "What should we do with him?" Christian said.

I looked at Liam because he seemed like the person who would know, but he was typing something into his phone. "We need to question him," he said. "See what he knows."

"Should we go after the others?" Christian said to Liam.

Liam pocketed his cell phone. "No. We were lucky we had the element of surprise, but next time they'll be ready." He looked over at us three girls. "Thanks for coming to help, even though," he glanced at me, "I believe I specifically told you to stay home."

Christian looked at me, his brows drawn together.

"I think they did great," one of the twins said, speaking for the first time.

We all turned and looked at them.

Liam nodded his head toward them. "This is Arik and Aaron."

"Who's who?" I asked, but Liam didn't answer. He had turned around and was walking away, scanning the ground for something.

"I'm Arik," the twin on the left said.

"And I'm Aaron," the other said.

Their voices were just as large as their muscular frames.

"Nice to meet you," I said. "I'm Llona, this is Tessa, and the fire-thrower is May."

They dropped Jackson and shot their hands out in front of Tessa and May. "Nice to meet you," they said.

"So are you guys like half giants or something?" May asked.

The twins laughed; the sound would've been frightening if they didn't have smiles on their faces. "Our kind come from the trees," Arik said.

May and I looked at each other.

"Long story," Aaron said. "Let's just say we're hard to knock down."

"I've heard of your kind," Tessa said.

Christian joined Liam on the other side of the clearing. They spoke softly, and by the looks of it neither of them was happy. "One second," I said to May and the others. Christian and Liam stopped talking when they saw me approaching. "What's up, guys?" I said.

"Jackson didn't bring anything," Liam said. "I was expecting some kind of trade."

"What does that mean?" I asked.

"If he didn't have any blood with him, then that means it's still back at Lucent."

"And?" Christian said.

Liam looked at both of us. "I'm worried the Vykens are planning on going inside to get it." His words hung in the air, making it feel heavy.

"They wouldn't dare enter Lucent," Christian finally said.

Liam looked annoyed. "Why not?"

"Because the place is guarded by Guardians."

"Jackson is a Guardian. How many more have switched sides?"

Christian didn't answer, but by his bulging jaw muscles and white-knuckled fists, I knew he was upset. I placed my hand on his back and let it warm with Light. He quickly moved away. "Don't do that."

"I just—"

"I know, but I need to feel this anger. I need to be upset. Things are not okay."

Christian was right, of course, but I hated seeing him so serious, as if he were doubting his own skills. It made me scared.

"I've got to get back," Christian said. "I need to see who's still on the good side."

"I have to go too," Liam said. "Arik, Aaron, grab Jackson and let's go," he said loud enough for them to hear.

The twins turned around but didn't move.

"Seriously, guys. Let's go," Liam said again.

Arik and Aaron slumped their shoulders and each grabbed an arm of Jackson's.

Liam turned to me. "Clear your head tonight. Use Light. Do something positive. I can tell you're buzzing hardcore."

Christian looked at me, waiting for an explanation, but instead I said to Liam, "You stopped me, with your voice."

"Stopped you from what?" Christian said.

"Back in the woods. We ran into a couple of Vykens, and we were about to fight them, but I heard Liam's voice. How did you do that?"

Liam looked up at the moon and then back to me. "It's sort of a thing I do with wind. It carries sounds to or from me."

Arik and Aaron began dragging Jackson. The motion stirred him awake. "What?" he mumbled. "Hey, let me go!"

"Shut up," a twin said.

Jackson looked around. "Taking me is pointless. They'll come for me."

"Nobody cares about you," the other twin added.

Jackson's gaze settled on Tessa. "Hello, Lizen. Hasn't your kind been warned to stay out of this?"

"Get him out of here," Liam said. The twins picked up their pace. This time Jackson didn't argue, but he didn't look worried either.

I moved over to Tessa. "What's he talking about?"

Tessa was pale. "A while ago the Lizens got a letter. We don't know who it was from, but they warned us not to get involved in upcoming events between the Vykens and Auras. They said there would be consequences."

Liam turned to her. "Why didn't you tell me this? I would never have involved you."

"It's my choice," Tessa said quietly.

I put my arm around her as did May. "Everything will be

okay," I said, but when my eyes met Liam's and I saw his concerned expression, I wondered if I'd just lied.

THIRTY-ONE

I WASN'T SURE WHAT TIME IT WAS WHEN MY CELL PHONE started vibrating, waking me up, but when I opened my eyes and saw the gray beginnings of morning's light shine through my window, I guessed it was around 6:00 a.m. I turned and looked at the clock. Close. 6:30. I'd been asleep for two hours.

After I'd parted ways with the group, who all looked exhausted except for Liam, I didn't go to bed like everyone else. Instead I ran on the track for almost an hour, trying to burn off some energy. I tried using Light, like Liam had suggested, but I just couldn't get it to come. My body demanded something physical. Maybe if I could've calmed my mind . . .

I picked up the phone. "Hello?"

"Is Tessa safe?" It was Liam, and he sounded frantic.

I rubbed my eyes. "Tessa? I think so, but I just woke up. Why?"

"Did she make it there safely last night?"

"Yes. What's this about?"

"After you guys left, we took Jackson to my cabin to question him, but he wouldn't say jack. I told the twins to take him to the Deific because they have better ways of getting someone to talk than I do, but on the way there they were attacked. Their car was totaled and Jackson was taken."

I sat up straighter, thinking. "How long ago was this?"

"The accident happened about three hours ago, but I just got the call."

"Why didn't they tell you sooner, especially since he threatened Tessa?"

"The Deific didn't know about the threat yet," Liam said, his voice full of regret. "I was going to tell them this morning when they questioned Jackson."

"What's everyone doing now?"

"They're looking for him. I'm going to help too, but I wanted to check on Tessa first."

While he was talking, I was already getting dressed. "I'll go check now and get back to you." I slipped my bare feet into shoes. "Are the twins okay?"

"They'll be fine. Call me soon."

I hung up the phone and rushed out the door, going straight for the dining room where I hoped I'd find Tessa in the kitchen.

The dining room was mostly empty. A few girls had come early and were sitting quietly reading books while a couple of Lizens set the tables. I pushed the kitchen door open and froze. Huddled in the corner were several Lizen women. When they saw me, they stepped back until I had a clear view of Lilly, Tessa's mother. She was crying.

"Tessa's missing," she said.

It took me a second to find my voice. "For how long?" I asked and wondered how much her mother knew about Tessa's activities.

She wiped at her nose. "A couple of hours maybe. Her bed was empty when I went to wake her this morning."

I moved forward and gave her a hug. "Have you told Sophie?"

She nodded.

"Good. I'll start asking around too. We'll find her, I promise." As I walked away, a plan formulated in my mind. It was time to talk to the Big Bad.

* * * * *

Alone in my room, I pulled out the cell phone and called Liam. He answered on the first ring. Before I could say anything, he said, "Please tell me she's okay."

"Tessa's missing."

There was a long pause before he said, "For how long?"

"Not sure. She was gone when her mother woke up." Liam was quiet. "Liam?" I asked.

He started talking. "No clues on Jackson yet, but I still have a few more contacts to see. You do what you can there. Ask around. Talk to the teachers."

"Actually," I hesitated, my pulse quickening, "I'm going to see Cyrus."

He paused again. "You'll be doing it alone."

"I know."

"It could be dangerous."

"I know."

"You have one advantage."

"What's that?"

"He doesn't know that you know about the pills. You have to keep pretending that he's not a Vyken."

"Right."

"Don't be scared."

"Not me."

"Keep my phone with you."

"I will. And will you tell Christian, I mean, about Tessa?" There was no way I was going to tell Christian I was about to see Cyrus. He'd freak out, especially after I told him and the others about the Shadow, and my suspicions of Cyrus last night.

"He won't be happy."

"I'll text you his number."

"Call me when it's over," he said. "I want to know you're okay."

"Will do. Later." I hung up, but before I pocketed my phone, I texted him Christian's number. Bells chimed. No way was I going to class today. I had to find a way into Cyrus's office, and I had a feeling it wasn't going to be easy.

I left my room, nerves shaking and a lump in my throat the size of an apple. Instead of going straight to Cyrus's office, I went to the dining room to tell May and Kiera what was going on. I found them at a table by themselves. May was in the middle of telling Kiera all about the night before. Kiera looked pale. No smiles this time.

"Hey, guys," I said and sat down.

May sort of smiled, but Kiera didn't acknowledge me. "I had no idea," she said, her gaze fixated on a plate of French toast in front of her.

"About what?" I asked.

She looked at me. "I mean, I know you guys have been talking about Vykens taking our blood, and them basically drugging us, but I guess I didn't realize how serious it was until May told me. Fifteen Vykens?"

"At least." I looked around the room before I lowered my voice and said, "Something bad has happened, guys. This morning—"

Kiera took hold of my arm, startling me. "You've got to teach me. About fighting, about how to use Light, about everything."

I shook my head, although I should have been happy. I'd been waiting forever for an Aura to say that, but the timing was all wrong. "Fine. I will, but first I have to tell you—"

"Good," Kiera interrupted again. "Because I don't want to be a sitting duck."

"Would you let her finish already!" May said.

Kiera looked at her and had a moment of awakening. "Right," she said. "I'm over it now. I'm listening."

I took a deep breath. "Last night the twins were attacked while taking Jackson to the Deific. He escaped and now Tessa's missing."

May brought her hand to her mouth.

"I've got to go talk to . . ." I hesitated, unsure how they'd feel about me talking to Cyrus alone, especially after telling them about Cyrus and the Shadow. "Some people about Tessa," I finished. It was just a conversation. Nothing was going to happen.

"What can we do?" May asked.

"Ask around. Talk to the students and teachers. See if anyone's seen her."

"You can count on us," Kiera said.

I nodded and hurried off to Cyrus's office. Instead of taking the stairs, I took the elevator to make sure I wouldn't chicken out. When the doors opened I just stood there, staring at the long hallway.

Ms. Crawford appeared when she walked out from one of the offices. "Llona? What are you doing here?" she asked.

I forced myself forward, my eyes scanning the name plaques on the wall. "I'm just looking for Ms. Smitty. She said to meet her here."

"But she's probably at breakfast."

I looked away, trying not to panic. *Think, Llona!*

"Are you okay? You look upset?"

A sudden thought occurred. I looked back at her, my eyes big, and I hoped glass-looking. "Some of the girls were giving me a hard time. About my mother. Ms. Smitty wanted to talk to me about it before class."

Ms. Crawford pulled me into a hug. "Don't you worry about those girls. Your mother was a special woman. If only we all could've been as brave as her."

I pulled away, startled. "You mean that?"

"Of course. I always admired your mother. You come from a long line of independent women. It's just unfortunate that others don't appreciate it as much as myself." She patted me on the arm. "You go wait in her office. I'm sure she'll be along soon."

I nodded and walked past her. Ms. Smitty's office door was open so I flipped on the light and sat down. The walls were a pale green color. Nature photos, some of forests and others of mountains, hung at eye level, but I couldn't get near them because the room was also filled with plants. They were everywhere, making me feel like I was in a jungle.

Several minutes passed before I dared to leave. Other than Ms. Crawford, I hadn't seen anyone else.

I stood up and peeked into the hallway toward Cyrus's office. Coast was clear. I went toward the heavy wooden door; it seemed to grow larger the closer I came to it. I stopped in front of it and reached up to knock, but as I did so the door opened. My legs almost gave out, and my head spun as if I'd just stepped off a merry-go-round.

In front of me, staring at me with a stern expression behind black-rimmed glasses, was Cyrus's assistant, Jameson. A Vyken. Jameson was the Vyken, not Cyrus. This sudden information rocked my frame, but I forced myself to stay upright. "I need to see Cyrus," I said, trying hard to sound forceful.

"He can't be bothered right now," Jameson said, his gums exposed.

"I just have to ask him some questions. It's important."

"Then come back between four and five. He visits with students during that time." He moved to close the door, but I put my foot into the door jam.

"It can't wait."

"Let her in," I heard Cyrus say.

Reluctantly, Jameson opened the door wide. I moved into the room and away from Jameson, hoping the nausea would leave me, but it didn't go away. It grew stronger.

I glanced behind me at Jameson and then back at Cyrus, realizing the predicament I'd just put myself in. I was now alone in a room with not one, but two Vykens.

THIRTY-TWO

I REACHED, AS CASUALLY AS POSSIBLE, TO THE NEAREST CHAIR to steady myself. "Thank you for seeing me, Cyrus," I said, trying hard to keep my voice from cracking.

From behind his desk, Cyrus grinned, slow and deliberate. An angel's smile on the devil's face. I could see why everyone trusted him so much.

"Llona. It's good to see you again. I trust everything has been resolved since our last conversation?"

Other than his lips, he didn't move. No shifting, no ticks, or movement of his hands. I don't think he was even breathing. "Um, yes, sorry about that. I was confused. You know, from everything I've been through." I looked down, away from his gaze that seemed to see right through me.

"It's quite understandable. Have a seat."

I eagerly accepted. One second longer and I might've fainted.

Cyrus examined me for a minute before he said, "I knew your grandmother and your great-grandmother. Did you know that?"

I took a deep breath and tried to clear my head. I gulped and said, "I assume they attended Lucent Academy?"

"They did. Rebels they were. Like your mother."

The fog in my head cleared real quick.

When I didn't say anything, he said, "Now, what seems to be the problem?"

I was vaguely aware that Jameson had positioned himself behind me. My muscles tensed. "I'm worried about my friend," I said.

"And who's your friend?"

"Her name's Tessa."

He moved. A fraction of an inch. "I don't think I've heard the name."

"She's a Lizen," I said.

His eyebrows rose. "Auras are making friends with Lizens now?"

This comment, on the tail of what he'd just said about my mother, sent a surge of anger, black as night, pulsing through my veins, but I forced myself to remain calm. For now. "Yes," I said, my nails digging into the upholstered chair.

"Strange," he said, "but I guess that's to be expected from you. So what's wrong with your friend, the Lizen?"

"Tessa," I said. "Her name's Tessa, and she's missing." The Vyken's dark poison inside me burned, and I wanted nothing more than to jump across the table and strangle him.

Just then a beeping sound filled the room. I glanced behind me. Jameson removed a cell phone from his pocket and looked at it.

Cyrus looked from Jameson and then to me. "Missing? For how long?"

"A few hours."

Cyrus laughed, but when he saw my serious expression, he coughed. "I'm sure it's nothing. A rebellious Lizen teenager, no doubt, but I'll promise you this, if no one hears from her by tonight, we'll look into it."

I was about to argue when Jameson interrupted, "I need to speak with you, sir."

"I'm visiting with a student, Jameson. Whatever it is can wait until we're finished."

"It's important."

Cyrus stared at Jameson. By the look of Jameson's paler-than-normal complexion, I would've guessed he was about to tell Cyrus his house had burned down. Now Cyrus was breathing. His chest rose and fell. Once.

Cyrus stood up. "I'll be just a moment." He followed Jameson out of the room and closed the door behind him.

I inhaled deeply; the tension in my muscles relaxed, as I was no longer controlling the nauseating effect the Vykens had on me. I focused my hearing, trying to listen in on their conversation, but I couldn't hear a thing. They must've gone into the stairwell.

Several minutes passed. I was too afraid to get up and explore the room, not that I was sure I'd find anything. The only thing I was interested in looking at was a thick row of leather-bound books on a shelf nearby. I hoped I'd find information about the Lizen's history to give Tessa.

The sound of an old clock, hanging high on the wall behind Cyrus's desk, ticked and tocked. Its steady beat reminded me of how tired I was. *Tick. Tock.* I closed my eyes. *Tick. Tock.* And then . . .

My eyes snapped open. *What was that?* A sound beyond the clock's mesmerizing tone. Very faint, but definitely there. I stood and moved behind Cyrus's desk.

Tick tock.

I pressed my ear to the wall. Muffled voices too faint to make out, but someone was clearly beyond the wall. As far as I could tell, the placement of Cyrus's office was in the corner, which meant he should have two windows, one on the north side and another on the east like all the other corner rooms in the school, but Cyrus's office only had one window.

I knocked on the wall softly. Hollow.

Just then I heard the doorknob turning. "Have him call me tonight," I heard Cyrus say just outside the door. I hurried back to my seat and dropped into it just as the door swung open. I tried to slow my breathing, but Cyrus still looked at me funny.

"Everything okay?" I asked, hoping my face wasn't flushed.

"Yes, of course." He went behind his desk and scanned the items as if checking to see if anything was missing.

I stood. "So, you'll look into Tessa's disappearance?"

He looked up. "What?"

"Tessa. The missing Lizen."

"Of course. I will do all that I can."

I turned to leave, but he stopped me. "Miss Reese, you come from a long line of strong Auran women, but they had a habit of getting themselves into trouble. I hope that won't be you."

I placed my hand on the door and looked back. "I abhor trouble, sir. Have a good day." I smiled and closed the door, reeling over what I'd just discovered.

I was about to start down the hallway when I heard the elevator door open. I dove into the nearest empty office next to Cyrus's. The lights were off, and, as I crawled beneath a desk, I wondered if I was making a mistake. I hadn't really thought of a plan, but I had to see what was beyond that wall. If there was even the slightest chance that Tessa was back there, I had to take it.

Whoever came out of the elevator, probably a teacher, went into an office across the hall. They were there for about ten minutes, shuffling papers and typing on a keyboard, before they finally left. I glanced at my watch. In a few more hours teachers would most likely come to this hall for their lunch break. I couldn't stay here forever. One hour, I decided. I would wait one hour to see if Cyrus and Jameson left the room. If they didn't, then I'd have to return at night, which I really didn't want to do.

I kept my ears tuned for sounds in Cyrus's office. Twenty minutes passed and I hadn't heard a word, not a rustling of papers, or even a chair leg sliding against wooden floors. This struck me as odd. What if no one was in there? What if they had escaped through the wall while I was listening to whoever had gone into the office across the hall?

I waited another ten minutes, listening to nothing but the slow, steady hum of an air conditioner somewhere in the building. I crawled out of my hiding spot and glanced down the hall. No one.

Very slowly, I turned the doorknob to Cyrus's office. I froze when the latch clicked, but no one said anything or rushed to the door. I cracked it open and looked inside. I opened the door farther. The office was empty.

I moved quickly to the wall behind Cyrus's desk and felt around for some kind of notch or other object that looked out of place but found nothing. It had to open somehow. I dropped into Cyrus's seat and swiveled around. I felt under his desk, opened his drawers; I even clicked a few pens thinking maybe it was some sort of remote control. Finally, after checking everything, I swiveled back to face the wall. I stretched my legs out and noticed my shoelace was untied. But that wasn't all I noticed.

At the base of the wall, where the floorboards came to meet it, part of the floor was slightly raised. I wouldn't have noticed the deformity by looking down on it. I stood up and pressed my toe onto it. I heard a clicking sound and a section of the wall sunk in. I pushed on it and felt it give.

I was about to push it all the way open but stopped as I remembered all the horror shows I'd watched with Jake. A common mistake of victims was never telling anyone where they were going. I didn't want to be a victim. I pulled out Liam's phone and texted: "Found secret room in Cyrus's office, behind desk. Latch on floor. I'm going in." I hit send.

Before I got a response back, I pocketed the phone. I could probably guess what Liam would say, but there just wasn't time to wait for someone to come with me, nor would I risk anyone else's life.

I pushed on the door until it was wide enough for me to slip in. It was dark and cold and the air smelled faintly of rusted copper pipes. I produced a ball of Light. Just in front of me was a narrow, metal stairwell that spiraled down into darkness. I swallowed and gripped the railing. *Here goes nothing.*

I wasn't sure how far I'd gone, but by the change in the temperature, I guessed I was beneath ground level. A little bit farther and the stairs finally ended at the beginning of a long hallway. On each side were doors with small windows covered by bars. It reminded me of an old, abandoned psychiatric hospital. *I really have to stop thinking of scary movies*, I thought. I pushed the images from my mind and continued forward.

At least there were lights down here—two light bulbs hanging from a wooden slat ceiling. Occasionally a drop of water would find its way between the warped boards and fall to the concrete floor. Parts of the floor had a greenish-blue hue as if mold had taken root. That would explain the pungent smell.

I avoided the green areas and stopped only long enough to peek through the bars of each closed door. Up ahead, I heard faint voices. I worked quickly. Other than metal beds, some of them turned upside down, the rooms were empty.

I thought my efforts had been a waste of time, but then I looked into the last room. Tied to a chair and head slumped forward was a person sitting motionless. Although her head was covered by a black cloth, I knew by her tan pants and black shirt that it was Tessa.

I tried the doorknob and exhaled when I found it unlocked. I carefully opened the door to avoid any creaking of what looked like a two-hundred-year-old door. Tessa remained still. I didn't allow myself to think that she may be hurt. I just needed to get her out of here.

After I closed the door behind me, I went to Tessa and lightly touched her back. She jerked as if doused by water and thrashed back and forth. "Be quiet, Tessa. It's me," I whispered. I removed the head covering.

She blinked several times. "What are you doing here?" She glanced behind me toward the door.

"Saving you."

Not far off another door opened.

"Hide!" Tessa said.

I looked around. My only option was under the bed. I moved to dive under it.

"Wait! The hood," Tessa whispered.

I scooped it off the floor and pulled it back over her head. Just before the door opened, I slid under the bed. The concrete floor was cold and wet in the corner.

Three people—or I should say Vykens by the way my body was reacting—walked into the room. For several seconds no one said anything. Then, "Someone's been in here," I heard Jameson say. "I can smell it. Search the room."

There was only one place to look in the cramped room.

Black boots shifted in the doorway. If they found me, they'd surely kill me and Tessa. I looked around helplessly. The dim light in the room reflected off an oily water puddle just in front of me. The surface of it contained all the colors of the rainbow, shifting slightly by the commotion in the room.

Footsteps walked the floor.

A rainbow.

My mother.

I guessed I had about ten seconds before I was discovered. I flexed every part of me as if I were lifting a two-ton car and wished to be invisible. *Be invisible. Change!* Sweat broke on my brow.

Boots approached the bed.

I imagined my skin shimmering, transforming into actual Light. My nails dug into my palms. *Change!* My body began to vibrate, rattling my insides until I thought I'd break in two.

A knee joined the boots on the floor.

Be invisible! I was shaking so hard I thought I might be having a seizure.

And then a burst of Light exploded in my brain and raced through my body. The shock of it felt like my skin was on fire, and the only thing that stopped me from screaming was the sight of Blade's head looking under the bed only a foot away. His black eyes swept the area, completely passing over me. I would've been relieved except for the fact that I'd never been in so much pain in all my life.

Blade stood up. "Room's empty."

As much as I was dying to let go of whatever power was making me invisible, I felt it was too soon.

Someone must have shoved Tessa because she grunted.

"Who's been in here?" Jameson said.

"What? Huh?" Tessa made it sound like she was coming to.

There was a shuffling of feet and Tessa made a strangling sound as the chair she was sitting on lifted. "Who's been in here?" Jameson said again.

She didn't answer, couldn't answer because she was still gagging. Her chair dropped and rocked backward. "No one," she finally coughed.

"It was probably Jackson or one of his boys," the other Vyken said.

Jameson must have accepted this because he said, "It was brought to my attention that you stole some of the Auras' pills. I want to know what you did with them."

"I didn't—"

He slapped her. "Tell me the truth! Where are the pills?"

Tessa was crying. "I, I took them," she stammered.

"Where are they?"

"I swallowed them."

"Why?"

"I thought they would make me special. Like the Auras."

There was a small pause before they all broke out into laughter. Jameson spoke first. "That is the most pathetic thing I've ever heard. A pill will never make you special." He paused before saying, "But it will make you dead."

"When?" Blade said.

"Wait until tonight. We can throw her body out with the trash."

Another Vyken laughed and said, just before the door closed, "I don't think the dumpster will be able to hold all the dead bodies. Maybe we should have the garbage truck come early." The others joined in his laughter.

As soon as the door closed, I let go of whatever power was keeping me invisible. A sound exploded in my ears and my vision blotched black.

I barely heard Tessa say, "Llona?"

Stay conscious, I commanded myself. I tried to slide out from under the bed, but I seriously felt like I'd been run over. Every part of me hurt. "One minute," I said, but even speaking proved difficult.

"What's wrong?" Tessa whispered.

I heard the worry in her voice, but it didn't make me move any faster. I couldn't. Arm over arm, I crawled toward her. Each movement sent mind-numbing pain up and down my body.

"Llona?"

"Hurt," is all I could say. I reached the back of her chair

and rolled onto my back. Through double vision I could just barely make out Tessa's bound wrists. I blinked a couple of times, trying to clear my line of sight. It didn't work.

I raised my hands, wincing because of the pain the action caused. I felt the ropes around her wrists. They were wet and slippery. I hoped it was from sweat and not blood, but when I squinted I saw red. This made me move faster.

"I'm so sorry," Tessa said. She was crying again.

The ropes were tight, but after a minute I was able to get them loose enough to where Tessa could free herself. She swiveled onto the ground next to me. "What did they do to you?"

"No. Me. Invisible." My vision was completely gone now. Only empty black space existed.

"I don't understand." She squeezed my hand. I tried to squeeze it back, but I had become paralyzed. No matter what I tried I couldn't move. "Help," I said with my last bit of strength.

"Llona?" Tessa sniffed, then waited. "I'm going to get help; don't worry." The last thing I heard was the sound of something heavy sliding along the floor, and I hoped it was Tessa stuffing me back under the bed.

THIRTY-THREE

My eyes opened. Blackness again. I thought I might still be under the bed, and I began to panic.

A voice said, "You're safe. I'm here."

My vision adjusted to the darkness. I was in my room, and I was familiar with the person sitting in a chair next to me. "Christian?"

He stroked my head. "You really scared us."

"Is Tessa—"

"Yes, Liam has her. They snuck her out."

"Is she okay?"

"A little bruised, but she'll survive."

Anger swelled within me. "Does her mother know?"

"Tessa wrote her a note. Can you move?"

I wiggled my toes. No pain. My fingers were next. When they felt fine, I lifted my arm. It took great effort, but it didn't hurt like before. After I finished assessing the damage, I became angry. The pain Tessa and I had experienced was caused by Cyrus and his followers. And Jackson. Darkness returned inside me. And I let it. "How did you find me?"

"Liam called. He told me where you were going. I ran into Tessa on her way out, and she led me to you."

"Did anyone see you?"

"As far as I could tell the place was empty, even Cyrus's office. We were lucky." His fingers laced through mine. I wanted to pull away, tighten my hands into fists.

Christian spoke softly. "Tessa told me what happened. I can only guess the reason you weren't caught is you figured out how to turn invisible."

I nodded.

"That was extremely dangerous. It nearly killed you."

I tried to sit up. It was difficult, but I let my anger and hatred for the Vykens force me upright. "Don't worry about it."

Christian ignored my curt tone and helped me into a sitting position. "You don't need to rush it. Go slow."

I turned toward the window. Just a glimmer of moonlight stole through the glass. "What time is it?"

"Almost nine. Liam should be here soon."

"Inside Lucent?"

"Hardly anyone's here. They all went to the city to see some musical. Besides, Liam wanted to see for himself that you're okay."

This made me madder, but I didn't know why. "Call him. Tell him not to come." I slid to the edge of bed.

"Relax, Llona. Why are you so worked up?"

"Because I need to go kill someone." Anger was burning my insides. I touched my forehead. Was I burning up? I stood too quickly and stumbled. Christian moved to help me. "Don't touch me! I can do this," I snapped.

"I'm just trying to help."

"No, you're babying me, so lay off."

Christian reached for me. "What's going on?"

I shoved his arm away. All I wanted to do was kill something, rip someone apart, but Christian was always in the way. "You are such a—"

My bedroom door swung open. Liam stood in the doorway.

He walked straight to me and took hold of my shoulders.

"Hey," Christian began, but Liam spoke only to me.

"You've got to calm down, Llona. It's eating you."

I pushed him away, my strength fully restored now. Liam stumbled back.

"What are you talking about?" Christian said.

Liam stared at me. "I could hear the poison in her voice from the first floor."

"I'm fine," I said, telling him what I thought he wanted to hear. I pulled on a beanie from off my dresser, anxious to leave. "I just need you two to leave me alone."

Liam took a step toward me. "I know you're scared. I know you're mad, and hurt, and probably a lot of other things, but you have to think this through."

I exploded. "You weren't there, Liam! They hurt Tessa and said horrible things to her. They were going to kill her and throw her body out with the trash. And me too, if they would've found me."

"I understand what you're feeling, but you have to control it."

"Llona?" Christian said, and I could tell by his expression that he had no idea what was going on. How could he?

I looked back at Liam, directly in his eyes. "I've never been more in control, and this feeling inside me is more powerful than anything I've ever felt. And it, more than any of your touchy-feely exercises, is going to help me kill Cyrus, so get out of my way!"

Liam relaxed. "Fine. But if you leave, I'll kill Christian."

Christian and I froze.

Liam continued, "Go, Llona. Get your revenge."

I looked at him and then at Christian, who had gone from confused to tense. Both of us were trying to decide if he was serious or not. "You're a horrible liar," I said and moved toward the door.

Before Christian and I could react, Liam was standing behind Christian, his arm around his neck. Christian gasped for breath.

"What are you doing? Stop that," I said.

"Make me."

Christian tried to swing a fist up, but Liam tightened his grip, forcing Christian to use all his energy on just trying to breathe.

Liam's actions surprised me, but I couldn't be fooled. "Sorry, Liam, but I know you won't kill him, you're wasting my time." I touched the doorknob.

"You're right," Liam said, and I turned back around. "I won't kill him, but I will hurt him." In a move that frightened me, Liam shoved Christian to the floor, and jammed his knee into his back. At the same time, Liam jerked Christian's arm back to an unnatural angle. Christian cried out, and I knew by his expression that it was no act.

"Stop me, Llona," Liam said.

I tightened my grip on the doorknob.

"Go, Llona," Christian said. "This guy's crazy. I can take care of—"

Liam punched the side of his face; blood splattered onto the floor.

"Stop me, Llona!" Liam said again. I stared at him, at his angry expression, but his eyes reflected a deep sadness. I didn't want to fight him. I was itching to rip apart someone else, but then Liam pulled at Christian's arm again until something popped. Christian screamed into the carpet.

"No!" I said. Light exploded into my palm, and I tossed it hard at Liam. It hit him square in the chest. I made three more balls and drilled each one at Liam, who was trying hard to keep quiet, but I knew they were hurting him.

When I was sure Liam had been rendered temporarily

useless, I went to him and kicked him hard in the stomach until he curled up and ceased to move. My hands burned bright with Light, and I pressed them to his back. This time he couldn't hold in the pain. He cried out as Light spread throughout his whole body.

I thought I might actually kill him, but then something peculiar began to happen. The rush of Light, which wasn't just consuming Liam but me too, began to absorb the Vyken's darkness inside me—the part that thirsted for revenge and the lifeblood of every living thing. And it was a different kind of Light than what I was used to using, one that was filled with concern and love for Christian. My mind became clear for the first time in a long time, and I was able to see how the Vyken's poison had worked itself into my heart. It scared me to realize how much control it had over me. I let go of Liam and stumbled back onto the floor. "I'm so sorry," I said, mortified.

Christian scooted over to me, protecting his left arm. "What happened? Why are you apologizing?"

My voice was quiet. "The poison. I thought I was controlling it, but . . . I'm an idiot. Liam saved me." I looked at Liam. He was lying flat on his stomach; his face etched in pain, but he did manage a smile. Just barely. "You knew. You knew I needed to use Light."

"But you have been using it," Christian said. "Just the other night."

I shook my head. "I needed to use it out of love. I haven't done that for a very long time. Not since Tracey died. All the other times, even just now when I wanted to go kill Cyrus, I thought my actions were out of love for my friend, but they weren't. I wanted to fight him, and everyone, because I love the feeling of contention, and because I yearn to kill." I glanced at Christian to see his reaction. His face was blank.

"I still don't understand," Christian said, and I knew he never would.

I crawled over to Liam. "How bad is it?"

"I'll survive."

"I'll make it up to you somehow."

"Just remember what you've learned. Only use your power for good." He took a deep breath like it was painful to breathe.

I touched him lightly. "I will. I promise."

THIRTY-FOUR

The next morning I woke early. I looked around for Christian, thinking he might've returned after helping Liam outside of the school, but my room was empty. Poor Christian. He hadn't understood what had happened and was upset that I asked him to help Liam.

"I should be trying to kill him, not helping him walk," Christian had said. He softened a little when Liam popped his shoulder back into joint and told Christian he could have three free hits as soon as he recovered.

Before I left my room, I glanced out the window. I didn't recoil from the bright morning sun like I usually did. Instead it gave me hope. I breathed in deeply, feeling better than I had in a long time.

At breakfast I told May and Kiera what had happened to Tessa. Both of them were shocked and really freaked out. "You have to get Sophie to close Lucent," May said, clasping her hands together tightly. "Even if it's just for a little while. Someone needs to figure out what's going on before anyone else gets hurt."

I looked around the crowded dining room. All these girls: sitting, laughing, eating, having no idea that their world was about to be ripped apart. They were the victims in all this.

I sighed. "I know. That's what Liam and Christian said too." Both of them were visibly upset after I told them what the Vyken had said about dead bodies filling the garbage.

"Do you think Sophie will listen to you?" Kiera asked. Dark circles were under her eyes, and I wondered how much sleep she was getting.

"I hope so. I guess I can always call in a bomb threat or something if she doesn't."

* * * * *

I waited all through breakfast for Sophie, but she never showed. I looked for her in the halls in between classes but didn't see her there either. At lunchtime I decided to skip lunch to go in search of her. I found her in the teacher's lounge standing at a microwave that hummed softly. By the smell of it she was cooking an Asian dish. Something with curry in it.

"Hello, Llona. How are you today?" she said.

"Fine."

"I haven't seen you in awhile."

"I've been busy."

"That's good. You should study as much as you can."

I laughed. *If only.*

"Is something funny?"

I cleared my throat and made my face go serious. "I need to talk to you," I said. "It's important."

The microwave beeped. "Okay. Come to my office with me while I eat. You want some?"

"No thanks."

Holding a container of steaming rice and chicken in one hand and silverware in the other, Sophie went to her office. I followed her.

"Mind if I close this?" I asked, my hand on the door.

"Go right ahead."

I closed the door and sat down while Sophie sifted through the rice with a fork. I thought carefully before I spoke, knowing any wrong word would shut Sophie off from me for good. "So," I began, "remember how you told me that my mother was too trusting? That she let people into her life too easily?"

Sophie mumbled an "Uh-huh" through a bite.

"I don't remember much about my mother, but from everything my father said about her she was trusting, but she wasn't stupid. She always tried to do the right thing. I'm sure you knew that my parents also moved around a lot."

Sophie put her fork down and stared at me. I couldn't tell by her blank expression if she was angry or just simply listening intently. I continued, "It took some time for Lander to scheme his way into their lives. My parents were manipulated. It could've happened to anyone, even another Aura."

Sophie shifted her position in the chair. More upright. "I don't know about that."

"Sophie, do you trust me?"

She didn't say anything, but her lips tightened and twisted like she was having a really hard time coming up with an answer.

I rolled my eyes. "Come on, Sophie. Do you think I would ever do anything to purposely hurt you or your reputation?"

"Of course not, but sometimes I think you can be impulsive. And when you're impulsive, you unknowingly hurt those around you."

I shook my head, realizing I was about to get into a debate I didn't want to have. "Look, I just need to know that you'll believe what I'm about to tell you. I have no reason to make it up."

"How about you start telling me what's going on, and we'll go from there, okay?"

I took a deep breath. On my exhale, I began telling her about the pills. This conversation led into Cyrus and his assistant and how they were Vykens. I ignored Sophie's skeptical expression, and even her occasional smile, and kept talking even though she tried to stop me several times. I told her about how they were taking our blood and selling it to Vykens, and how they'd kidnapped Tessa. And finally I ended by telling her about the attack on the school sometime in the next few days. The only thing I didn't tell her about was the Shadow. *Resolve one problem at a time.* "What I need you to do, Aunt Sophie, is tell all the girls to go home for the rest of the week. They can't be here. It's not safe." Finally, I was quiet.

Sophie leaned back in her chair. She said nothing for almost a full minute. I opened my mouth to say something else, maybe she needed more convincing, but she stopped me. "That's quite a story you've told," she said. "Do you have any proof?"

I thought for a moment. "I'd show you the blood bags that have been replaced with Vyken blood, but because you've been taking the pills, you won't be able to tell the difference. I guess I could have you talk to Liam, but you might think he's lying. Same with May and Kiera."

"You got them involved in this?" For some reason this seemed to upset her more than anything else. "Who else have you spoken to?"

"Are you saying you believe me?"

"I don't know what I'm saying just yet."

And then I remembered something. "Of course I have proof. The secret room in Cyrus's office where I found Tessa."

"You are the one that found Tessa?" She shook her head. "Wait, what secret room?"

I nodded excitedly and told her about what had happened, but I conveniently left out the part of me going all invisible. That was something I didn't want to share quite yet since it just didn't seem as important as everything else.

"The first chance I get I'll check it out," Sophie said.

This alarmed me. "But you must be careful. In fact, maybe you should have me go with you. If any Vykens found you, I know they would kill you."

Sophie laughed, and I couldn't tell if it was because she didn't think I could protect her or that a Vyken could kill her. "Why are you laughing?" I asked.

She cleared her throat. "So dramatic, Llona. Just like your mother."

I sunk into my chair. "You don't believe me."

"No, no. I do believe there is something to your story. I mean, it's so elaborate, how could you make it all up? And there is the fact that Auras are being attacked outside our school. No, something strange is going on, but there's no way Cyrus is a part of it. If something's going on, it's without his knowledge. Let me conduct my own investigation. And for your own piece of mind, I'll be careful."

"Please do. It's important. I don't want to lose you too."

Sophie stood and walked around her desk. She leaned down and gave me a hug. I hugged her back, inhaling the smell of cinnamon laced with curry.

"Nothing's going to happen to me. I promise," she said. After a short moment, Sophie let go and looked at me. "You may not know this, Llona, but I'm good at adapting. This skill has put me where I'm at today."

"What do you mean?"

Sophie just smiled, like she knew some great secret. "I'll talk to you soon, Llona."

* * * * *

I left Sophie's office feeling conflicted. I wasn't sure what she was going to do, and it didn't seem she believed me about Cyrus, but it was a start. If she wasn't convinced by tomorrow, then I'd call in that bomb threat—every day if I had to.

The rest of the day went quickly. After school I worked with Kiera, trying to teach her all I knew, but there just wasn't enough time. I wished I had a few months. When we were finished, I spoke to Tessa. She was staying at the Deific office in New York. The way she spoke about the place and the people, I couldn't wait for the opportunity to find out more about them.

When we were done talking, Tessa handed the phone to Liam. He sounded weak and tired, but he assured me that he would be back to normal within a day.

I saw Christian that night; the two of us shared a quiet dinner in my room. Kiera was watching May practice with Dr. Han, hoping she could pick up on an idea or two that might make her Light stronger. All of us were trying to prepare, but tonight I didn't want to think about it anymore. I just wanted to be here with Christian, as if we were the only ones in the world.

"What are you thinking about?" he asked. We were sitting next to each other, leaning against the wall. A box of half-eaten pizza lay next to us.

"Just wishing we could do this every night."

He squeezed my hand. "We will. Soon you'll leave Lucent. We'll get married. Move to the coast. Have children. Maybe a dog." He paused. "Why are you looking at me like that?"

I wasn't sure how I looked, but I did know my heart had stopped beating. "What did you say?"

"Um, that we'd have a dog? You don't like dogs? Maybe we could get a—"

"No. The part about us getting married."

"Oh. Well, we will, won't we? I mean, I know I haven't

officially proposed, and we're both still young, but I just can't imagine spending my life with anyone else. You're my plan, Llona. Wherever we go, whatever happens, I want to be in your life. Always."

When I didn't say anything, he quickly added, "When the time's right, of course. No need to rush things." His face turned red. "I freaked you out, didn't I? Sorry. I just—"

I threw my arms around him. "I love you."

"I love you too, Llona." He hugged me back. I sunk into him and rested my head on his chest.

"You're my forever, Llona," he said and kissed my forehead.

And I believed he was mine.

* * * * *

The next morning, earlier than normal, chimes sounded, but they weren't the normal chimes signaling mealtime. They were the "mandatory meeting" chimes. I slid out of bed and got dressed. After combing my hair to my "bad" side, I pulled on a beanie and left my room. The halls were crowded and filled with excited voices.

"I bet we're having another dance," one girl said as I passed. Another said, "Maybe we're getting some new teachers."

I dodged in and out of the girls until I found May.

"What do you think this is about?" May said.

"Maybe my talk with Sophie actually worked." I hoped.

Other than being more crowded than usual, the dining room was the same as always. Lizens carried trays of food to Auras who were huddled around the tables, looking happier than they had been in a long time. It made me ill. The smell of pancakes and citrus circulated throughout the room. Comfort food.

Kiera waved us over from across the room where she had

saved two seats. On the way over, Tessa's mother caught my attention. She smiled and mouthed the words, "Thank you."

When I reached the table, I didn't sit down right away. I glanced around the room looking for Sophie. I found her at the front talking to several teachers. She met my gaze and acknowledged me with a nod.

Kiera pulled me into a chair. "What's going on?" she said.

"We'll know soon enough."

A few minutes later Sophie walked to the front podium. "Can I have your attention? Girls, please. Sit down. I have an announcement."

The girls hurried toward a seat and waited expectantly. Just then Cyrus walked in. I think it was the first time I'd seen him in the dining room. It must have been a first for the others too, because they looked just as shocked. Cyrus went straight to Sophie and whispered something in her ear. She shook her head and motioned for him to sit down. He did not look happy.

Sophie began, "You girls are so special. Has anyone ever told you that?"

A wave of laughter and giggles filled the room. May and I looked at each other and rolled our eyes.

"Because of this," Sophie continued, "I want to give you a surprise. Something we've never done before in the summer."

Everyone leaned forward.

"We're giving you a week off from school starting today."

May and I looked at each other and stared.

THIRTY-FIVE

THERE WAS A COLLECTIVE GASP FROM THE AUDIENCE FOLlowed by cheers and high fives. Cyrus stood up and stormed over to Sophie. I tried to listen to what they were saying, but even my great hearing couldn't weed out their voices over the celebration. A few seconds later, Cyrus sat back down looking seriously mad. Sophie motioned with her arms to quiet the crowd. "Be quiet, please. I have more to say."

When loud voices quieted to whispers, she continued, "Because of the short notice, I know many of you won't be able to leave, as your families may be away. For those of you who can't leave or who want to stay, we will have activities planned every day. And not the normal ones. We have several field trips planned."

Excited voices rose again. I shook my head, wishing Sophie hadn't added this last part. We needed the girls to leave, not want to stay.

"An official announcement has already been emailed to your parents," Sophie said. "When we are finished here, you will be allowed to call your parents. All phones, including in the teachers' offices, will be made available. And finally," Sophie paused, waiting for the girls to quiet down again, "all Lizens will be given the week off too."

A blanket of silence dropped on the room. No one said anything. I don't even think they were breathing, including the Lizens. Three tables over, Ashlyn stood up and raised her hand.

"Yes, Ashlyn?" Sophie said.

"But if the Lizens are allowed to leave, who will take care of us if we choose to stay?"

Sophie's jaw tightened briefly before she said, "You will take care of yourself. You know how to do that, right?"

Shocked, Ashlyn glanced around, clearly looking for support, but no one said anything.

"Any other questions?" Sophie asked into the microphone. When no one said anything, she said, "Good. Now get moving."

May turned to me. "This is good, right?"

"It's the best we could've hoped for." I stood. "I'll be right back."

I pushed my way to the front until I found Sophie. She embraced me before I could say anything. When she pulled away she said, "I found the room. I can't believe Cyrus didn't tell us about it."

"So you believe me?"

"I do believe Vykens were in the school and kidnapped Tessa, but I searched Cyrus's office and found no proof that he was involved, or proof of any kind of a plot involving our vitamins or selling our blood. I mean, really, Llona, the whole thing is just very fantastical."

I shook my head. "But what about the secret room and the fact that Cyrus and Jameson disappeared into the very same place we found Tessa?"

Sophie kept her voice even. "They could've come out and slipped by you into the hallway. You said yourself that you were hiding under a desk."

I closed my eyes. This woman was crazy, but . . . "Whatever. Believe what you want for now. I'm just glad you're sending the

Auras home. There will be time enough for me to convince you of the rest."

Sophie patted me on the arm. "Everything will be fine. You'll see. In one week everything will be as it should."

I forced a smile, knowing it would never be normal again.

Sophie returned to the teachers, who bombarded her with questions. I was about to return to May and Kiera when a cold hand gripped my arm. My legs went weak, and I would've fallen if it weren't for the tight grip holding me up. I turned and came face to face with Cyrus. He looked at me with a puzzled expression, like he was trying to figure out why I was having a difficult time standing.

When I didn't say anything, he said, "We still haven't found your Lizen friend, but we will. She can't be far." I wondered if this was the first time he'd ever told the truth. Him and the other Vykens were probably mystified as to where Tessa went.

"That's good," I stuttered. *Pull it together!*

His eyelids drew down thin. "How have you been feeling, Llona?"

"Fine, sir. I'm fine."

"Have you been taking your vitamins?" His nails bit into my arm, and I knew that he knew.

With my free hand I took hold of his arm and shoved it away. "You mean your drug?"

Cyrus towered over me, and I couldn't help but take a small step backward. "You think this will work?" he whispered. "Protect them? You are a stupid, silly girl."

I was caught off guard by his sudden confession. Gratefully I didn't have to say anything. Dr. Han appeared. "Llona, Abigail's looking for you so you can use her phone to call home."

"Right." I followed him out of the dining room, ignoring Cyrus's death stare.

I thought we were going upstairs to Abigail's office, but instead Dr. Han led me outside. He looked over his shoulder at me and said, "Follow me."

I obeyed. First, because I was curious what he was up to, and second, because I was too afraid to say no. The man was powerful.

He led me across campus and inside Risen Auditorium. As soon as we were in his office, Dr. Han closed the door. His office was the complete opposite from the others. The walls were a pale white, and other than his desk and a couple of chairs, only weapons occupied the room. Blades and spears hung on the wall or were piled in a basket on the floor. I looked at them nervously. He must've noticed because he said, "You have nothing to be frightened of. I've spoken with Liam."

This surprised me. "You know Liam?"

"Yes."

"How?"

"We've worked on various projects for the Deific over the years." He moved to the window and peered out the blinds. "A few days ago Liam contacted me and told me all that has happened. You were smart to tell Sophie, although she thinks you're a very troubled teen."

"Awesome. Thanks."

He looked back at me. "But she cares for you. Otherwise she wouldn't have sent the students away." That's what he said, but the words lacked feeling. It was as if he were trying to make me feel better.

"How long have you known?" I asked.

"Known what?"

"About Cyrus? About him being a Vyken?"

Dr. Han crossed the room and sat down. "I didn't know, still don't, but I trust Liam. And I trust you."

"Why?"

"Because of your bloodline. I fought side by side with your great-grandmother Mary."

I leaned forward. "I haven't heard about her."

"You wouldn't have. She was part of a movement in the thirties that hunted Vykens. No one talks about that time."

"You were there?"

Although he was looking right at me, his gaze seemed to go beyond, to another time, perhaps, and for the first time I saw emotion in his face. "I was with her the day she died." He paused and his focus returned. "I believe even Liam worked with her on an occasion or two."

"Liam?"

"With such a small circle of supernatural creatures, it's hard not to cross paths when you fight on the same side."

I shook my head. Something was nagging at me. Mary in the thirties, hunting Vykens and working with Liam and Dr. Han. I looked up at him. "The Shadow," I said. "She was the one who destroyed it, wasn't she?"

"It's true," Dr. Han said, and I noticed that he didn't look surprised that I knew about the Shadow. Liam must've told him about what Mr. Steele had said. "The Shadow was under the control of a Vyken named Darius," he continued. "Once Mary gave her very life to destroy the Shadow, I was able to kill Darius."

My heart swelled with pride when I thought of Mary and all that she'd done, but the feeling faded when I realized we were now in the same predicament she was. "But the Shadow's back. How is that possible?"

"I don't know, but believe me, I won't rest until it's sent back to hell where it belongs."

THIRTY-SIX

I LEANED BACK IN MY SEAT, WONDERING IF THINGS COULD GET any worse. I looked at Dr. Han. "Why do you believe me about Cyrus when my own aunt doesn't?"

"Because I saw your reaction that day when you first met Cyrus and Jameson. It's the same reaction Mary and a few others used to have. I didn't know what I was seeing at first, as it had been so long since an Aura had reacted like that, but after I thought about it and spoke to Liam, I knew."

Leaning forward, I said, "Didn't you ever wonder why Auras could no longer sense Vykens?"

"I didn't get involved with Auras until the early thirties when I met Mary. And by then, many of the Auras already had their senses dulled. Liam said the drug was introduced in the twenties, correct?"

I nodded.

"I'm sure it was introduced slowly. So slowly that after enough time passed, Auras forgot. The ones who could still sense Vykens thought it was a gift only they had. But, looking back, I can see that they were just the ones who didn't drink tea. Mary hated it." He actually smiled.

I slumped into my seat, feeling exhausted. So many years had passed with people ignorant to the truth. "What about May's blood? Why did you take it?"

He hesitated briefly. "I wanted to test it. To see what would happen if a Vyken's poison infected a Fury's blood."

"Why didn't you just use yours?"

His jawline tightened. "I wanted the blood of an innocent Fury. One who hadn't awakened the Fury darkness inside them."

I stared at him, wondering what challenges he had overcome. Maybe there was something in his past that could help me. But not now. Too much to do. "And what did you discover?"

Dr. Han faced the window in a thoughtful expression. Finally he said, "Furies are immune."

"How is that possible?"

"Furies already have their own evil to contend with. A Vyken's poison does nothing but add to it."

"But May. There's not a bad bone in her body."

"Like I said before, she hasn't been tested. But be assured, it's in her, and one day she'll have to fight it."

I leaned back, a deep ache in my gut. I couldn't bear the thought of May going through anything like I was.

"What now, Llona?" Dr. Han said.

"You're asking me?"

"You are the leader, are you not?"

"I'm an eighteen-year-old girl who wants this to all go away. I'm no leader."

"Leaders never choose their destiny. It's handed to them. And what they do with it will either lead them and their followers into victory or defeat. Which direction will you lead us in?"

The air in the room felt cold and heavy.

"You remind me of her," he said, and I looked up. "She was like you. Always doubting her abilities, and yet she always made the right choices."

"My mother?"

He shook his head. "No. Mary."

"What about my grandmother? Did you know her well?"

Dr. Han smiled. "I did. Sarah had the same rebellious spirit as her mother, but when Mary died, she took that spirit with her. Sarah wasn't herself ever again, but I did notice a light return to her when she had your mother."

"What happened to Sarah?"

"She was killed with her husband in a car crash. No one knows the details, but there was a huge blizzard the night she died. Their car was found on fire at the bottom of a ravine."

I closed my eyes. So many deaths.

"But now there's you, Llona. You are like Mary. You can change people's minds with your voice and your actions. Already you have an Aura on your side, Kiera. I've watched you with her."

"And Sophie," I added, opening my eyes.

His lips tightened briefly then relaxed. "Yes. And Sophie. Don't despair, Llona. Change takes time."

I shook my head. "But we don't have any more time."

"Then what do we do?"

I glanced up at the clock, a plan forming in my mind. "Tonight. At six."

"Where?"

"In your training room. And bring whoever of the teachers you think will go along with us." I stood.

"What about Sophie?"

"She needs to be there. And can you tell her before she meets with Cyrus? I'm worried what he'll do to her if she confronts him."

"I'll go talk to her now."

Outside his office, May and Kiera were waiting for me. They must've seen us leave together and followed us.

"What did he want?" May said.

"He spoke to Liam and is going to help us."

Kiera squealed. "Yes! A Fury is on our side."

"Um, hello," May said. "I'm a Fury too."

Kiera's smile disappeared. "I know. I just meant an experienced Fury."

"I have to call Liam and Christian," I said. "We're all going to meet at six tonight in Dr. Han's training room. You two try to convince everyone to leave today. Say whatever you have to, but make this week sound like it's going to be completely boring."

They nodded and left through the front doors, leaving me alone in the hall. I took several deep breaths until my lips began to tingle. The weight of what was happening pressed on my chest. *How can Dr. Han expect me to lead? A year ago, I didn't even have friends.*

I thought of my great-grandmother; what sort of person she must have been. She sounded so strong. If only she were here to talk to. *But she's not, Llona*, I thought and looked up into my reflection in the glass door. *There's only you.* I shoved back whatever pity I was feeling and pushed open the door.

It took some time, but eventually I made it back to my room. By the many conversations I eavesdropped on, most students were planning on leaving. I called Christian first and told him about the meeting and how the school was shutting down for a week.

"I heard," he said.

"What about the Guardians? What have they been told to do?" With the phone to my ear, I went to the window and looked out. Already the driveway was starting to fill with cars. The richest of the rich probably had paid a Lizen to drive their child home.

"As soon as the announcement came, I'd say about a third of the Guardians just disappeared. I have no idea where they could've gone."

"Do you think they're with Jackson?"

"Could be, or maybe they're scared. Many of them have never been in a real fight before." He was silent for a few seconds, then said, "But the rest of us are ready to defend Lucent. Do you know who else will be at the meeting?"

"Not yet. I'm calling Liam after you, and hopefully he can rally some troops from somewhere."

"Good. I'll come meet you for lunch, and you can fill me in then."

"Deal."

"Llona?"

"Yes?"

"I love you." But his tone held so much more than those three simple words.

"I know. I love you too." Reluctantly I hung up, took a deep breath, and called Liam. He sounded better.

"I have good news," he said. "Not really good news, actually, but information."

"What is it?"

"In three nights. That's when the Vykens are coming into the school using the secret entrance in Cyrus's office."

My pulse quickened. "And they're coming for the blood?"

He didn't say anything for a few seconds, but then asked, "How are you doing? Are you feeling better, not so Jack Ripperish?"

"I'm fine," I said, annoyed by the comparison, although it was probably true. "Just tell me."

He took a deep breath. "Yes, they're coming for the blood."

I frowned. "But why not just sneak it out? Why a dramatic entrance?"

Liam's voice lowered when he said, "They want the girls too. Every last one of them."

I dropped the phone.

THIRTY-SEVEN

After I recovered, I bent down and picked up the phone. "Say that one more time." My voice was shaking.

"They want to take you all to a facility where they'll use the Auras as their own never-ending personal blood bank. But it's not just the blood, Llona. They also want to change some of you."

I didn't know which horrifying discovery to address first. "But changing Auras, won't they all end up like Britt?"

"They've done something to the blood. Less potent, I guess."

I leaned my head against the cool glass. "How do you know all of this?"

"Last night the twins and I went out. We caught ourselves a Vyken and made him talk."

"But you were so weak!"

"Sometimes you just have to man up."

I sat on my bed, listening to his quiet breathing. So many people were going to get hurt.

"Llona?"

I forced myself to speak. "There's a meeting tonight at Lucent, about what's going on. At six. Bring whoever you can."

"Will do."

"Oh, and Liam?"

"Yes?"

"Cyrus knows that I know."

It was Liam's turn for silence.

After a moment, I said, "Liam?"

"Is Christian there?"

"No, but he will be," I glanced at the clock, "in one hour."

"Good. Whatever you do, don't be by yourself. Stay in public by May and whoever else. Got it?"

"Got it. See you soon."

I hung up before he could say anything else. Liam's tendency for bluntness was the last thing I needed right now. I was scared enough.

I found May and Kiera in the commons area talking to several of the girls. I pulled them away from the crowd and into the corner of the room. "What's everyone deciding to do?" I asked.

"A lot are going home today," May said. "They can't wait, actually. Sometimes I wonder if they sense the tension in the air." She was looking around the room as if she could feel it too.

Kiera said, "And a bunch more are leaving tomorrow."

May lowered her voice. "If I had to guess, I'd say less than twenty percent are staying the rest of the week."

"That's too much," I said, still frustrated with Sophie for planning fun activities during the break. Maybe I could get her to cancel those as well. "Let's keep campaigning. I'll talk to Sophie about stripping some fun out of the schedule later."

Despite the warning from Liam, we split up. There wasn't enough time to get everything done if we didn't. May and Kiera were more successful than I was, as I was still considered a troublemaker, but I didn't give up. If only I could tell them the truth: *if you stay, you might die, or worse, become a Vyken*. But no one would've believed me even if I did. I was an outsider.

"Hey," a voice said.

I spun around and smiled. "Christian."

"What a scene," he said, looking around. "Everyone's pretty anxious to get out of here, aren't they?"

A girl rushed by us, flinging her backpack over her shoulder. It barely missed me. "I know. Lucent's never done anything like this before. The girls seem excited, but every once in a while, I see a flash of fear in their eyes. They're scared."

"Are all the girls leaving?" Christian said.

"Most of them. What are the Guardians up to?"

"Come see for yourself." He pulled me toward the window, and I looked down. The sun was shining bright, reflecting off a slew of car windshields. I waited for my eyes to adjust to the brightness. When they did, I saw a bunch of Guardians loading bags for Auras into the trunks of their cars. "You've got to be kidding," I said. "Can't we do anything for ourselves?" I looked back at Christian. "How did we let ourselves get so wimpy?"

"I think that was the point, but don't worry. We'll change things."

"Come on," I said. "Let's get some lunch and wait for things to settle down."

We passed by Abigail's office when I heard, "Llona!"

I turned around.

Abigail was standing in the doorway, smiling big. "Do you want to use my phone? It's available."

I stared at her, trying to understand what she was saying. There was so much to do.

"My phone. So you can call your uncle. I bet he'd love to have you home for a week."

Jake. Just the mention of him made me homesick.

"Call him, Llona," Christian said. "It might make you feel better."

He was right, of course. There wasn't a person alive I'd rather speak to right now. "Thanks, I'd love to." I went into her office and picked up the phone. While I dialed, Christian started up a conversation with Abigail about all the excitement. Jake answered on the third ring. I relaxed into Abigail's chair at the sound of his voice. "Man, I miss you," I said.

"Tink? Is it really you?" he said. "I was beginning to think you forgot about me."

"Never."

"I figured I'd hear from you today. So when are you coming?"

"You got the notice then."

"Of course, but I'm surprised you called. I figured you'd be on the first flight out as soon as you heard. I can't wait to see you. Heidi and I already have some awesome things planned."

"I'm not coming, Jake."

He didn't say anything for a moment, then, "How come?"

"I need to stay here. You know, take care of stuff."

"What stuff?"

"School stuff."

"You don't care about stuff."

"This stuff I do."

"What's going on, Llona? I hear it in your voice. You're scared."

I swallowed. "I'm okay. Christian's with me."

"That makes me feel a little better, but do I need to speak with Sophie?"

"No, not at all. It's nothing like that. Really, I'm fine. But how are you? And tell me everything. I really miss you."

Jake and I spoke for twenty more minutes. After I hung up, I felt better. And worse. Better because Jake had made me laugh, and I really needed that, and worse because I wanted to go home, and that made me feel guilty.

By the end of the day, about a hundred girls remained, and about half of those would be leaving tomorrow. I wished it were more. Through all the commotion, I occasionally caught sight of Sophie. She was on the phone mostly, talking with parents, arranging rides and flights.

May came and found me in the lobby. "Kiera's already at the meeting. You ready?"

I nodded and followed her over to Risen Auditorium. I remained by the door, waiting for Liam and the others to arrive while she continued toward the Fury training room.

The sun was just setting, changing the sky to a deep purple color. I hoped it was dark enough for Liam. I hadn't thought about that when I'd chosen the time. I guess he would've told me on the phone if it were a problem.

A moment later, Liam arrived wearing a black baseball cap, sunglasses, and a long trench coat. He looked ridiculous, but I knew it kept him sheltered from what little light was left. Behind him were the twins. They looked even bigger in the light. They said hello as they passed me. Liam stopped at the door. "Why are you alone?" he said.

"Why do you look like a serial killer?" I asked. When he didn't smile, I said, "Everyone's just inside. I was waiting for you."

"And the Auras?"

"The ones who are left are outside near the track field. Sophie set up an outdoor movie."

"How about the Lizens? Where are they?"

"Sophie gave them the night off. They should all be inside Lambert House."

"Good. Let's get started." Liam waited for me to go first before he closed the door.

I went into the training room and looked around. On the left of the court, May and Kiera sat on a long bench against the wall. Both looked deep in thought. Near them, more toward the middle of the room, Christian and several of his Guardian friends spoke quietly. To my right, Liam was shaking Dr. Han's hand, and I was pleasantly surprised to see Ms. Crawford standing next to him. She was glancing around nervously and fidgeting with her hands, especially when she saw the twins. But where was Sophie? It was almost six—maybe she was late?

I waited a minute before I cleared my throat. Everyone turned and looked at me. I suddenly felt very small in the great big room. I looked at Christian. He nodded at me encouragingly. "First, thanks for being here," I said. "Seriously. I can't imagine going through this without your help, so thank you. Second, I guess everyone knows why we are here." I took a deep breath. "In just a few days' time, the school's going to be attacked by Cyrus and other Vykens. Thanks to Liam and his group, we've learned that Cyrus has a facility where he plans on keeping the Auras. The ones still alive, anyway."

The group broke out in cries of disbelief. I let them wrap their heads around what I'd just said and turned to Liam. "Where's Sophie?"

He looked around. "I don't know. One second." He walked over to Ms. Crawford. Over the commotion I heard him ask, "Where did Sophie go?"

She looked over his shoulder at me. "She went to see Cyrus. I told her to wait for Llona, but she said she couldn't wait anymore."

A lump formed in my throat, and my eyes slowly turned toward the door. Before I realized what I was doing, I was moving forward. And then I was running.

THIRTY-EIGHT

Christian called my name, but I was already out the door. At the last second I heard Liam tell Christian to go after me.

I ran fast, past the clock tower that chimed six o'clock, and into Chadni Hall, not slowing for anything, even Christian, who was still calling me. I took the stairs three at a time until I was on the fourth floor. I could tell by the smell of cinnamon that Sophie had just passed by here.

Christian caught up and stopped me. "What's going on?"

I shushed him and pointed to Cyrus's open office door. I could hear Sophie's voice saying, "Cyrus, I'm glad I caught you before you got too busy."

I hurried down the hall and into the room, panting. I took in the scene. Three men and two women were talking to Cyrus near his desk. A wave of nausea washed over me. Not humans. Vykens. I stumbled to Sophie, who was just inside the doorway, and gripped her arm. "Let's go, Sophie," I said.

Christian moved behind me, keeping his hand on my lower back. I glanced back at him. His lips were pressed tightly together, and his skin looked pale, or maybe it was the lighting. Why was it so dark in here? I glanced around nervously, searching for the Shadow, but if it was here, it remained hidden in the darkness.

Sophie turned around, looking very annoyed. "What are you two doing here?" She shook her head when I tried to speak. "Never mind. I just want to get to the bottom of this." She turned back to Cyrus. "What is going on, Cyrus, and who are these people?"

Cyrus looked at me and nodded his head once, before he acknowledged Sophie. "Sophie," he said, "I'm so glad you stopped by. I've been wanting to talk to you, but with all the excitement today, I just couldn't find the time."

"Who are these people, Cyrus?" Sophie demanded again. I held her from moving forward.

The five Vykens all looked at Cyrus, waiting for him to answer. Cyrus smiled. "There's been a terrible misunderstanding, Sophie."

"I would agree," she said.

"I didn't mean to get upset with you this morning, it's just that I had something else planned." He looked back at the others. "I was going to tell the students today that we have some transfer teachers from Ellie Academy who will be introducing new classes to the curriculum."

Sophie frowned. "I don't understand. Why wouldn't you have told us?"

"Honestly, I didn't think they would be coming until the fall, but then I received word from Ellie that it would be much sooner. I meant to talk to you about it yesterday. I hope you'll forgive me."

This was getting ridiculous. "Don't listen to him, Sophie. He's lying."

Cyrus looked at me, innocence radiating from his light blue eyes. "I'm not sure why you say things like that, Llona. I'm beginning to think you really are a disturbed, young Aura." He turned his attention to Sophie. "I have the paperwork if you'd like to see it. It bears Professor Hurley's signature."

Sophie took a step, but I tightened my grip. "Don't do it, Sophie."

"It's just on my desk," Cyrus swept his arm toward it, as if to say, "After you."

Sophie brushed at my hand. "Let go, Llona."

"No way. We have to get out of here," I said.

"Llona's right," Christian said. His whole body was tense, and his hand was no longer pressing on my back, but was gripping my shirt tightly. I could tell by the way he kept looking toward the open door that he knew what I knew: there was no way we could fight this many Vykens. Our only chance was to run.

Sophie whirled around on us. "No. Llona is *not* right," she snapped and then looked at me. "I'm sorry, Llona. I know you've suffered a lot so it makes you question everything and everyone. I understand, I do, but you're wrong about this."

"Well said, Sophie," Cyrus said. "Now if you'll just come read the letter, this whole matter can be put to rest."

"Please, Sophie," I said, trying one last time.

"I did as you asked, Llona, sending the Auras away, but I just can't accept the other." She pushed my arm away and went to Cyrus. When she drew near, he extended his other arm as if to embrace her, but instead of looking at her, he was looking at me with an assassin's smile.

"Sophie, no!" I yelled and moved toward her.

But it was too late.

Just as Sophie reached for Cyrus, his hands struck forward and took hold of her head. He wrapped her up like a snake, his hand cutting off her airway.

I ignited Light in my hands, and Christian stepped forward. The other Vykens also moved forward.

"You do it, and she dies," Cyrus said. Sophie's eyes bulged from the pressure on her throat.

Christian's head swiveled around the room, and I knew he was trying to think of a way to get everyone out safely. I, on the other hand, was willing to do whatever Cyrus wanted if it meant he'd let Sophie go. I extinguished the Light in my hands. Christian looked at me, his eyes sad, and shook his head. "We'll come back for her, I promise, but right now we need to go." Christian began tugging me backward.

"Actually, Christian," Cyrus said, "*You* need to go. You weren't invited to this party." The Vykens in the room began to fan out.

Christian pushed me aside and settled into a fighting position, but it didn't matter. Two of the male Vykens, and one female, attacked him at once. But they weren't just fighting him, they were shoving him out of the room. And they won. The door slammed shut, leaving the two males outside with Christian.

"Christian!" I yelled and ran to the door, but the female Vyken stopped me. She took hold of my arms. Her hands were icy cold, stinging my skin, and when I looked down, I noticed my skin was turning blue. I looked at her, and she smiled, a row of yellow, broken teeth. I recognized her then. The Vyken who had chased me into the water and who had caused ice to form beneath her footsteps. But she looked normal now with long black hair and dark eyes, everything but her yellow teeth.

"That's enough, Eira," Cyrus said.

The Vyken, Eira, let go of me and walked next to Cyrus. Sophie's face was turning blue.

"Please let her go," I begged. Out in the hall, Christian called my name. His voice was followed by the sound of something crashing into a wall. I prayed it wasn't him.

Cyrus barely released his grip and nuzzled his head next to Sophie's. "I won't do that. She's my insurance."

"For what?"

"To ensure you embrace your new identity. Embrace your Vyken half or she dies." Sophie's eyes turned to Cyrus and then to me. "That's right, Sophie. Your sweet niece was bitten. What do you think of her now?"

Sophie, her hands hanging on to Cyrus's arm as if to keep her upright, choked, "Help me, Llona!"

I glanced around the room. Eira stood directly next to Cyrus, watching me closely. The other two Vykens stood to the left and right of me. I had never felt so helpless in my life. "What can I do?" I asked her, my eyes pleading.

"You can join me," Cyrus said, and I turned to him aghast. The secret door in the wall behind him began to open. "You've been a pet project of mine for some time now."

"Why? Why me?"

Cyrus began to back up toward the opening, dragging Sophie with him. "It's no fault of your own really. I'm just fulfilling a promise." He looked down at Sophie and smiled. "Besides, Llona. You're one of us now."

"I'm nothing like you. I am an Aura."

Cyrus tilted his head. "Then why aren't you with them now, trying to save them?"

I stared at him, trying to process what he'd just said. Cyrus motioned his head to the back wall. The Vykens around me moved behind him until they disappeared into the opening.

"I'm going to give you some time, Llona, while you think about what side you're on. Meanwhile, she and I are going to spend some quality time together." When Sophie struggled against him, he raised his hand and punched the side of her head. She fell limp in his arms.

"No!" I yelled and moved to attack him, but suddenly I tripped. I fell hard to the ground, and when I looked back to see what had caused my fall, a long, thin stretch of a shadow retreated back into the corner of the room. I scrambled backward, toward the door, realizing I didn't know what I was up against.

"Time's running out," Cyrus said. "Your poor friends."

I glanced at the door and then back at Sophie in frustration. Just then the shadows in the room began to shift, left and right, growing longer and longer until they detached and fell from the ceiling and lights, slid from the walls, and slithered out from beneath the chairs, all moving in the direction of Cyrus. A cold chill raced up my spine when the shadows came together behind him, forming into what looked like the shape of a tall man, if that man was wearing a long cloak. The room had brightened considerably.

"I feel sorry for you, Llona," Cyrus said. In his arms, Sophie's hair floated and twirled, and her skirt billowed as if the shadow's movements had stirred the air. "You're going to suffer so very much."

THIRTY-NINE

I didn't let him say anymore. I was already out the door and running down a hallway covered in ash and, gratefully, no blood. The stairwell was empty, and I raced to the bottom, practically stumbling down most of the stairs. *Find Christian, save the girls, get Sophie back*, I thought over and over.

I was nearing the clock tower when Liam, May, Tessa, and everyone else who had been with them, came running out of Risen Auditorium. I stumbled to my knees when I saw Christian trailing behind. His head was bleeding, but he was alive. I almost laughed, and then I cried—sort of both.

Liam knelt by me and placed his hand on my back. "Are you all right?"

I choked on a sob.

All of a sudden, Dr. Han shoved Liam aside and said in my face, "Pull it together, and tell us what's happening!"

Liam pushed him away. "Give her a minute."

I looked up at Liam. He looked angry, angrier than I'd ever seen him before, and I recognized the darkness rising in his eyes. I needed to do something and quick.

Before I could, Christian came to me, and I stood, throwing my arms around him. He squeezed me tight. "I've never been happier to see you," he said." He pulled away and stroked my face. "We were just coming for you. What happened?"

Shoving all emotions to the back of my mind, I let go of Christian and looked around, my eyes settling on Liam. "They're coming. Not in a few days. Now."

Everyone looked at each other. Kiera grabbed May's hand. Mrs. Crawford gasped. The twins straightened; one of them cracked his knuckles. "Get all the Auras into the dining room," I said. "We can protect them better there." Nobody moved. "Now! Come on, let's go!"

I took off running toward the track field. Footsteps pounded behind me as I ran to where the girls were watching a movie on a giant screen. A black-and-white Dorothy was singing "Somewhere over the Rainbow." At the sight of me, several teachers stood up, looking alarmed.

"I need everyone in the dining room right now. This is an emergency," I said.

The girls turned around. A few of them laughed while others continued to eat popcorn.

"What's this about?" Ms. Smitty said.

Dr. Han caught up to me. "Llona's right. Everyone in the dining room. There's not a second to spare."

This made them react. Teachers jumped up and began to herd the students away in a flurry of commotion and voices. I turned around and addressed the twins and the Guardians who were with Christian earlier. "You guys lead them in. Go through the Lizen entrance straight into the dining room. The Vykens won't be expecting that. The rest of us will bring up the rear."

Just as I finished, two Vykens appeared around the corner of Chadni Hall. The others followed my gaze. I stepped backward. Three more came, and still more. I stopped counting at twenty.

"Let's go!" Christian said, tugging on my arm.

"Move!" Dr. Han said. "I'll hold them off. Secure the Auras!" Two balls of fire appeared in his hand. May stepped next to him, producing her own.

I looked at her. "Are you sure?"

She nodded. "Go." She was trying so hard to look strong. I would have given anything at that moment to make it all go away. As I left her alone with Dr. Han, I heard Dorothy singing after me, "If happy little bluebirds fly beyond the rainbow, why, oh, why can't I?"

I followed Christian into the dining room and froze just inside the door to stare at the chaos. Many of the Auras were screaming and huddling together. Only the last few waiting outside the door had seen the Vykens coming, but that was enough to stir the rest into a frenzy. Teachers were yelling at them to stay calm, but they didn't seem to be talking to anyone directly. They were freaking out as much as the girls. Ms. Crawford was right there, trying to take control.

On the far side of the room, the twins and Guardians had already barricaded the doors with several of the tables. Liam came out from the kitchen with a handful of knives to use for weapons. In his other hand he was talking on his cell phone, asking someone to send more people.

"We want to help. What can we do?" a voice said behind me.

Christian and I turned around. Several Lizen men stood ready, their expressions full of anger and an intense passion I'd never seen in them. Combined with the scales on their faces, they actually looked kind of scary.

Christian placed his hand on a Lizen's shoulder. "We're honored to have you. You guys can help barricade the doors. This way." Christian hurried them to the front of the dining room.

The rushing sound of flames through air, followed by

screams, drifted in from outside. Some were female. I tried not to think about them being May's. Instead, I stood on top of a table and whistled. This caught some of the girls' attention. I yelled "Hey!" to get the rest.

With all eyes on me, I said, "I'm sure you've already heard by now, but Lucent is under attack. Vykens are here, and they want your blood. You must do what you can to protect yourselves. Do you understand?"

"How?" someone called.

"We can't fight," Ashlyn said to the left of me.

I wish there would've been time for me to explain how stupid that idea was, but there wasn't. "Don't worry about fighting. Just protect yourself with Light. Use it any way you know how."

A rattle on the inside double doors made everyone jump. The sound was followed by pounding. Vykens were in the school.

I jumped from the table and returned to the outside door to check on May and Dr. Han. Their backs were to me, and they were scooting backward behind a wall of fire that they had to constantly recreate because Vykens were coming through. Some cried out as their flesh bubbled, but in less than a minute they returned to normal. With how quickly they were healing, I wondered if they had recently fed on Auran blood and a lot of it.

I ran next to May, whose legs were shaking, and added Light to their fire. Just like in the forest, the fire turned an ice blue. Now any Vyken that tried to walk through it turned to ash. My hands began to shake trying to maintain a wall of this size.

"We can't hold them much longer," Dr. Han said.

I glanced behind me. The door was about twenty feet away. "We can make it if we're quick," I said.

May grunted. "On three?"

I said, "One, two, three!"

The firewall flickered and then dissipated as we turned and bolted for the door. May went in first. I came next followed by Dr. Han. Just as he closed the door, a Vyken's arm jammed through it, preventing the door from closing. May and Dr. Han leaned against the door, which looked like it was taking every ounce of strength they had, while I took hold of the Vyken's trapped arm and lit it up. He cried out and withdrew it from the door, which finally clicked shut.

While they secured the door, I hurried back to join the others. The twins and Guardians were losing their battle with the main doors. One side was torn open, and they were stabbing at any Vyken who tried to come through. The Lizen men were there too, shooting their toxic spit several feet into the doorway, burning any part of a Vyken it touched.

I glanced around for Kiera. She was with a group of girls, giving them a crash course on creating a tangible ball of Light. I appreciated her efforts, but there just wasn't enough time.

Liam jogged over to me. "The doors are going to give. We need to get the girls into the kitchen. Lock them in there while we fight the Vykens out here."

"But there's too many of them," I said.

"I have help coming, but they're several minutes out. We need to buy some time."

I nodded and went to Kiera, trying to squeeze my way into her circle. "We need to get the Auras into the kitchen," I said. "And figure out a way to light up the door once it's closed." Ashlyn was behind her, looking terrified. I turned to her. "Help Kiera. Help them all. They need you." She nodded weakly.

Kiera grabbed her hand. "Let's go."

"Llona!" Christian yelled from across the room.

I ran to him, weaving in and out of frightened girls as they made their way to the kitchen.

"I want you to go with them," Christian said when I reached him. Sweat dotted his forehead, and he was breathing heavily.

"I'm not leaving you guys."

"I figured you'd say that. It was worth a try. We need—" his words were cut off by the sound of wood splintering.

The dining room doors had completely fallen, and Vykens began pouring through. Behind them, I saw Jackson. In his arms he held a limp Auran girl with long blonde hair. It reminded me of my own. Jackson's eyes met mine, and he winked.

"I'm going to kill him," Christian whispered, but he didn't have time to do anything about it. There were just too many Vykens.

Liam rushed by us, wielding two long butcher knives. He fought the first few who entered and was successful in decapitating them. His ability to spin like a whirlwind made him much faster than the Vykens.

Other Vykens, who were climbing—some leaping—over the broken tables and chairs that had been pressed against the doors, were met by the twins, several Lizen men, and Guardians. I pushed my hands forward, sending three bursts of Light into the doorway. Several Vykens cried out and fell to the side, but they were only replaced by more.

Another splintering sound, just as loud as the other, drew my attention behind me. May and Dr. Han were slowly backing away from the rear door. I went to them, hands ready to blast whatever came in.

"We can't use fire in here," Dr. Han panted. "We'll burn the place down."

I glanced toward the kitchen; the last of the girls were going through. "May, go with Kiera, please."

"I'm staying with you," she said.

There wasn't time to argue. The back door flew open, and four Vykens came through it. One of them was Eira, the Vyken who could produce ice. I blasted her with a steady stream of Light, but she avoided it by creating a wall of ice in front of her. She escaped around it and darted to the side, her sights set on the Auras escaping into the kitchen.

I turned my attention to the other Vykens and blasted each one, temporarily dazing them. Dr. Han attacked the first one. He was an incredible fighter, spinning, jumping, and kicking like a ninja warrior. In less than a minute he managed to get behind a Vyken and snap his neck. The Vyken fell to the ground, not dead, but in pain and waiting for his body to heal. Dr. Han didn't give him the chance. He withdrew what looked like a pocketknife from inside his jacket pocket.

I didn't get to see how Dr. Han finished him off; I was too busy tossing Light at the other two. One of them broke away and, faster than either May or I could move, bolted behind May and wrapped his arms around her chest. May grunted and gasped for breath.

I turned just in time to dodge a blow from Blade. I wasn't even sure where he'd come from. I spun away from him and jumped behind the Vyken gripping May and wrapped my hands around his face. I jerked his head back at the same time Light flowed from me to him. He exploded within a few seconds, but this gave Blade enough time to kick me hard in the leg. Something inside it snapped. I hoped it wasn't a bone, but the moment I put weight on it, I knew it was. I collapsed in agonizing pain. May fell too, gasping for air.

Blade jumped onto my stomach. May saw and struggled to her feet. I wished she would've stayed, but I couldn't tell her this because I was too busy feeling a meaty fist smash repeatedly into my face. The pain was severe. I blocked what I could, and even tried to get in my own punches, but it was useless. Fighting on my back wasn't going to work.

Just then May jumped onto Blade's back and turned her hands a fire red. Before it could have any effect, he snapped his elbow back, hitting her square in the face. She fell to the side of us, unconscious.

FORTY

I STARED AT MAY, THEN TURNED TO BLADE. "YOU'RE SO dead." I clasped my hands together and brought them up on his nose hard. It spurted with blood. My fists opened and Light shot out, but Blade had seen it coming. He rolled off me.

I tried to sit up, but the pain in my leg slowed me down, giving Blade enough time to get behind me. He jerked my head back hard, splitting my vision. I tried to summon Light to my palms, but they sparked and fizzled like an empty lighter.

Focus! I yelled at myself.

While I fought to keep his face away from my neck, time slowed. Through blurry vision I saw the chaos around me. Dr. Han was to my left, fighting two Vykens. A fire was spreading up the wall next to him, filling the room with smoke. The twins and a few of the Guardians were each battling one, sometimes two, Vykens. I watched in horror as a Vyken stabbed a Guardian in the chest.

Where was Christian?

In my attempt to locate him, I saw Liam fighting near the kitchen door. The door was lit up by a bright glowing light, and on the floor in front of it were two young Auran girls. They weren't moving. I was numb to it all. The only thing I felt was a deep throbbing pain pulsing from my leg. I'd gladly feel this over anything else.

With one of my hands, I was holding Blade's forehead back, barely keeping his teeth from puncturing the skin on my shoulder. I needed to do something and quick. The only thing I could think of was to turn invisible, but that would render me useless. The sharp spike of teeth grazed my skin.

Be invisible, I began to think, but just then I saw Christian sprinting through the smoke toward me.

Blade must have noticed too, because his head came up, and his grip relaxed as if he were going to move away, but he didn't have time. Christian dropped to his knees and slid along the marbled floor while I ducked. From behind his back, Christian withdrew a long knife and sliced Blade's head off, covering me in dust and ash.

"That was for Britt," I whispered.

Christian scrambled over to me. "Are you okay?"

I opened my mouth to answer but was interrupted by the sound of clapping. We both turned around. Cyrus was standing in the doorway, looking down on us with a tight smile. "Who says chivalry is dead?" He looked up and gave a low whistle. Three Vykens, one of them Eira, stopped fighting and followed him out the door.

Christian started after them. I took hold of his arm. "What are you doing?" I said.

"I'm going to finish this." He shook free of my grip.

"No! Christian, you can't. He's too powerful."

Christian looked back at me. "I have to try. If I don't, he'll only hurt more people." His shoulders slumped, and he looked so very tired. "I love you, Llona." He turned and rushed out the door.

"Christian!" I struggled to get up but fell back down again when my injured leg gave out. I frantically looked around for

Liam. He wasn't far away, battling two Vykens. He seemed to be winning the battle.

"Liam!" I yelled. "I need you!"

He glanced over at me between blows, and then spun, turning himself into a small, yet powerful, whirlwind. It knocked the two Vykens into the wall. Liam rushed to me. "What is it?" he said out of breath.

"Christian went after Cyrus. You have to stop him." I was pulling on his arm, half begging and half trying to get myself into a standing position.

"You're hurt," he said and helped me to stand.

"Just go after him!"

He glanced around, his face saddened by what he saw. "I can't. I'm needed here."

"Please. I'm begging you, Liam. Christian can't face him alone."

I looked behind him. The two Vykens who had crashed into the wall were now beating down the door to the kitchen. Every other second or so, the door would flicker with Light. Like the rest of us, the Auras were growing tired.

Liam saw what I was looking at. "I'm sorry, Llona. Christian's on his own." He sprinted away.

"Liam, no! Please!" The words stung my throat.

Liam didn't turn back.

Using every ounce of strength and willpower I had left, I forced myself to take a step toward the door. A biting pain shot up my leg and into the rest of my body until it rattled my brain. I fought a wave of nausea and took another step. And then another. I paused when I reached May. She was still out, but at least she was breathing steady. I continued on, my steps quickening just a little. I think the numbness in my heart was spreading to my limbs. *First Sophie and now Christian.*

I went outside and was shocked by what I saw. Part of the

lawn looked like bombs had gone off; chunks of grass laid upside down, and deep, uneven holes almost made the lawn impassable. I stumbled my way through the great mounds, following the destruction.

The sky looked swollen and bruised. It's dark purples and grays screamed rain, making me think the sky was in as much pain as I was.

Beneath my feet, the earth rumbled and I almost fell. *Cyrus.* I'd never seen such destruction before. I looked up ahead. The carnage seemed to go around the corner of the building and to the front of the school. I hurried faster. The sounds of my ragged breathing reminded me of the panic attack I'd had the day my father died. Tears stung my eyes. I blinked through them. *Don't panic. Move faster.*

I turned the corner.

And fell to my knees.

The sky released its pain.

Mine would forever remain.

Christian was standing thirty yards away, his head lowered. Blood covered the side of his head, neck, right shoulder, and arm. Drops of it dripped from his fingers, staining the ground red. The rain pouring from above only made the crimson puddle bigger.

But this wasn't what frightened me. It was the wall of dirt, at least ten feet high, rushing toward Christian from the side. He didn't seem to see it.

"Christian!" I yelled. Cyrus was off to the side, his hands outstretched as he controlled the moving wall of earth. Next to him were Jackson and Eira, but no Sophie. Where was she?

Christian slowly looked up at me, eyes empty. Like the dead.

I forced myself up and began to run despite the pain. Two Vykens I hadn't noticed before sprinted toward me from behind

Christian. I shot a spray of Light from each palm, hitting them both in the chest. The force of it was enough to knock them back several yards into the side of the school where they fell limp. I turned to Cyrus and shot at him, but Eira produced a wall of ice in front of them that I couldn't penetrate.

The moving wall of earth was almost to Christian. "Move!" I screamed, but he just stood there. Why wasn't he moving?

I was almost to him but realized I still wasn't going to make it in time. I shot one more blast of Light. It hit Christian in the chest and began to lift him into the air and back. *He'll be okay*, I told myself. *Christian will live.* I almost smiled.

Out of nowhere another wall of dirt rose behind him, stopping his body from moving out of the way. He bounced off it and fell to the ground. At the last second his head raised and our eyes met. The rushing wall of dirt crashed down upon him, sending a spray of dust into the air despite the rain.

I ran into the dirty mist and began to dig. "No, no, no. Please, no!" I dug fast, reaching into the ground as far as I could. Tears and rain fell from my cheeks. Any second now I'd feel an arm, a leg, his hair, anything to hold onto. I called to him with my mind and prayed for a response.

Using both my arms, I shoved dirt aside, back and forth, pushing the growing mud away. Upheaved roots and broken tree limbs thwarted my efforts by tearing at my skin and nails. I gritted my teeth and swiped my rain-soaked hair from my eyes with the sleeve of my shirt. If I could just find him, give him all of my Light to save him. *Oh, Christian, please!*

I continued to dig until something hard crashed against the side of my head. I fell over onto my back and blinked into the rain, but my fingers kept moving through the earth, still searching. *Must find Christian.*

A Vyken's dark form stepped over me, and he held something shiny in his hands. I tried to focus on it, but my head was spinning. Whether from his presence or the fact that he'd just bashed my head, I couldn't be sure. The Vyken knelt down beside me and laughed. It was Jameson. He raised the object; rain slid down its silver edge.

Even though I was on my back, I kept digging, both hands clawing into the earth and bringing up handfuls of only dirt. No Christian.

Jameson brought down the knife, but before it could pierce my heart, I rolled to the side. Jameson's knife plunged into the ground. I swung my good leg around hard and brought it down on his spine, making him collapse to the ground. I scurried onto his back and screamed as I took hold of his head and snapped it back hard. Light filled my arms and hands and spread to Jameson until his head burst into a million pieces, followed by the rest of his body.

With Jameson no longer under me, I fell to the ground and blinked rain from my eyes. And something warm. A drop of dark blood fell from my cheek. I continued to dig. At least I think my fingers were moving. I felt nothing, and I was struggling just to remain conscious.

I stopped only when I heard my name. A faint whisper. *Christian!*

"Llona." The voice was louder. I raised my head. It was Cyrus, still standing next to the school. "Join us," he said.

Anger rose inside me, but it wasn't like before, not dark and demanding. It was only the overwhelming urge to stop the pain and suffering of my friends. To stop anyone else from dying, and to repay what he did to Britt. I raised my hand and flung it forward. A single ball of Light, full of every emotion inside me, left my palm, fast and furious.

Before I lost consciousness, I saw it smash through the wall of ice Eira had created and continue on its path toward Cyrus, but at the last second, he took hold of Eira and jerked her in front of him. The ball of Light hit her between the eyes, and she exploded into dust.

FORTY-ONE

Lights flashed. I opened my eyes and closed them. I was so tired. My body was being carried. I opened my eyes again, but they closed just as quickly. Liam was carrying me.

"She's coming to," Liam said.

I tried to speak. *Christian. Someone had to help Christian.*

"What is it, Llona?" Liam said.

I tried again. "Christian." I couldn't hear my own voice, but Liam heard.

"They're looking for him," he said.

"Under dirt," I said. It hurt to speak, but not physically.

Liam paused, listening to my silent pleas. "We'll find him." A second later I heard him say to someone else, "Tell them to look under the dirt where we found Llona."

Liam continued carrying me.

"Hang on, Llona," I heard May say from somewhere close by. "We're taking you to the nurse. You've lost a lot of blood."

Lost blood meant I'd need blood. I began to struggle. "No! No blood," I said, my eyes opening and closing.

"Let us worry about that," Liam said. "We'll make sure it's safe."

Before I fell unconscious again, I said, "Get Kiera."

*   *   *   *   *

I'm not sure what time it was when I woke, but it was dark. But not as dark as I felt. I blinked at the blackened window and tried to figure out where I was. By the tan decor and floral bedspread I knew I was still in Lucent. I rolled over and grunted when pain shot up my leg.

"You're awake," May said. She was sitting at the foot of the bed. Her left eye was black and blue, and her hands were bandaged.

"Are you okay?"

She nodded, just barely. "I'll be fine."

"What time is it?" I asked, wincing from the pain of speaking. By how tight the skin felt on my face, I knew it must be swollen.

"Almost midnight." She sounded exhausted.

"Where am I?"

May looked around. Her good eye was red and puffy, like she'd been crying. "One of the bedrooms. The nurse's office is just around the corner. She's attending to others right now."

A lump formed in my throat. "How many were injured?"

"Several Guardians, a few Lizens, and, the last I heard, twelve girls. The ones who were in their rooms when the attack began."

I hated asking the next question. "How many died?"

May paused. "Five Guardians, two Lizens, and three Auras, but six are missing. There wasn't enough time to get to the girls who weren't at the movie."

I rolled onto my back and pulled the covers up to my chin. I was so cold. "How's Liam? Kiera?" I said, but it came out a whisper.

"They're both fine."

I felt her place another blanket on top of me. "And Arik and Aaron? Dr. Han?"

"They'll survive."

"And Sophie?"

She swallowed hard. "Still missing."

There was still one more person I needed to ask about, but I couldn't bring myself to say his name.

May touched my shoulder lightly and said in a quiet voice, "We found him, Llona. I'm so sorry. He didn't make it."

I sucked in air, but my lungs wouldn't expand fully. My breathing quickened, cold, short breaths, and the whole world began to spin. "May?" I gripped her arm tightly, looking for an anchor.

"I, I don't know what to say," she stuttered, and then she began to cry. Tears I didn't know I had left joined hers. I stared at the ceiling, gasping for air.

"I don't know how," May said, "but we'll get through this. You'll get through this."

I tried to nod, but I don't think I did. How could I get through this?

A soft knock at the door made me wipe at my eyes. The door opened. Liam stuck his head in. "Can I come in for a minute?"

May sniffed and stood up. "Of course." She looked at me. "I'm going to go get Tessa and Kiera. They wanted to know when you woke up."

"Thanks, May," I said.

As soon as she was gone, Liam moved to the side of my bed. His dark hair looked crusted and matted. By the red smear on his cheek, it was probably from blood. I also noticed he was limping. "You look terrible," he said. "How do you feel?"

I didn't answer him, but my chin quivered when I said, "Why didn't you help him?"

He didn't say anything for a moment, then, "A choice had to be made."

I exhaled. The air barely passed through my tight chest. "I don't know how to get through this."

Liam looped his finger through the chain on my neck. He pulled it out of the blankets and stared at the ring the chain held. "Christian gave this to you, didn't he?"

I nodded.

"The symbols. Tell me what it means."

My chin quivered. "Endure to the end."

He let go of the necklace. "That's how you'll deal."

"I don't know if I can." Sophie was missing, and Christian was gone. The blankets on top of me provided no warmth.

"You will. In time."

I turned to him. "How can you be so sure?"

Liam crossed the room to the door and looked out its window into the hall. Finally, he turned around. His green eyes were glassy, like a stone at the bottom of a lake. "A long time ago, Vykens held me captive and made me watch as they killed my parents, my two younger sisters, and," he swallowed and adjusted his jaw, "my wife. We'd only been married for three days. I know about loss, Llona. I know what it feels like to wish for the worse kind of torture over what you're feeling now. But it gets better. Duller anyway, with time."

My eyelids drooped, and my chest felt like it was collapsing within itself. "Why? Why so much sorrow?"

"I asked myself that same question every day for over a hundred years, and you know what I came up with?"

I shook my head and wiped at my eyes.

"Nothing. There's no reason for it. Horrible, unexplainable things happen all the time."

"How do people go on?"

He looked steadily into my eyes. "They find a purpose. Mine was helping others through the Deific. Doing what I could to make the world less miserable for everyone else."

A knock on the door interrupted him.

When Liam opened the door, Tessa and Kiera rushed to the bed and hugged me. They looked good, no injuries. For that, I was grateful. May stood behind them, her lips tightened together.

"Are you okay?" Tessa asked.

"I will be," I said, my eyes meeting Liam's behind them. "I think."

The door was still open, and Dr. Han came into the room. He closed the door.

"Where's Sophie?" I asked right away. "Please tell me you know something."

Dr. Han looked at Liam, and I noticed the girls had tensed. "What?" I said.

"The Deific is looking for her," Liam said.

Dr. Han moved next to him. "I'll admit they don't have much to go on, but it's still early. Every man available is helping. We'll find her."

"And Jackson? Cyrus?"

Liam bristled. "They got away, but we got a few of the other Guardians who had turned. They were the ones rounding up the girls left in the school."

"I have to ask, Llona," Dr. Han said. "What happened outside the school?"

I stared at the dirt beneath my fingernails. "Christian fought Cyrus. I didn't see it though. Only saw Cyrus bury him." I swallowed and nearly choked. "I tried to save him, but he was too far under. Then Jameson attacked me. I killed him." If I had said this last week, I would've been thrilled, reveled in the fact, but I felt no joy now. Only sadness.

The room was quiet until Dr. Han crossed the room to my bed. "I want you to know that I will do everything in my power to get Sophie back and make sure Cyrus pays for his crimes, but, please, right now focus on getting better. How's your leg?"

May touched my arm with her bandaged hand.

I looked at Dr. Han, shaking my head. "There's so much more to worry about than my dumb leg. It will be fine, but who knows if Sophie or the other Auran girls will be."

"Getting them back is our top priority," he said. "And, starting immediately, things are going to change around here. The pills, for example. The Deific has already replaced them with a placebo. Within a month, the girls should be back to normal."

"Why a placebo?" I said. "Just cut them off. Tell them everything that's been going on. Tell them how they've all been fooled. Tell them their true potential!"

Dr. Han was shaking his head. "Change takes time. We have to ease them into this or no one will believe us. Remember, Llona, this has been the Auran way of life for decades." He glanced back at Liam, then to me. "But I want your help to change it. I need someone who can help Auras find the strength they once had. I need you, Llona."

"To do what?" I looked at the girls. Tessa and Kiera were both smiling, but May still looked sad.

"I want you to teach. This fall I'm going to introduce some new classes. One of them will be teaching Auras to fight. We won't call it that, of course. We'll have to be very subtle."

"Even after what just happened? Aren't the Auras, the Council, up in arms about this?"

"The Council is divided. An emergency meeting has been scheduled to decide how to proceed. With your help, I hope to change their way of thinking. Help them to see the power within them."

May looked down at me. "What do you think, Llona? I know you'll make a great teacher."

"I'll think about it." The room fell quiet. I looked again at the dirt on my hands and under my nails. Something on my arm caught my eye, and I was surprised I hadn't noticed sooner. A white cotton ball covered by a single piece of clear tape. "I was given blood," I said.

"It was mine," Kiera said quickly. "Vyken-free."

"What about the rest of it?" I asked, feeling a little relieved. I don't know what would've happened to me if I had been given more of their poison.

Liam said, "Most of it was taken, but some of what was left was used on injured girls."

"You let them use it?"

"It happened before we knew what was going on," Liam said.

"Was it poisoned?"

"I don't know yet."

I sunk into the bed. "Is there any good news?"

"What happened tonight could've been so much worse," Liam said. "Sophie saved a bunch of lives by sending girls home. That is the good news."

"But there's still the other thing," I said, looking back and forth at Liam and Dr. Han. "I saw it. The Shadow. It was there."

Dr. Han tensed. "Are you sure?"

"There was no mistaking it. It came together from the shadows of the room and formed behind Cyrus."

Dr. Han looked at Liam. "He's in control of it. This is bad, Liam."

"We'll deal with it tomorrow."

I forced a yawn, not wanting to think about anything else bad right now. I just wanted to sleep.

"Are you still tired?" May asked.

"Yeah, I think I'd like some time alone. Rest and stuff."

"Sure. Of course," Tessa said. "We're going to go check with

Abigail. See if we can help." They left the room with Dr. Han.

Before Liam left too, he said, "The next several months, possibly years, are going to be very difficult for you. Just remember, though, that you're never alone. You still have your uncle, your teachers, your friends. And me. We care about you."

I nodded, but no matter how hard I tried, I couldn't force a smile. Just as Liam was about to close the door, I said, "Wait!" He looked back at me. "Will you stay? I want to sleep but don't think I can do it alone."

He nodded and closed the door. "Of course."

FORTY-TWO

My eyes opened. The room was bright; light spilled in between the slits in the blinds. It took only a second for me to remember everything. I swallowed hard, unsure how I was going to deal with today. "Liam?" My throat was dry, and my body ached, especially my leg, but at least I could move it now.

He moved into my line of sight. "I'm here." He looked the same as last night. Blood caked his matted hair and on the side of his face, and his shirt was torn. He looked terrible. I was touched that he had stayed the entire time.

"Thanks for staying," I said.

"It was nothing. How are you feeling?"

It took me a moment to answer. "Better." While Liam spoke, I moved into a sitting position. "I thought of something else last night."

"What's that?"

"Dr. Han said Cyrus is controlling the Shadow. If that's true, why did the Shadow, or really Cyrus, save Christian in the tower? Especially if he was only going to kill him later?"

Liam shook his head. "I don't know. Maybe he wanted you to have more time with Christian, to cause you more pain." His voice sounded bitter.

I looked down at the bedspread, remembering Cyrus's last

words. I needed to get stronger, and fast. Before he could hurt me anymore. I thought of my friends. And Jake. "What next?" I asked.

"We hunt down everyone involved. The Deific has already begun. They've been questioning the captured Guardians all night."

"What about the Shadow?"

He shook his head. "I don't know anything yet, but we'll deal with it. Whatever happens."

I looked toward the window. "Will you take me to him?"

He knew exactly whom I was talking about. "They are shipping his body today, back to his father."

"I'd like to say good-bye."

"Of course."

Twenty minutes later, Liam was wheeling me down the hallway and into the elevator. I kept my eyes straight, but I could hear others being attended to inside many of the rooms. As soon as the elevator doors closed, I said, "I could've walked."

"The chair was available." Liam didn't say anything else until he wheeled me into a small room just off the main office on the first floor. I gasped when I saw a pine box sitting on top of a table. "Do you want me to stay?" he asked.

I shook my head, my eyes burning.

"I'll be outside." Liam closed the door.

I stood up and limped to the box. I imagined Christian inside, alive and well. His blue eyes, the color of a shimmering dragonfly's wing, and the never-ending dimple in his cheek. Trailing my hand across it's top, I said, "I'm sorry, Christian."

Memories flooded my mind. I thought of the first time we met, when I'd fallen on the bleachers and he caught me. The times we trained together, laughing, sharing our deepest fears and regrets. I remembered how he taught me to use Light in ways other Auras wouldn't dream of. I thought of our kisses, his letters, and finally his words of love and our future. It was too much. I rested my head on the box and cried.

I stayed like that for a long time. I knew the moment I left this small room I would never be near Christian again. This thought left a hole in my heart, one that would never heal. But I was a survivor. I stood and wiped at my eyes. I would endure to the end, as Christian would want, but I wasn't going to just endure. I was going to live life, starting by taking control.

I came to Lucent with the desire to learn what I could and then get out. I never wanted to be a part of the Auras. Their way of life used to repulse me, but after all I'd learned, and I had learned a lot, I realized that they had been manipulated by someone they trusted. We were the same.

No. I wasn't going anywhere. Lucent was my home, and I was an Aura.

Special Sneak Peek

Fractured Truth

by

Rachel McClellan

Coming Soon From Sweetwater Books

One

Pain burst in my head into a spectrum of colors, and a wave of nausea buckled my knees. *Four minutes and twenty-two seconds. I can endure this pain for that long,* I thought, trying to convince myself.

The small plane's engine roared, a high-pitched sound different from the steady hum of the last twenty minutes. Everyone had boarded a while ago. It was a silent crowd, not one that liked to converse with each other.

I shifted my weight in the plane's cramped closet. I could've come out since I'd just turned invisible, but I wanted to wait until the speed of the plane increased, covering any sounds the closet door might make when I opened it.

It was shortly after Cyrus kidnapped Sophie from Lucent Academy that I began to teach myself to turn invisible. I practiced every day, sometimes for hours, until I could do it without all the paralyzing weakness. And although the pain hadn't gotten any better, I was able to increase the time I could maintain invisibility to several minutes. I'd accomplished all this in just the four short weeks since Christian's death.

"You have four minutes," Liam said through a microphone in my ear.

Just then the plane lurched forward, picking up speed on

the runway. I opened the door and peered into the plane's small kitchen. When I saw that it was empty, I quietly slipped out and closed the door behind me.

The front wheels of the plane were starting to bounce.

I looked in the cabin. As I suspected, it was full of Vykens sitting in their seats, their backs to me, as if they were regular passengers. Except for one. Jackson. He sat three rows up to the right of the center aisle.

Through the help of the Deific, Liam had finally received a tip on Jackson's whereabouts. It was the closest we'd come to finding out where Cyrus was keeping Sophie. I glanced to my left, to the emergency exit. By the way the plane was vibrating, I knew it was close to taking off.

A Vyken stood up and came into the aisle. I pressed myself against a seat to keep him from bumping into me. I had yet to learn how to let matter pass through me. That may have been a trick only my mother knew how to do.

After the Vyken passed by, I went to Jackson. He was looking down at his hands, staring at bloodied knuckles. I wondered how that could've happened. Jackson used to be a Guardian. He, and a bunch of others who had followed him, had joined the Vykens against the Auras months ago. I'd been training harder than ever to stop them all and restore the Auras to their former strength. The strength only a few knew about.

I felt the plane lift. Still plenty of time to make my move.

I reached down, careful to avoid touching Jackson, and undid his seatbelt. He glanced down surprised. I smacked the back of his head hard. He turned around and stared at the Vyken behind him. "What's your problem?" he said.

The Vyken ignored him.

Jackson stood and confronted the Vyken again. "I'm talking to you," he said again.

The Vyken slowly looked up from the sports magazine in

his hand. "I know Cyrus said we can't kill you, but he didn't say I couldn't hurt you. Sit down, Guardian."

Liam's voice spoke again in my ear. "Hurry up."

The sound of his voice this close to so many Vykens drew attention. Several of them looked around to see where it had come from. *Time to pay for your crimes, Jackson.* I drew my fist back and punched Jackson in the face. His hand came up to his nose. "What the . . . ?" he looked around.

Several Vykens stood up.

I punched him again. He stumbled back toward the exit, arms out stretched to steady himself. "What's going on?" he yelled.

I kicked him in the chest. It took just a second for him to recover before he started blindly throwing punches. "Someone help me!" he said.

The Vykens looked around as if they didn't know what to do.

I dodged Jackson's fist and punched him again. He was in position. I took hold of the emergency latch and pulled it as hard as I could. The door flew open, sucking air from the cabin. Papers and all kinds of debris flew past me. Jackson moved backward, his eyes darting around as if searching for help, until he was pressed against the wall separating the kitchen from the cabin.

The other Vykens stood alert and ready to fight the unknown attacker.

Grabbing Jackson, I spun him around and faced him toward the open door, his clothes and hair whipped around violently. And he was stuttering.

I chuckled, glad he was afraid. I was about to reveal myself to him, so I could see the surprise in his eyes, but then I heard Liam's voice in my ear, "Get out of there now!"

Jerking into action, I wrapped my arms around Jackson's chest and jumped from the plane, spiraling into a black abyss.

About the Author

Rachel McClellan was born and raised in Idaho, a place secretly known for its supernatural creatures. When she's not in her writing lair, she's partying with her husband and four small children. Her love for storytelling began as a child, when the moon first possessed each night. For when the lights went out, her imagination painted a whole new world. And what a scary world it is . . . Currently she lives in Rhode Island, where the graveyards are as enchanting as the forests.